THIS BOOK BELONGS TO

_____

365 DAILY DEVOTIONS

LIVE
HOPE
MINUTE

MARK SMEBY

BroadStreet
PUBLISHING

BroadStreet Publishing Group, LLC
Racine, Wisconsin, USA
BroadStreetPublishing.com

LIVE HOPE MINUTE

ISBN-13: 978-1-4245-5567-3 (hardcover)
ISBN-13: 978-1-4245-5568-0 (e-book)

Stock or custom editions of BroadStreet Publishing titles may be purchased in bulk for educational, business, ministry, fundraising, or sales promotional use. For information, please e-mail info@broadstreetpublishing.com.

Cover design by Chris Garborg at garborgdesign.com
Typesetting by Katherine Lloyd at theDESKonline.com

Printed in China

17 18 19 20 21 5 4 3 2 1

Greetings!

I grew up going to church and learned all the right things to do and say. I got good at being good. But it never felt right—even while it appeared to be working for all the happy, firm-handshaking people at church.

I justified my disappointment by thinking I wasn't supposed to be living for any level of joy in this temporal life, but merely for the eternal next.

Fortunately, I woke up one day and realized my best intentions had turned me into a depressed, fear-driven, score-keeping, self-righteous man, living in glass-bubble isolation, lacking compassion and any idea of what grace was all about. I decided to search for the meaning underneath it all and landed on what I'm calling *hope*, a word I want to reclaim as the true anchor for our souls—something tangible we can dive into and make our own.

This journey to knowing the essence of hope and exploring how to live it can change a person from the inside out. It's made my relationships with other people less tangled with expectations and disappointments, my relationship with myself more peaceful and present, and my relationship with God more intimate and stunningly beautiful—which is what I have been hoping for all along.

You are brave for starting down this road.

Here's to the hope awakening!

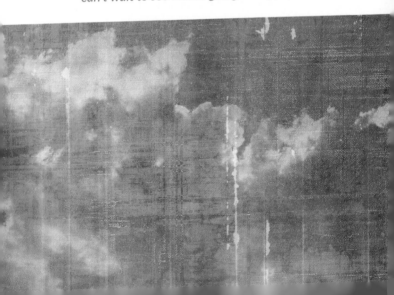

JANUARY

Hope says, *God, I can see that you're writing a grand story in the world and in my life. And I can't wait to see what's going to happen next.*

Three Parts of Hope

I'm on a quest—perhaps you are, as well. I'm really wanting to discover what hope is—you know, beyond the cliché, finger-crossed wishing that I hear a lot of people mention. This quest has uncovered a couple ideas I'd like to offer as what might be an easy way to understand hope.

Hope is made up of three parts—faith, love, and vision. Faith says God is in this—it's trusting, it's the knowing beyond knowing; it's the spirit part. Love is the action—knowing you are loved and then declaring the worth of every single person you meet. This is the heart of hope, its motivation. And vision is looking ahead with desire—it's the *why*. It has a goal in mind ("I'm building God's kingdom"). This vision is what guides us and keeps us living day to day with great expectancy of what God will do.

These three elements, when combined and working together, can guide us throughout this year into a life of hope.

> Since we have such a [glorious] hope and confident
> expectation, we speak with great courage.
>
> 2 Corinthians 3:12 AMP

▸▸ *What additional elements of hope might you add to the formula?*

▸▸ *How can you best adopt a posture of hope and live rooted in it?*

Hope = Grounded in Faith + Fueled by Love + Guided by Vision

Is *Hope* an Overused Buzzword?

*D*oes the McDonald's Happy Meal really give hope as their commercial suggests? Advertisers use the allure of hope to get us to do what they want. But true hope is deeper than anything a consumeristic transaction could ever promise.

So what is it really, this hope? I want to know true hope—hope that is rooted in something real. But more than trying to define something as mysterious and spiritual as hope, I want to explore what it means to live hope—to actually live life fueled by, driven by, and infused with hope.

Hope says this is not all there is. This pain, this struggle, and these circumstances don't solely define us. Our story is not finished being written. And, in fact, the best is yet to come.

> May the God of hope fill you with all joy
> and peace in believing, so that by the power
> of the Holy Spirit you may abound in hope.
> ROMANS 15:13

▸▸ *Why do businesses and politicians like to use hope as a way to advertise?*

▸▸ *How do you define hope?*

Are You Struggling to Find Hope?

*A*s I travel the country, I constantly meet people who are struggling to find hope. Life is difficult for many people. So many of us feel alone, tired, defeated, broken, or victims of our circumstances. We long to have some light break into our darkness, to experience hope amid our pain.

Light can come from a variety of places—from something you read, a phone call with a friend, an inspirational song, a meaningful Scripture, or a stranger's kindness. That glimmer of light—however small or large—is the first sight of hope and tells a person, *I can continue.* This is something we can help each other with.

The greatest truth, which I believe to be our great hope, is that we are not alone—that God is with us, Emmanuel.

> "Therefore the Lord himself will give you a sign.
> Look! the virgin is with child and she is about to give birth
> to a son, and she shall call his name 'God with us.'"
> ISAIAH 7:14 LEB

▸▸ *Where do you see the light of hope breaking through?*

▸▸ *Who is someone you could reach out to today with a touch of hope?*

Hope = Grounded in Faith + **Fueled by Love** + Guided by Vision

Where Do You Find Hope?

*A*sk anyone where they find hope, and after they struggle to try to figure out what you mean, they may say, "I don't know." Some of them may say they find hope in their family or their kids. Some may even say their job or their education or maybe even God. But what would you say?

Hope has a major element of looking forward within it—our vision needs to be placed on something to live lives of hope. And as we choose to keep our eyes on Jesus as the source of hope, the things in the world around us will, as the old hymn says, "grow strangely dim." As we see more clearly God's plan for the world and our lives, the old way of living just doesn't cut it any longer.

If you're frustrated by how the world keeps letting you down, perhaps it's time for a hope readjustment.

> "And you will feel secure, because there is hope;
> you will look around and take your rest in security."
>
> JOB 11:18

▸▸ *In what ways do the things of this world let you down?*

▸▸ *What does it mean for you to put your hope in God?*

How Do You Demonstrate Hope?

I grew up thinking I had to present a picture of perfection to everyone I met, mostly because I wanted people to see the perfection of Jesus in me. I had to smile and show that I had it all together, or, at least, that Jesus had put me all together. It was exhausting! I was missing out on something quite profound about God.

Second Corinthians 1:3–4 says, "Praise be to the God and Father of our Lord Jesus Christ, the Father of compassion and the God of all comfort, who comforts us in all our troubles" (NIV). God longs to comfort us in our pain, our struggles, and even in our imperfection. God says, "It's okay, I've got you. It's okay to struggle, to not be perfect." That's good news.

We live hope when we show how God comforts us through our struggles and imperfections.

> Even though I walk through
> the valley of the shadow of death,
> I will fear no evil,
> for you are with me;
> your rod and your staff,
> they comfort me.
>
> PSALM 23:4

▶▶ *How does God comfort you during your struggles?*

▶▶ *How can you show hope to others through your authenticity?*

Hope = Grounded in Faith + Fueled by Love + Guided by Vision

When It Hurts So Much

*M*any people are going through challenging circumstances, whether health related, financial, or relational. Where is hope found in the midst of pain and struggle? Second Corinthians 1:4 says that God comforts us "so that we can comfort those in any trouble with the comfort we ourselves receive from God" (NIV).

Our pain can keep us focused on ourselves and how difficult our circumstances are. Or we can focus on the comfort that God promises to us so we can make it through anything. Then we are better able to share what we have received with other hurting people. Hope is found when you let your pain make you more compassionate to the world around you.

> Blessed be the God and Father of our Lord Jesus Christ, the Father of mercies and God of all comfort, who comforts us in all our affliction, so that we may be able to comfort those who are in any affliction, with the comfort with which we ourselves are comforted by God.
>
> 2 CORINTHIANS 1:3–4

▸▸ *What have you been through that has equipped you to reach out to someone else?*

▸▸ *Why is it so easy to focus on our pain rather than God's promise of comfort?*

How Do You Live Hope?

*W*e all know people who seem to be able to walk around with a great attitude, always hopeful about the days ahead. I don't know if you're anything like me, but sometimes I just don't feel that way. Sometimes I can't see through the darkness right in front of me, even the very next step. This is why hope is such an important topic for me.

Hope is one of the great promises of God. But it's also my responsibility—my opportunity—to live in that hope. It's a choice every day for me to say, "God, I trust you. You've got me. And, as it says in your Word, you have a good plan for my life; a plan to prosper me and not to harm me; to give me hope and a future. I accept that for my life, both for today and forever." That's when I truly live hope.

> "For I know the plans I have for you,
> declares the LORD, plans for welfare and not for evil,
> to give you a future and a hope."
>
> JEREMIAH 29:11

▸▸ *Why is hope an important topic for you?*

▸▸ *What is a prayer you could pray every morning to commit to living with hope?*

Hope = Grounded in Faith + Fueled by Love + Guided by Vision

In the Midst of the Darkness

*H*ope is such a big word with a lot of different meanings for different people. I love hearing from people all over the country about what hope means to them. Mary (Florida) told me that hope is the beautiful unknown, yet it has the strength to get one through. She told me about the day her mom died. She knew it was her time and was grateful she could be with her mom during her final moments.

As sad it is was, Mary said that when the sun rose the next day, there, as bright as could be, was a stunning rainbow in the distance. As she worked to get through all the details surrounding her mother's passing, the rainbow said, *Yep, all is well*. I love that so much. Just like in Genesis 9, God's promise to Noah and his family came through in vivid colors.

> "I have set my bow in the cloud, and it shall be
> a sign of the covenant between me and the earth."
> GENESIS 9:13

▸▸ *How do you see hope in the darkness?*

▸▸ *Has God provided you any specific signs of his presence?*

Christ in You, the Hope of Glory

*C*olossians 1:27 says, "Christ in you, the hope of glory." I'm curious what that means for you. As believers, we know that Christ is within us, that we are, as the word *Christian* has been translated by some, "little Christs." It means that we are sons and daughters of God. It means that we can share in the life of Christ, a life that was before time and will always exist. And as C. S. Lewis said in *Mere Christianity*, "the whole purpose of becoming a Christian is simply nothing less."

Knowing that I share in the life of Christ, not only in how he lived and loved his Father, but also in his death, and ultimately in his glory and resurrection—this is what gives me great hope.

> "Nor will they say, 'Look, here it is!' or 'There!' for behold, the kingdom of God is in the midst of you."
>
> LUKE 17:21

▸▸ *How does Christ in you give you hope?*

▸▸ *How does the truth of living forever change the way you live today?*

Do You Have a Favorite Hymn of Hope?

*O*ne of my favorite hymns is "Great Is Thy Faithfulness." A woman from Minnesota wrote it was hers as well. She said, "Over the last year, I have faced many times when I didn't know how I could go on. … In the third verse of this hymn, Thomas Chisholm writes—strength for today and bright hope for tomorrow, blessings all mine with ten thousand beside!"

She continues, "I have prayed this prayer to God so many times and have also prayed it for other family members and friends going through trials. These words and thoughts give me so much peace and comfort, knowing that I'm not doing this on my own but that it is God who gives me strength for today and bright hope for tomorrow."

Next time you sing this song, remember that you are not alone and that God is strengthening you for whatever you're facing.

> Humble yourselves, therefore, under the mighty hand of God so that at the proper time he may exalt you, casting all your anxieties on him, because he cares for you.
>
> 1 PETER 5:6–7

▸▸ *What is your favorite hymn of hope?*

▸▸ *What does it mean for you to have bright hope for tomorrow?*

Hope = Grounded in Faith + Fueled by Love + Guided by Vision

If Life Is a Journey, Where Are We Going?

*A*s followers of Jesus, we are going somewhere. We are following Jesus to our actual home, which is being prepared for us right now. Hebrews 11 talks about the heroes of our faith and how they admitted they were foreigners and strangers on earth. Verse 14 says, "People who say such things show that they are looking for a country of their own"—they are longing for a better country, a heavenly one.

I know that feeling—that nagging feeling that things aren't exactly like they're supposed to be; that indeed, I've been made for another place. We are not there yet, but we are on our way. There's great hope in the idea that life is a journey, which means your story is still being written. And it's a good one.

> For we know that if the tent that is our earthly home is destroyed, we have a building from God, a house not made with hands, eternal in the heavens. For in this tent we groan, longing to put on our heavenly dwelling.
>
> 2 CORINTHIANS 5:1–2

▸▸ *How does longing for heaven impact your life now?*

▸▸ *What's the best way to engage this world, knowing eternity is coming?*

One of the Most Important Things You Need

I love the idea that we are all on the road to our actual home-land—that we realize we are meant for something more than this temporary, superficial, broken world. But many days are more difficult than we ever imagined. For some of us, leaving the house requires great courage.

Do you know how a runner needs a coach to tell him or her not to give up, to keep training, to keep working out, because it's all going to be worth it? I'm the same way. I need people in my life to stay in my face, telling me to not give up, to keep pressing on. Let me encourage you with a favorite verse from Hebrews 12:1: "Let us run with endurance the race that is set before us."

> Not only that, but we rejoice in our sufferings,
> knowing that suffering produces endurance, and
> endurance produces character, and character produces
> hope, and hope does not put us to shame, because God's
> love has been poured into our hearts through the
> Holy Spirit who has been given to us.
>
> ROMANS 5:3–5

▸▸ *How does your hope journey require patience?*

▸▸ *What tempts you to give up and quit the race?*

Hope = Grounded in Faith + Fueled by Love + Guided by Vision

Are You Making Your Own Choices?

*W*e make hundreds of choices each day—to enjoy the ride and see the beauty in the world around us, or to live in a prison of resentment and fear, wishing others would give us the life we deserve. For most of my life, I chose a twisted cocktail of these two. I enjoyed times of beauty and fun that crossed my path. But when times were tough, I thought about all the people who hurt me. I felt miserable most of the time. And I could not figure out why.

Then I realized I could choose. I could live my own life, or I could let other people live it for me. Living my own life means continually choosing hope instead of despair, faith instead of fear, and forgiveness instead of resentment. And it means refusing to let the actions or attitudes of others determine the outcome of my life.

> Aspire to live quietly, and to mind your own affairs,
> and to work with your hands ... so that you may walk
> properly before outsiders and be dependent on no one.
>
> 1 Thessalonians 4:11–12

▸▸ *How have you let other people control your life?*
▸▸ *Has the blame game held you back in any way?*

Creatively Showing Hope

God has given each of us unique gifts and talents for a couple of reasons. First, we can experience significant joy in the expression of our talents. And secondly, our talents can to be used to bring life and hope to the world around us.

Personally, I believe music can change a life. If we hear a certain song at a certain moment, something powerful can occur. That's what I hope to be a part of with the music I make—creating moments where people who are just about to give up hope don't. Or people who feel completely alone realize they aren't. To be a part of that is perhaps the greatest honor I could attain.

The possibility that somehow, somewhere, someone will be encouraged or inspired to take one more step on their own journey allows me to keep pushing forward.

> Therefore encourage one another and build
> one another up, just as you are doing.
>
> 1 Thessalonians 5:11

▸▸ *How have you been impacted by someone else's creativity?*

▸▸ *In what ways have you been uniquely equipped to show hope?*

Losing Yourself in a Good Story

*A*re you enjoying the story God is writing with your life? A good story lived over several chapters can be a great example of redemption and hope. Have you ever read a book like this? Sure, you can find all kinds of books written specifically about hope. But that's not what I'm talking about. I'm talking about a real page-turner—a book you just can't put down.

For me, losing myself in a wonderful book is one of the great joys of life. The author has managed to create a scenario where I can't wait to see what's going to happen next, and I trust that reading the whole book is going to be worth it. This is what it's like to live a life of hope.

Hope says, *God, I can see that you're writing a grand story in the world and in my life. And I can't wait to see what's going to happen next. But more than anything, I know that it's all going to be worth it in the end.*

Trust in the LORD with all your heart,
and do not lean on your own understanding.
In all your ways acknowledge him,
and he will make straight your paths.

PROVERBS 3:5–6

▸▸ How is God writing a grand story with your life?

▸▸ How can you live with anticipation for what God is doing next?

Hope = **Grounded in Faith** + Fueled by Love + Guided by Vision

You're a Star

*T*here's a song by Coldplay called "Sky Full of Stars." I find that interesting, considering Philippians 2:15, which says, "Then you will shine among them like stars in the sky" (NIV). If you get a chance, find the darkest place you can, away from any city lights, and sit in awe of the brightness of these glistening diamonds held up by the hand of God. Not only can a starry night be a breathtaking sight, but it's a great analogy.

I find great hope in seeing the family of God as a "sky full of stars." We live in a dark world, but the light of Christ is shining through us. Matthew 5:16 says, "In the same way, let your light shine before others. that they may see your good deeds and glorify your Father in heaven" (NIV). You can show bright hope to the dark world by letting the light of Christ shine through you.

> But the path of the righteous is like the light of dawn,
> which shines brighter and brighter until full day.
>
> PROVERBS 4:18

▸▸ *In what ways do you let the light of Christ shine through you?*

▸▸ *How do we shine as a family of God?*

Is Life with God a Dance?

I just read how author Jean Rhodes wrote about the word *guidance*, how she kept seeing the word *dance* at the end. And then she saw *g*, *u*, and *i* at the beginning and thought, *God, you and I dance.* Cool, huh? She says, "When two people try to lead in a dance, nothing feels right. When one person realizes that and lets the other lead, both bodies begin to flow with the music. The dance takes surrender, willingness, and attentiveness from one person and gentle guidance and skill from the other."[1]

Are you looking for hope in the midst of your circumstances? Let me encourage you that God is with you, with his gentle hand of grace, love, and comfort wrapped around you. He is guiding you. And he's never going to let you go. Even if you feel like he has, the truth is that he hasn't. Hanging on to this is how you start dancing to the song of hope in your life.

> Your word is a lamp to my feet
> and a light to my path.
>
> PSALM 119:105

▸▸ *How do you feel God leading you?*

▸▸ *How can you increase your attentiveness to how God is leading your dance?*

Are You in a Smiling Contest?

*A*s a kid, I was taught to smile big all the time, that my happiness would be the way to attract people to Jesus, because "you might be the only Jesus some people ever see." This is true, but to be honest, I didn't always feel happy, and I didn't always feel like smiling. Maybe you feel the same way.

I had to get to a place where I was so convinced of God's unconditional love for me that I couldn't worry about what other people thought about me. Trusting that God's love would overflow to others—and more than happiness or a big smile, others would know that they are loved by God, regardless of what they think or feel. Jesus knew he was loved by his Father. As we that soak in, hope will come alive in ways we've never imagined.

> "If you keep my commandments, you will abide in my love, just as I have kept my Father's commandments and abide in his love."
>
> JOHN 15:10

▸▸ *Why is there value in putting on a happy face even when you don't feel like it?*

▸▸ *How can you abide in the love of God?*

Are You a Prisoner or Are You Free?

*I*f Christ came to set the captives—you and me—free, why do so many people still live as if they're in prison? Probably because it's difficult to know how to live like a free person. This means that I'm free to be loved by God and by others, and, in turn, I'm free to show that same kind of unconditional love to others.

Here I am today, telling you that you are free. You no longer need to be imprisoned by your past or held captive by the unknown future. You are free to live today, completely loved, perfect in God's eyes because of his Son. Now it's your chance to live hope by telling someone else this good news.

> "The Spirit of the Lord is upon me,
>   because he has anointed me
>   to proclaim good news to the poor.
> He has sent me to proclaim liberty to the captives
>   and recovering of sight to the blind,
>   to set at liberty those who are oppressed,
>   to proclaim the year of the Lord's favor."
>
> LUKE 4:18–19

▸▸ *How have you been held back from freedom?*

▸▸ *What does true freedom feel like?*

It's Easy to Point Fingers

S ociety likes to push people to the margins. We see those who aren't living like us and look for ways to live without them interfering in our lives. For anyone who has ever been pushed aside, told you weren't good enough, or made to think that because you might be different, there is something wrong with you—this is for you. Jesus continually went after the outcasts, the ones the religious people were marginalizing and pushing to the side. These are the ones Jesus chose to spend time with.

If this is something you've experienced, I'm sorry. You are uniquely qualified to show hope to the world. Because you know what it's like to be marginalized, look around you to find others who have been pushed aside and demonstrate the love of Christ by showing the compassion you've been uniquely trained to offer. That is living hope.

> "What man of you, having a hundred sheep,
> if he has lost one of them, does not leave the
> ninety-nine in the open country, and go after
> the one that is lost, until he finds it?"
>
> LUKE 15:4

▸▸ *What prevents you from connecting with people different from you?*

▸▸ *How have you been uniquely equipped to minister?*

Hope = Grounded in Faith + **Fueled by Love** + Guided by Vision

Can You Conjure Up Hope at Will?

I hear the word *hope* swirling around all over the media and in daily conversations. It seems to make people come alive, to perk up, to give people a little spring in their step. But it remains a bit intangible. I'm on a quest to understand more what it really means to have hope—to live hope.

I'm convinced that hope isn't an emotion. Even though we tend to describe it in terms of being an emotion, hope is a posture—I can choose to look at all of life through the lens of hope. I don't have to wait until a particular circumstance clears up or the weather gets better or I get some money in the bank. It is not rooted in circumstances or in fear, failure, or even success. I can choose to have hope today.

> But this I call to mind,
> and therefore I have hope:
> The steadfast love of the LORD never ceases;
> his mercies never come to an end;
> they are new every morning;
> great is your faithfulness.
>
> LAMENTATIONS 3:21–23

▸▸ *How do you choose to live hope, despite your circumstances?*

▸▸ *If having hope is a choice, is hopelessness also a choice? Why or why not?*

Hope = **Grounded in Faith** + Fueled by Love + Guided by Vision

Are You on a Pilgrimage?

I love the poetic imagery invoked by the word *pilgrim*—though I don't mean turkeys, knickers, or buckles on wide-brimmed hats. We are all familiar with the pilgrims of Thanksgiving fame who sailed from England to the New World in 1620 to live in religious freedom. We even celebrate their arrival with an annual celebration of football and turkey.

Webster's defines a pilgrim as someone who journeys in foreign lands, someone who undertakes a pilgrimage. This is traditionally a visit to a place of some religious or historic significance; a considerable distance is often traveled. We are all on a great journey—one that has religious significance. Jesus said, "In my Father's house are many rooms. ... I go to prepare a place for you" (John 14:2). While there are days this world seems crazy, I find great hope knowing this world is not our final home, but we are on our way there.

> I press on toward the goal for the prize
> of the upward call of God in Christ Jesus.
>
> PHILIPPIANS 3:14

▸▸ *What tries to steal your hope along your journey?*

▸▸ *Who is someone you could encourage today that may need some hope?*

Hope = Grounded in Faith + Fueled by Love + **Guided by Vision**

A Long-Distance Race

*H*ave you ever run a 5K, or perhaps a half marathon? A few years back, I signed up for a half marathon in Chicago. I wasn't a runner; in fact, I hated running. I set out on the twelve weeks of prescribed training and did my best to do everything the experts said to get prepared for the 13.1 miles. I learned a ton about myself over the course of those three months.

I learned that nearly all the limits I place on myself are set in my head, not in my body. I learned that if I set my mind to something, I can do it. But it took training, patience, and great hope. My hope was based in the fact that no matter what happened during the training or the race, I would get something valuable out of the experience. Without hope, I never would've finished.

> Therefore, since we are surrounded by so great a cloud of witnesses, let us also lay aside every weight, and sin which clings so closely, and let us run with endurance the race that is set before us.
>
> HEBREWS 12:1

▸▸ *What is something meaningful you could work toward?*

▸▸ *What limits have you placed on yourself?*

One Word Makes All the Difference

*M*ost people are aware of how various Bible translations use different words to communicate the meaning of a verse. Terry from Pennsylvania sent me the verse that he says gave him hope through the darkest hours: Isaiah 40:31. I learned the verse as, "But they that wait upon the LORD shall renew their strength." But the version Terry sent me said, "Those who *hope* in the LORD …" (NIV).

This version changes the verse from a passive waiting, like you're waiting for a bus, to a more active expectancy. Having hope in the Lord implies a focus and direction, a heart and mind-set. And it seems to fit more with the action implied in the rest of the verse: "They will soar on wings like eagles; they will run and not grow weary, they will walk and not be faint" (NIV).

> But he said to me, "My grace is sufficient for you,
> for my power is made perfect in weakness." Therefore
> I will boast all the more gladly of my weaknesses,
> so that the power of Christ may rest upon me.
>
> 2 CORINTHIANS 12:9

▸▸ *Do your weaknesses allow God's power to shine through?*

▸▸ *How does hope give you strength?*

How Much Hope Do You Have?

*I*f I were to ask you, *On a scale of one to ten, what is your hope level?* what would you say? Some may say a ten and then give me a high five; some may say only a one or two. Your capacity for hope is connected to how intimately you believe God is involved in your life. Journalist and author Norman Cousins said, "The capacity for hope is the most significant fact of life. It provides human beings with a sense of destination and the energy to get started."

If you are looking for a way to increase your hope level, try reading in the Bible how intimately God was involved in the lives of his people. Ask another believer how intimately she feels God is involved in her in life. And then ask God how intimately he wants to be involved in yours. Tell him how much a part of your life you'd like him to be. I'm convinced you'll see hope show up in these beautiful moments of honesty.

> Even though I walk through
> the valley of the shadow of death,
> I will fear no evil,
> for you are with me.
> PSALM 23:4

▸▸ *How does God show up in your life in intimate ways?*
▸▸ *How can you increase your hope level?*

Hope = Grounded in Faith + Fueled by Love + Guided by Vision

Letting Hope Flow through You

*I*f I asked you if you'd like to be a vessel of hope, I'm sure you would say, "Of course!" But if I asked you how to do that, it might be difficult to come up with an answer. This is why so many Christians are discouraged today—they rarely see hope show up in their lives. So what's the answer?

If you're hungry for hope and longing for it to show up in your life, the best thing you can do is show hope to someone else. For example, Isaiah 1:17 says, "Learn to do good. Seek justice. Help the oppressed. Defend the cause of orphans. Fight for the rights of widows" (NLT). If you were to pick one of these four items and begin showing hope to others, you would discover the hope you've been looking for right in front of you.

> He has told you, O man, what is good;
> and what does the LORD require of you
> but to do justice, and to love kindness,
> and to walk humbly with your God?
> MICAH 6:8

▸▸ *How has hope been shown to you?*
▸▸ *How could you live hope to the world around you?*

Do You Want to See the Future?

I love the song "Mary, Did You Know?" in which the singer asks Mary if she had any idea of all the things her little baby would end up doing during his lifetime. It's such a profound song, knowing what we know about Jesus, juxtaposed with the innocence and hope of her newborn baby. Of course, she had no clue—just like we have no clue about what's yet to come in our lives.

Sometimes I'd love to know what's going to happen tomorrow, or next week, or next year. That's a normal desire. But the reality of life is that we can't see beyond the present moment. That's all God gives us—combined with faith enough for the day. So we're faced with the daily choice of worrying about the future or living in the hope for today.

> "Therefore do not be anxious about tomorrow,
> for tomorrow will be anxious for itself.
> Sufficient for the day is its own trouble."
> MATTHEW 6:34

▸▸ *How can faith overturn your desire to know the future?*

▸▸ *Can you trust God with your future and still have goals and dreams?*

Hope = Grounded in Faith + Fueled by Love + Guided by Vision

Tempted to Give Up on Your Dreams?

*I*t can be difficult to have a dream—a goal that you are trying to reach—especially if there are people in your life who think you should give up. I've been told on more than one occasion that I should dream more realistically. There's not anything realistic about a dream—if there is, you're probably not dreaming big enough! But it's important to have hope to hang on to.

I love what author Ayn Rand wrote: "Do not let your fire go out, spark by irreplaceable spark, in the hopeless swamps of the approximate, the not-quite, the not-yet, the not-at-all. Do not let the hero in your soul perish."[2] We should not give up just because we haven't reached our goal. Hope says that this story is still being written and it's going to be something good because God's in it. Don't quit just because you can't see the finish line. It might be around the next corner.

> Jesus looked at them and said, "With man it is impossible, but not with God. For all things are possible with God."
>
> MARK 10:27

▸▸ *What's the benefit of giving up on your dreams?*

▸▸ *What do you think God thinks about your dreams?*

Hope = Grounded in Faith + Fueled by Love + Guided by Vision

Feeling Far from God?

I was talking with a friend last week who felt far away from God. When I asked him if something happened, he said, "Not really. It's just a feeling of being left alone." Is this something you can relate to?

Sometimes we rank our relationship with God on a scale, based on how we feel. I'm thankful for those moments when I have sensed God's intimate presence and his powerful hand working in my circumstances. This is where hope comes in. The Bible says that God is our Father and there is nothing we can do to separate ourselves from his love. We can't make God stop loving us—even when we don't feel it.

Base your hope on God's love for you and that he's pleased with how he made you. There's nothing you can do about it!

> For I am sure that neither death nor life, nor angels
> nor rulers, nor things present nor things to come,
> nor powers, nor height nor depth, nor anything else
> in all creation, will be able to separate us from
> the love of God in Christ Jesus our Lord.
>
> ROMANS 8:38–39

▸▸ *To feel closer to God, should you work harder or rest more?*

▸▸ *Is your hope rooted in circumstance or relationship?*

Hope = Grounded in Faith + **Fueled by Love** + Guided by Vision

Fueled by Love

I'm committed to exploring the topic of hope and helping people understand more fully how to live it out. One of the main elements of living hope is being fueled by love. Everything I do needs to come from a foundation of love.

The foundation of all I do and all I am is firmly rooted in the great love of God. Once that foundation is laid, I can then go out into the world with love as my fuel. God loves me so that I can love others: "Since God loved us that much, we surely ought to love each other" (1 John 4:11 NLT).

The amount of love you have for others will be in direct proportion to the amount of love you believe God has for you. When I am focused on declaring the inherent worth and value of every person I meet, I see hope.

> "This is my commandment, that you love one another
> as I have loved you. Greater love has no one than this,
> that someone lay down his life for his friends."
>
> JOHN 15:12–13

▸▸ *How do you show value and worth to people you meet?*
▸▸ *How do you fill up your love tank?*

Tired of Trying to Do Good?

I often hear people say they are burned-out, tired, and exhausted from all they're supposed to be doing. Perhaps you're one of those people. Maybe you're tired and thinking about quitting. Let me give you some hope from Galatians 6:9: "Let us not grow weary in doing good, for in due season we will reap [a reward]." Though sometimes it doesn't feel like I have much control over how weary I get while waiting.

If I'm neglecting to take care of myself—physically, emotionally, spiritually—then it's no wonder I'm going to wear out. I also should remember why I'm serving others in the first place. It's not to get God to love me more than he already does—that's impossible. But my outward actions are a response to all I've been given. Thank God continually, and you'll find the energy and desire growing inside you to keep serving others.

> So we do not lose heart. Though our
> outer self is wasting away, our inner self
> is being renewed day by day.
>
> 2 CORINTHIANS 4:16

▸▸ *How can you say thank you to God with your life?*

▸▸ *In what way do you need to take better care of yourself?*

FEBRUARY

Hope is found when you grow in your understanding of how deeply and unconditionally loved you are by God.

Would You Like to Change the World?

*H*ope plays a huge part in our ability to change the world. A big part of living hope is having a clear vision for how things can be better, and then taking practical steps in that direction. You can start today! How? Anne Frank put it so well when she wrote, "How lovely to think that no one need wait a moment. We can start now, start slowly, changing the world. How lovely that everyone, great and small, can make a contribution toward introducing justice straightaway. And you can always, always give something, even if it is only kindness."[3]

If you want to change the world instead of being overwhelmed by the magnitude of the task, find something you can do today. Start small and don't give up. The early steps you take will fuel you to keep taking more courageous steps.

> Do not neglect to do good and to share what you have,
> for such sacrifices are pleasing to God.
> HEBREWS 13:16

▸▸ *How do you want to use hope to change the world?*

▸▸ *What is something small you could start doing today?*

Hope = Grounded in Faith + Fueled by Love + **Guided by Vision**

An Emotion or a Decision?

*A*lot of people love the idea of having hope—they are looking for it all around—but very few know where to actually find it. I'm convinced that hope is less of an emotion and more of a decision, a posture one can adopt when you wake up in the morning and through every moment of each day. Romans 12:12 says, "Be joyful in hope." This verse implies that hope is a destination we choose to go to. And then when we're there, we are to be joyful.

I love how Eugene Peterson translates this verse: "Be cheerfully expectant" (MSG). Choosing to live hope in day-to-day life is an important decision you make. Our hope is rooted in faith, fueled by love, and guided by vision. And as a result, we live with great expectancy, filled with joy, looking ahead to see what God is going to do.

> But if we hope for what we do not see,
> we wait for it with patience.
>
> ROMANS 8:25

>> *What attitude would you like to choose each morning?*

>> *How can you more intentionally look for God to work in your life?*

Are You a Control Freak?

I have the capability of being a control freak. I like to plan how I want things to go and then take the required steps to make sure everything happens that way. Unfortunately, that also means trying to maneuver people to get what I want—like a good salesperson. I don't want to be that kind of person. But the reality of life is that things rarely go as planned.

Psalm 37:7 says, "Surrender yourself to the LORD, and wait patiently for him" (GW). Waiting on God is a huge part of hope; it means I trust him. It's faith, which is thankfully a gift from God. I don't have to muster it up. Faith fills in the blanks when we can't see the future, and it lets us rest and wait patiently for what's ahead. That's when hope shows up.

> Therefore, as you received Christ Jesus the Lord,
> so walk in him, rooted and built up in him and
> established in the faith, just as you were taught,
> abounding in thanksgiving.
>
> COLOSSIANS 2:6–7

▸▸ *What or whom do you need to surrender control over?*

▸▸ *How would your prayers change if you surrendered your own desires?*

Hope = Grounded in Faith + Fueled by Love + Guided by Vision

One Thing You Can Do

$\mathcal{S}$ ometimes I face challenges with a blank stare, unsure how to take the first step. Sometimes worry feels like the best option when I face the unknown. If I worry about it, I feel like I'm actually doing something—like I'm working through the problem in my head, trying to find an answer. But the bitter consequence of worry is a feeling of anxiety—head spinning and heart racing. I don't want to live that way.

Philippians 4:6–7 speaks some hope into my mess: "Be anxious for nothing, but in everything by prayer and supplication, with thanksgiving, let your requests be made known to God; and the peace of God, which surpasses all understanding, will guard your hearts and minds through Christ Jesus" (NKJV). Next time you feel worry or anxiety creeping in, thank God for being in complete control of your life. Ask for his help. Figure out one thing you can do to address the problem, but then rest in the peace that passes all understanding.

> Cast your burden on the LORD,
> and he will sustain you;
> he will never permit
> the righteous to be moved.
>
> PSALM 55:22

▸▸ *What is the difference between worry and anxiety?*
▸▸ *To what extent do you believe God is in control of your life?*

Hope = **Grounded in Faith** + Fueled by Love + Guided by Vision

Living Unbroken

*O*ne of the best books I've read is *Unbroken*. It is a biography about Louis Zamperini, a former Olympic track star who survived a plane crash in the Pacific during World War II, spent forty-seven days drifting on a raft, then survived more than two and a half years as a prisoner of war in several brutal Japanese POW camps. The power of his story is not only found in his remarkable strength and resiliency, but also in his ability to later go back and offer forgiveness to his former captors.

I'm struck by the hope he held on to and the hope that his family held on to. Despite all reports, Louie's family believed he was alive. Hope grows deep roots in the face of unbearable circumstances, just as a house built on the solid rock stands firm in the face of great storms. I'm thankful for Louie Zamperini and how he lived hope.

> "Everyone then who hears these words
> of mine and does them will be like a wise man
> who built his house on the rock."
>
> Matthew 7:24

▸▸ *How long would you be willing to hold on to hope for a miracle?*

▸▸ *Why does hope seem so unreasonable at times?*

Hope = **Grounded in Faith** + Fueled by Love + Guided by Vision

Hope through Forgiveness

My buddy told me about a friend of his, Jeff, who has been in prison for thirty years, serving a life sentence. Each time he was up for parole, one of his victim's family members was there to speak against his release. Until this time. Yes, the victim's sister was still there, but something had changed. She believed it was time for him to be released. That it was time for her to forgive and move on. But she had one condition: Jeff was to check in with her once a month and let her know how he was doing.

This story of forgiveness and redemption cuts straight to the heart of the gospel. God doesn't want any of us to live in unforgiveness. Forgiveness doesn't happen when we deserve it; it happens when we don't deserve it.

Take a moment and offer forgiveness to someone in your life—someone who probably doesn't appear to deserve it but who desperately needs it.

> "For if you forgive others their trespasses,
> your heavenly Father will also forgive you, but if you
> do not forgive others their trespasses, neither will
> your Father forgive your trespasses."
>
> MATTHEW 6:14–15

▸▸ *How has unforgiveness taken root in your heart?*

▸▸ *How can you forgive another person even if they aren't sorry?*

Hope = Grounded in Faith + **Fueled by Love** + Guided by Vision

How Much Expectancy Do You Have?

A pastor asked his church full of farmers, "How many of you hope it rains today?" They all raised their hands, needing water for their crops. Then the pastor said, "How many of you brought umbrellas?" And—you guessed it—no one had.

First Peter 1:3 says, "Praise be to the God and Father of our Lord Jesus Christ! In his great mercy he has given us new birth into a living hope through the resurrection of Jesus Christ from the dead" (NIV). Not only is our hope focused on a person, but it can also have a positive effect—an opportunity for us to live with great expectation. I can't wait to see what God has for me and for you. It's going to be good, because his love for us is greater than we can understand. Does your hope have expectations? Did you bring your umbrella?

> For God alone, O my soul, wait in silence,
> for my hope is from him.
> PSALM 62:5

>> *How would you act differently if you truly believed God would answer your prayer?*

>> *How have unmet expectations affected your view of God?*

Hope = **Grounded in Faith** + Fueled by Love + Guided by Vision

Who Is Your Favorite Person?

I've had days when I didn't like myself very much. Sometimes it feels as if I can't do anything right, and I just end up messing things up. I'm thankful I don't spend too much time in that miserable place, but I've visited there frequently.

The more you dislike yourself, the easier it is for you to dislike the world and its inhabitants. But when you discover your own personal awesomeness, life becomes magical. Hope is found when you grow in your understanding of how deeply and unconditionally loved you are by God.

We are all wonderfully made. That uniqueness is so we can feel God's most intimate fingerprint on our lives, which is where true worth and value come from. We are then to take that uniqueness and use it to serve the needs of others. That's when life comes alive and you will be your own favorite person!

> For you formed my inward parts;
> you knitted me together in my mother's womb.
> I praise you, for I am fearfully and wonderfully made.
> Wonderful are your works;
> my soul knows it very well.
>
> Psalm 139:13–14

▸▸ *Why did God make you unique?*

▸▸ *How does a fear of arrogance make you think less of yourself?*

Living Hope in Prison

I'm confronted with the reality of hope on a regular basis while doing a weekly Bible study with a bunch of great guys in prison. It makes me think about where people find hope when every single detail of their life is out of their own hands, and consequently, how much hope I put in my own efforts. Some of these guys are locked up for justifiable reasons, while others are locked up for what seem to be illogical, unjust reasons. I wish the system was perfect, but it's not. So where do these guys place their hope?

My buddy Nick puts his hope completely in the hands of Jesus, trusting that even while he's working with his attorney to reverse his charges, God has him inside the walls for kingdom reasons—it very well might be to lead his cellmate to Christ. His hope looks like peace, confidence, and strength, based not in his own efforts, but in the saving work of God.

> And the peace of God, which surpasses
> all understanding, will guard your hearts
> and your minds in Christ Jesus.
>
> PHILIPPIANS 4:7

▸▸ *How would you hope differently if you had no control over life's details?*

▸▸ *Does helplessness drive you to despair or to hope?*

Hope = Grounded in Faith + Fueled by Love + Guided by Vision

This Isn't Our Home

*I*t doesn't take much these days to see how things in our world are out of control. Does it ever feel like your faith and your hope isn't getting you anywhere?

I find great hope in Hebrews 11, a hall of fame of people who lived by faith, with their sights set on things greater than this world: "Now faith is confidence in what we hope for and assurance about what we do not see. This is what the ancients were commended for" (vv. 1–2 NIV). It continues, "All these people were still living by faith when they died. They did not receive the things promised; they only saw them and welcomed them from a distance. … They were longing for a better country—a heavenly one" (vv. 13, 16 NIV).

If you feel out of place, like this world really isn't your home, then let me encourage you that you're in good company.

> "But seek first the kingdom of God and his righteousness,
> and all these things will be added to you."
>
> MATTHEW 6:33

►► *How can we long for heaven, yet still live effective lives now?*

►► *How could you keep hoping now, if you knew you wouldn't see it come to pass?*

Hope = Grounded in Faith + Fueled by Love + **Guided by Vision**

What's Wrong with Hope?

*I*n a disturbing article about the benefits of giving up hope, the writer said hope keeps us in chains, subject to the powers we hope will intervene on our behalf. He proposed that giving up on hope would allow us to be more proactive to tackle the problems we see in the world, to protect what we love.

This is the flaw in his logic: when we face difficulties, whether from within or without, hope says, *I'm going to get through this. Even though I might not be able to see through this mess, I believe God is in this.*

Hope is one of the most courageous choices you can make each day for the rest of your life—to look beyond the hopelessness of what we see and believe that God is still in the business of making things right, good, and whole again, just as he intends.

And he who was seated on the throne said,
"Behold, I am making all things new." Also he said,
"Write this down, for these words are trustworthy and true."

REVELATION 21:5

▸▸ *In what way could hope be a bad thing?*

▸▸ *When has hope ever made you relinquish your responsibilities?*

Hope = Grounded in Faith + Fueled by Love + Guided by Vision

A Surprise Letter of Hope

A woman who recently attended one of my concerts wrote that she has been worried about her fifteen-year-old grandson, Steven, who is in a detention center. He is overwhelmed with rage and gets in fights. She heard me speak of my prison ministry during the concert and couldn't help but think about her grandson, whom she cares about but felt so helpless as to how to help him.

The day after the concert, she received a long-welcomed letter from him, telling her how much she means to him. Even though the letter was sent before the concert, she knew God was putting it all together so she could get the additional encouragement to be vigilant and continue to be there for Steven, instead of shrugging her shoulders and saying, "Oh well, he brought it on himself," as other family members have said. God is certainly in the hope business.

> But exhort one another every day,
> as long as it is called "today," that none of you
> may be hardened by the deceitfulness of sin.
> HEBREWS 3:13

>> *Is there someone you've given up on who could use a word of hope?*

>> *When is it justified to give up on encouraging someone?*

Will God Ever Intervene?

I went to a parole hearing for one of my buddies recently. As much as it seemed he was ready to get out, I had to go into that little room not knowing whether he'd be offered the opportunity to get out or if he'd have to keep serving additional time. I've seen it go both ways for seemingly incongruent reasons.

God was with us in that room. My hope was directed toward God, that he would intervene. But then there was a time when one must say, "Okay, God—it's all in your hands. I trust you with whatever happens." That surrender can feel like falling off a cliff. But I'm choosing to be a person who believes that God is completely in charge of the world—today and every day. (Thankfully, my friend was offered parole and was released after a short while!)

> In this you rejoice, though now for a little while,
> if necessary, you have been grieved by various trials,
> so that the tested genuineness of your faith—
> more precious than gold that perishes though it is
> tested by fire—may be found to result in praise
> and glory and honor at the revelation of Jesus Christ.
>
> 1 PETER 1:6–7

▸▸ *How do you keep hope alive when God doesn't appear to intervene?*

▸▸ *How does hope leave room for disappointment?*

Hope = Grounded in Faith + Fueled by Love + Guided by Vision

Ever Said You Can't Do Something?

*E*very day we face dozens of choices. Some we don't think about—we just naturally do them. We've done them in the past, and so we do them again. But what about when you're faced with something you don't think you can do? How do you respond? A major sporting-goods company said, "Impossible Is Nothing" to inspire people to believe they can do anything they set their mind to. Thomas Edison said, "When you have exhausted all possibilities, remember this: you haven't."

You might be facing something today and can't see any way through it, much like the friends of Jesus thought after they saw him nailed to the cross and sealed in a tomb behind a giant rock. Jesus basically said to them, "Don't lose hope—I'm going to see you again. Just give me a few days."

Whatever you're going through, hold on to hope that God is at work. With God, you have never exhausted all the possibilities.

I can do all things through him who strengthens me.

PHILIPPIANS 4:13

▸▸ *What is something you can attempt that currently seems impossible?*

▸▸ *How can hope fuel your efforts?*

Does a Little Child Have Hope?

I had a happy childhood—we always had food on the table, clothes in the closet, and plenty to do to stay busy, whether outside playing with friends or being busy with school or sports. Life wasn't perfect, but I didn't have much to worry about—thanks to my parents.

Jesus invites us to live that way today. He said, "Unless you change and become like little children, you will never enter the kingdom of heaven" (Matthew 18:3 NIV). Trusting, lowly, loving, forgiving—there is great hope in living that way.

A kid knows how to live in the moment. As we grow up and turn into serious, responsible grown-ups, somehow hope gets kicked out of us. We become less trusting, less loving, less forgiving. How can we get back to that frame of mind? I have to continually commit myself to trusting God as my Father, loving unconditionally and forgiving outrageously. And I have to get out and play in the yard as often as possible.

> And without faith it is impossible to please him,
> for whoever would draw near to God must believe that he
> exists and that he rewards those who seek him.
> Hebrews 11:6

▸▸ *How do you live like a child?*

▸▸ *What hinders you from living in the moment?*

Focused on the Future

*W*hen we say we have hope, I wonder if it's based too heavily on future optimism, a hope that something good will happen in the future? Pastor and author John Piper defines biblical hope as "a confident expectation and desire for something good in the future."[4] When I'm constantly looking ahead to what I hope happens, or living in the future fantasy of how great things are going to be one day, I miss the beauty of the present moment.

Tomorrow is not promised, so we must believe that this great hope can actually be found today. I live with hopeful expectation of the good God will do, knowing he is always good, whether I see it or not. Romans 8:15 describes the hope-filled life as "adventurously expectant, greeting God with a childlike 'What's next, Papa?'" (MSG). I want to live each day aware of God working in the present, no longer consumed with the unknown future.

> "Remember not the former things,
>   nor consider the things of old.
> Behold, I am doing a new thing;
>   now it springs forth, do you not perceive it?"
>
> ISAIAH 43:18–19

▸▸ *How does thinking about the future make you less present today?*

▸▸ *How much proof do you need before you can trust God?*

Join a Spiritual Movement

I'm curious if you'd like to join forces. I'm not asking for membership dues or even for you to buy anything. But when we join forces and combine our energy in a gospel-driven direction, we can seriously change the world.

Let me give you a few suggestions on how we can do this. First, we need to know the gospel. What is the good news of Jesus and what does it mean for you? Once you answer this question, then you can allow yourself to be changed by God. God promises to make you more like Jesus. Let him do that by his love. As this happens, you will be drawn to give it away. We've been loved so that we can love others. Commit yourself to loving others outrageously and impacting the world around you with your own unique gifts. Are you in?

> "But love your enemies, and do good, and lend,
> expecting nothing in return, and your reward will
> be great, and you will be sons of the Most High,
> for he is kind to the ungrateful and the evil."
>
> LUKE 6:35

▸▸ *How would you describe the gospel in one sentence?*

▸▸ *Who can you love today who you've thought didn't deserve it?*

What Defines You?

The world's definition of success is very different from God's definition. It's easy to think that what you allow to define your worth and value as a person is based on your accomplishments. It's even easy to allow yourself to be defined by what happens to you—the good or bad circumstances thrown at you. I want to live differently. I want to be defined not only by what God thinks about me but also by how I choose to respond to what happens to me.

Instead of looking at my achievements or my circumstances to tell me whether or not I should feel good about myself, or as an indicator of God's love, I'm going to continually choose to be a person of hope. I want to be defined by my posture rather than my performance. I'm calling myself to a whole new way of looking at life—not by what I get out of it, but who I choose to be amid it all—the good and the bad.

> But I will hope continually
> and will praise you yet more and more.
>
> PSALM 71:14

▸▸ *What makes you feel like you have worth as a person?*

▸▸ *How can you root your identity in what God says about you?*

To What Is Your Hope Fastened?

I don't consider myself a big history buff, though I do like to study how great figures in history lived, the choices they made, and the beliefs they held. I'm usually deeply moved and inspired.

For instance, four hundred years ago, a man named Samuel Rutherford grew up in Scotland, becoming a pastor, a theologian, and an author. He said, "Our hope is not hung upon such an untwisted thread as, 'I imagine so,' or 'It is likely' ... Our salvation is fastened with God's own hand, and with Christ's own strength, to the strong stake of God's unchangeable nature."[5]

Rutherford found his hope solely in who God is, not in what he may or may not do in the future. And he lived it out, constantly giving away God's love and the hope of salvation. It was said that Rutherford was constantly praying, preaching, visiting the sick, and always writing and studying. His tombstone ended with the words, "Acquainted with Immanuel's song." I love that.

> Every good gift and every perfect gift is from above, coming down from the Father of lights, with whom there is no variation or shadow due to change.
>
> JAMES 1:17

▸▸ *How much of your hope is based on what you hope God will do in the future?*

▸▸ *What is it about God that you can place your hope in?*

Hope = Grounded in Faith + Fueled by Love + Guided by Vision

When Someone Gets under Your Skin

*M*ax Lucado is one of my favorite authors. He speaks in such simple, yet stunning, language—explaining things of God to me in ways I've never heard.

I just read an entry in his *Grace for the Moment* devotional that struck me. He suggests that when people say or do things that get under our skin, we have a choice in how we're going to react. He writes, "At this point you need to make a choice. *Am I going to keep a list of these wrongs?* You can. … Or you can do something else. You can take those thoughts captive. You can defy the culprit. Quote a verse if you have to: 'Bless those who persecute you; bless and do not curse' (Romans 12:14 NIV). You are not a victim of your thoughts. You have a vote. You have a voice."[6]

Hope tells me I have a choice. I may not be able to choose my circumstances, but I can choose my attitude toward them.

> Finally, brothers, whatever is true, whatever is honorable, whatever is just, whatever is pure, whatever is lovely, whatever is commendable, if there is any excellence, if there is anything worthy of praise, think about these things.
>
> Philippians 4:8

▸▸ *What are you going through now that you could choose to view differently?*

▸▸ *What role have you let resentment and unforgiveness have in your life?*

Hope = Grounded in Faith + Fueled by Love + Guided by Vision

How Often Do You Sin?

I wonder if we too easily fall into the trap of believing that the measure of our success at being a Christian is directly proportional to how often we don't sin. This is interesting, since most of us came to be Christians when we made the realization that we were too weak to control our sinful natures and only through the great hope of God's grace could our sinful natures be purified.

Many Christians lose out on the fantastic power of a personal relationship with Jesus Christ. Instead of seeking that relationship, letting him be the one to remove the desire to sin, we spend our time trying to figure out how to remove the desire to sin, thinking that's how we can have a better relationship with him. Hope says all the work was done on the cross and that God wants you just as you are.

> For God was in Christ, restoring the world to himself,
> no longer counting men's sins against them
> but blotting them out. This is the wonderful
> message he has given us to tell others.
>
> 2 CORINTHIANS 5:19 TLB

▸▸ *What role does sin play in your life?*
▸▸ *How much focus on sin is healthy?*

Sunday Comics

I used to love the Sunday comics as a kid: *Peanuts*, *Blondie*, *Ziggy*, and *Family Circus*. As I have become older, however, I have grown to appreciate the intelligence of *B.C.*, especially when creator Johnny Hart would throw in creative religious references. In one Easter strip, he drew a caveman pointing to an empty tomb and shouting, "Yes!" I admired his courage.

Hart's prehistoric *B.C.* comic strip, which made its debut in 1958, is one of the most popular comics of all time. With *B.C.*, Hart put a caveman twist on everyday life. When he became a Christian in 1984, his newfound faith began to appear in his comics, varying from light-hearted comedy to moving and thought-provoking content. This is what it means to live hope. Does Johnny Hart's courage inspire you as much as it does me?

> And he said to them, "Go into all the world
> and proclaim the gospel to the whole creation."
>
> MARK 16:15

▸▸ *How are you expressing your faith in a courageous way?*

▸▸ *How does Hart's story inspire you to do something to infuse the world with the truth of the gospel?*

When Are Things
Going to Get Better?

I'm not one of those people who, like Chicken Little, walk around proclaiming, "The sky is falling!" even though times are tough for many people. But I wonder if the hard times might be the best time to do a little house cleaning—figure out what needs to go and what needs to stay. Perhaps that is what God is doing with us.

Pastor James Robison says, "This world needs more goodness. But if we try to do good in the world before first becoming good ourselves, we will not succeed. First we must *be*, and then we can effectively *do*." How can we be good? I believe goodness grows through prayer, study, journaling, healthy relationships, and having intentional conversations about God with others. Ultimately, our hope needs to completely be in Christ or else everything will look desperate.

> God is our refuge and strength,
> a very present help in trouble.
> Therefore we will not fear though the earth gives way,
> though the mountains be moved into the heart of the sea,
> though its waters roar and foam,
> though the mountains tremble at its swelling.
>
> PSALM 46:1–3

▸▸ *In what ways do you think the sky is falling?*

▸▸ *How might God be doing his own spring cleaning?*

Hope = **Grounded in Faith** + Fueled by Love + Guided by Vision

Do You Listen to Classical Music?

*L*istening to a beautiful symphony that was written several hundred years ago, I was blown away by the intricacy of the arrangement—it was sophisticated and beyond my comprehension! It was written before computers could assist musicians with their arranging. I pictured the composer with paper spread out, trying to write the right lines that would best feature all the different instruments, not knowing how it would all turn out until the end.

Hope allows people to act, to build something even when they can't see exactly how it's going to turn out. What is God asking you to create? What is it that you could do that can only be done with God's help? I'm starting to learn how to trust God for great things to be done through my simple hands.

> And the LORD will guide you continually
> and satisfy your desire in scorched places
> and make your bones strong;
> and you shall be like a watered garden,
> like a spring of water,
> whose waters do not fail.
>
> ISAIAH 58:11

▸▸ *What have you been hesitant to start since you can't see the finish?*

▸▸ *What would you love to see God do through you?*

Is It Possible
to Change the World?

*I*t's easy to get bogged down in the day-to-day routine. This makes it challenging to be a person who changes the world. Is there anything I can do, or should I not even try?

There is a story of a young boy walking along a beach that is covered with starfish, which have been stranded on the shore by the ebbing tide. One by one, the boy picked up the starfish and threw them into the water. An older gentleman cynically asked, "What are you doing? This beach is covered with starfish! There's no way you will be able to save all these starfish." The boy looked at him, smiled as he threw another starfish into the water, and said, "I may not be able to save all of them, but I saved that one!"

The best way to start making a difference is by doing one action. That's when hope shows up.

> For our boast is this, the testimony of our conscience,
> that we behaved in the world with simplicity and godly
> sincerity, not by earthly wisdom but by the grace of God,
> and supremely so toward you.
>
> 2 CORINTHIANS 1:12

▸▸ *What can do today to change the world for one person?*

▸▸ *What would be a simple mission statement for your life?*

Hope = Grounded in Faith + Fueled by Love + Guided by Vision

Ever Been through a Tornado?

*G*rowing up in the Midwest, I'm familiar with heading down to the basement whenever there was a tornado warning. As a kid, I never worried about what might be happening above. I never worried we would come out of the basement and the rest of the house would be gone! Now that I'm older, it is easier to be cognizant of the potential destruction of the weather, even while taking shelter and waiting for it to pass.

You might be hunkered down in your metaphorical basement, waiting for a storm to pass. Hope doesn't say that nothing's going to happen to your life or to people you love. Hope isn't ignorant of the horrible effects of life's most difficult circumstances. Rather, it believes that God is hunkered down with you, holding you close, reminding you of his love. When the sun returns and you climb out, he'll be there, helping you clear out all the rubble.

> We live within the shadow of the Almighty,
> sheltered by the God who is above all gods.
> This I declare, that he alone is my refuge, my place
> of safety; he is my God, and I am trusting him.
>
> Psalm 91:1–2 TLB

▸▸ *Where is your basement you go to during a storm?*

▸▸ *How can you have hope knowing destruction is swirling all around you?*

Hope = **Grounded in Faith** + Fueled by Love + Guided by Vision

How Much Television Do You Watch?

*T*he average American watches roughly five hours of television every day. That's thirty-five hours a week—1,825 hours in a year. That equals about seventy-six days. Compare that to the fact that on average, a little over thirty-eight minutes per week of meaningful conversation happens between a parent and a child.

A great way to live hope is to shut off the television, computers, or phones for one hour a day—for starters. Spend that hour in meaningful conversation or doing a fun activity together or exercising. Call it an hour of hope. The goal is to spend more time with those you love, less time brainlessly sitting in front of a screen.

Hope comes alive when we try to live intentionally, not passively. Television can entertain, but it can also be a great substitute when one can't think of anything else to do. Live hope with those you love, and turn off the television.

> For you were called to freedom, brothers.
> Only do not use your freedom as an opportunity
> for the flesh, but through love serve one another.
>
> GALATIANS 5:13

▸▸ *How do you live hope with your family?*

▸▸ *How could you change up your normal routine for the better?*

Planting a Hope Garden

*H*ave you ever planted a garden? When you put seed in the ground, you don't set it on top of the soil so you can keep your eye on it; you bury it under the dirt where you can't see it. And then, as tempting as it is, you don't go back and dig up the seed to see if anything is happening—that would destroy the process. You wait. You trust the sunshine, the rain, and your watering will all do its part to make something new out of the seed.

Not every seed will grow, but that doesn't make you a bad gardener. Some plants will grow fruit; others won't. It is not up to us to produce the fruit from the seeds we've planted. Our job is to plant the seeds, water them, and help them to get plenty of light—and wait with great expectation of what might emerge from the dirt.

> Be patient, therefore, brothers, until the coming
> of the Lord. See how the farmer waits for the precious
> fruit of the earth, being patient about it, until it
> receives the early and the late rains.
>
> JAMES 5:7

▸▸ *What tempts you to want to dig up the seeds you have planted?*

▸▸ *How can you water those seeds of faith?*

Last Inning and Down by Eight Runs

I've been on the same softball team for nearly twenty years. Last fall, we had a good game going before the other team had a great inning. It left us at the bottom of the final inning down by eight runs. I love the energy that we all found in the final at bat. I heard things like, "Come on guys, let's get some hits," or "We can do this." But the best thing I heard was, "We've done this before." He was right—we had come back from being behind even more runs and won. Remembering this is when hope appears.

It's easy to feel like you're facing the impossible. But hope comes in and reminds you that you've been through the impossible and survived. Even won. When you feel like hope is far away, remember how God has been faithful; thank him for carrying you through the impossible. And yes, we rallied and scored the needed nine runs to win. A sweet victory of hope.

> Let all that I am praise the LORD;
> may I never forget the good things he does for me.
> PSALM 103:2 NLT

▸▸ *How has God brought you through something in the past?*

▸▸ *What part does remembering play in your life of hope?*

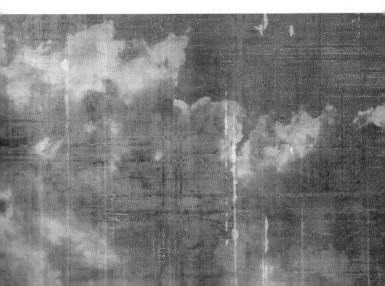

MARCH

To live hope, believe that rescue is near,
and the help you need will be available
as you keep your eyes and hands wide open.

When Tragedy Strikes

*W*hitney's world was shattered when she received a phone call that her husband was dead. The magnitude of not only his death but the way he died was so unbelievable that she didn't know if she was going to be able to survive. "It was Christmas, and I couldn't do anything for myself," she said. "But maybe I could for others. I decided to ask people to help find a family—in particular, a family that had lost someone. I ended up with three families for whom I bought some gifts. It meant more shopping for others and less time thinking about my own situation."

She also told me: "Once I opened up and listened to some of the people around me, I began to understand that others have also gone through tragedy and survived; they had similar stories of not sleeping, eating spoonsful of peanut butter just to get something in their stomachs, or wandering around random stores to pass the time and ease the loneliness."

Whitney discovered hope by bringing it to others. Today's *your* chance to live hope.

> Share each other's troubles and problems,
> and so obey our Lord's command.
> GALATIANS 6:2 TLB

▸▸ *How have you been equipped to help someone else?*

▸▸ *What have you been through that holds you back from knowing hope?*

Hope = Grounded in Faith + **Fueled by Love** + Guided by Vision

Finding Hope at Widow Camp

*W*hitney discovered a nonprofit organization called Soaring Spirits Loss Foundation (SSLF). In addition to providing a network of support for anyone grieving the loss of someone they love, SSLF offers a variety of programs, including Camp Widow. The camp encourages people to put together a support system that is unique to each individual and loss.

"The one thing that we all have in common at Camp Widow is that we have all lost the love of our life, our future, our best friends … that one person we thought would always be there," Whitney told me. "This support system I have built from Camp Widow has given me an outlet, a group of people who will be there whenever I need them, who will understand all my crazy and accept me anyway, and who will be my biggest cheerleaders when I have good days."

May you, too, be encouraged to reach out of your pain to find the support you need.

> "Ask, and it will be given to you; seek, and you will find; knock, and it will be opened to you."
>
> MATTHEW 7:7

▸▸ *Are you ever tempted to think no one would ever understand your troubles?*

▸▸ *Who could you help by coming alongside and fighting the battles together?*

America's Most Important Product

*H*arvey Mackay is a successful businessman and inspirational newspaper columnist. He writes: "The most important product that America has managed to produce is not the automobile, television, or computer. It is hope—not only for ourselves, but for the world. In these times of so much tension and divisive rhetoric, hope is what will sustain us. America is, after all, a country founded on hope."

Mackay continues: "Hope is the reason most of us find a way to keep on keeping on. Hope is what helps us get past the bumps in the road and find a better path. Hope is believing the best is yet to come. Hope is a gift we give ourselves. Hope is a gift we can share with others. Hope is free, yet losing hope comes at a great cost. Hope is within all of us. We just need to let it guide us to a better future."[7]

> "I have said these things to you, that in me you
> may have peace. In the world you will have tribulation.
> But take heart; I have overcome the world."
>
> JOHN 16:33

▸▸ *What is the basis for America's hope?*

▸▸ *How can hope guide you to a better future?*

Hope = Grounded in Faith + Fueled by Love + **Guided by Vision**

Finding Hope in God's Promises

*T*he Bible is filled with thousands of God's promises to hold on to, especially when we aren't feeling strong. There are many times I feel like I have no strength for the task in front of me. I like the promise in Isaiah 40:29: "He gives strength to the weary, and to him who has no might He increases power" (NASB).

Is there a struggle that seems to continually rear its head at you? Find a promise of God in the Bible and write it down, learn it, memorize it, and speak it out loud as a prayer when you need it. When you have hope in God's promises, it says in Romans 5:5 that hope "will never disappoint, because God's love has been abundantly poured out within our hearts through the Holy Spirit who was given to us" (NASB). Hope is as close as a prayer.

> But he said to me, "My grace is sufficient for you,
> for my power is made perfect in weakness." Therefore
> I will boast all the more gladly of my weaknesses,
> so that the power of Christ may rest upon me.
>
> 2 CORINTHIANS 12:9

>> *Why do we try to hide our weaknesses?*
>> *Who might benefit from knowing a struggle of yours?*

When Someone Is Hurting

*H*ave you been through a difficult time and someone said to you, "Just let me know what I can do for you!" It's often well intentioned, but putting the responsibility on an individual to let whoever is asking know what one needs usually gets them off the hook. Then I usually never hear from them. For example, when there's a death in the family, people come around for a brief time, and then it seems as if everyone disappears. Is there a better way to show hope to people who are going through something difficult?

One of the best ways to show hope is by showing up for another person. You don't have to have anything profound to offer. It might just be a pizza or flowers or a lawn mower to cut the grass. When we choose to live hope, we will think of creative ways we can show up for the people in our lives.

> Let each of you look not only to his own interests,
> but also to the interests of others.
>
> PHILIPPIANS 2:4

▸▸ *How do you wish people would have responded differently to something difficult you experienced?*

▸▸ *Who has been through something difficult you could offer hope to?*

Hope = Grounded in Faith + **Fueled by Love** + Guided by Vision

Know Anybody Different?

*I*t's easy to surround yourself only with people who are like you, which can make it difficult to understand or be compassionate toward people who are different. I've worked hard to step outside of the unfortunate boundaries of my homogenized upbringing and develop relationships with people from different backgrounds and experiences, even different perspectives and religions.

To live hope is to learn to love as God loves—showing unconditional love to all people, regardless of who they are, where they're from, or even what they've done. When I'm convinced of God's unbelievable love for me and how that love has nothing to do with my performance, it allows me to give that love away more freely to others. Not to change them, but to change me. That's truly living hope.

> And I pray that Christ will be more and more
> at home in your hearts, living within you as you trust in
> him. May your roots go down deep into the soil
> of God's marvelous love; and may you be able to feel
> and understand, as all God's children should, how long,
> how wide, how deep, and how high his love really is.
> EPHESIANS 3:17–18 TLB

▸▸ *What's the difference between loving with and without an agenda?*

▸▸ *How is God working to expand your boundaries?*

Hope = Grounded in Faith + **Fueled by Love** + Guided by Vision

Can You Make God Love You Less?

*I*t is interesting that most believers are convinced of the unconditional love of God. Yet they don't appear to live like it. Do you think that somehow your behavior can make God love you less than he already does? Many of us are so aware of our faults and shortcomings that if we can beat ourselves up about them, we assume we're showing God that we're truly sorry and repentant. If we're disappointed in ourselves, surely God must be disappointed too. Instead, because of Jesus Christ, we can say, "My sins are covered; I'm forgiven. I'm free from the weight of them."

Instead of focusing on your imperfections, focus on the perfection of God and how he loves you unconditionally. What you do doesn't affect how God feels about you, though it most certainly will affect how you think about yourself. Hope holds firm to Romans 8:38–39, which says nothing can "separate us from the love of God."

> "I, I am he
> who blots out your transgressions for my own sake,
> and I will not remember your sins."
>
> ISAIAH 43:25

▸▸ *How does your sin hold you back from experiencing God's love?*

▸▸ *What part does shame play in your life?*

Patient While Waiting

*H*ope optimistically looks forward into the day, the week, and your life, knowing God is in the middle of it all, bringing about good for those who love him. But a large part of having hope is waiting—for some, this is the hardest part since we live in a culture of immediate gratification. How can we learn to be patient while we're waiting on God?

First, trust that God is with you in your waiting. He's not out there in the future, distant and removed from all you're going through. Second, ask God for patience, and notice when impatience creeps in. Take a breath and let it out before reacting. As you do this, your automatic reaction to impatience will lessen.

As you wait for the job you need, as you're waiting to be healed of your sickness, as you're waiting for your relationship to be restored, keep your eyes on God the fixer and restorer. That's truly living hope, even during the most difficult circumstances.

> For in this hope we were saved. Now hope that
> is seen is not hope. For who hopes for what he sees?
> But if we hope for what we do not see,
> we wait for it with patience.
>
> ROMANS 8:24–25

▸▸ *When are you most tempted to be impatient?*
▸▸ *What inside work is God doing while you wait?*

Does Your Past Keep You from Hope?

*Y*ou can see it on some people ... the way they walk, talk, react to others. You can tell they've been hurt. They're the walking wounded. In a way, isn't that all of us? Many horrible things have happened to so many people, that sadness and brokenness are truly understandable.

We always have a choice about how much power the circumstances of the past have on us. God was with us, even when those bad things were happening. He promises to use everything for our good, even if we can't fathom that right now.

The enemy tempts us to focus on our past to keep us from looking ahead with hope to what God is going to do. Just like we can't drive a car by looking in the rearview mirror the whole time, we can't live that way either.

> I do not consider that I have made it my own.
> But one thing I do: forgetting what lies behind
> and straining forward to what lies ahead,
> I press on toward the goal for the prize of
> the upward call of God in Christ Jesus.
>
> PHILIPPIANS 3:13–14

▸▸ *What in your past have you needlessly focused on?*

▸▸ *What do you need to do to move beyond mistakes of the past?*

Hope = Grounded in Faith + Fueled by Love + Guided by Vision

Hope in the Cross of Christ

*H*ow can the cross give you hope? Jesus demonstrated incredible grace and patience during his final agonizing hours. He didn't put up a fight—he submitted to the torture, even though there wasn't any valid reason why it was happening to him. He knew that God was writing a bigger story than what he was going through. That's the same for you. God is writing a bigger story with your life than what you're currently going through.

Hope says God is in this, and he's not finished with you yet. Hope allows you to go through the trials of today, knowing it's not the end of the story. There is still so much yet to be written. Sometimes I wish the story God was writing with my life was more like I want it to be, but I need to continually look to God as the author and perfecter of my faith—maturing me to be more like Jesus.

> Not only that, but we rejoice in our sufferings, knowing that suffering produces endurance, and endurance produces character, and character produces hope.
>
> ROMANS 5:3–4

▸▸ *How has God matured your faith and character?*

▸▸ *Why do we seek to avoid suffering when it's so beneficial?*

Do Our Pets Show Us Hope?

*A*re you a pet lover? I sure am. I've had dogs all my life. My most recent dog, Kirby, was such a great companion. I was devastated when cancer took the life out of her.

Pets can teach us so much. They're so happy to see us. They don't hold grudges. They are fully present, simply wanting our presence, food, and trips outside. They don't think about how much better tomorrow is going to be because today is all they need. They fully enjoy the moment.

While it's easy to think about hope in terms of looking ahead to the future with optimism, a part of hope is like our pets. Hope lives today without expectations. It is fully present, knowing that God's got it all under control. Don't let your anxiety about the future steal your hope and joy. When you pet your dog, cat, turtle, or snake today, thank God for these beautiful examples of how we can live and love.

> Do not be anxious about anything, but in everything
> by prayer and supplication with thanksgiving let your
> requests be made known to God. And the peace of God,
> which surpasses all understanding, will guard your hearts
> and your minds in Christ Jesus.
>
> Philippians 4:6–7

▸▸ *What can you learn from your pet or others' pets?*
▸▸ *Why do we love our pets so much?*

Finding Something Missing

*H*ave you ever lost your keys, looking all over for them, only to find them out in the open, but you just couldn't see them? It's the strangest thing. I took a walk and saw the most beautiful sunset, but I almost missed it because it quickly went behind a building I was walking past. This made me wonder what else I might be missing, just because I'm not looking for it or because I'm distracted and looking the other way. Is God trying to show you something beautiful you may be missing?

To live hope means to live with your head up, noticing all the beauty around. It means continually looking for the hand of God at work. You'll be amazed at what you've never noticed before. As the old hymn says, "Turn your eyes upon Jesus, look full in his wonderful face. And the things of earth will grow strangely dim, in the light of his glory and grace."

> "Call to me and I will answer you, and will tell you great and hidden things that you have not known."
>
> JEREMIAH 33:3

➤➤ *What distracts you from seeing beauty?*

➤➤ *In what manner were you once blind, but now you see?*

Can Hope Help You Sleep?

*H*ave you ever had insomnia? I've been struggling lately with getting to sleep at night. You know how you just sit there and watch the clock go through its silent routine, picturing that everyone else in the world is asleep? How can hope help us sleep at night? Sometimes I get focused on all that I need to do and how exciting the future is going to be that I can't stop my mind from racing.

Hope looks forward with great anticipation. It also fully rests in the simplicity of today, no matter how much you have or haven't accomplished, but in knowing all that truly matters is that you're God's beloved. You are his child, and he couldn't be more pleased with you than he is right now. Hope trusts that God has the future completely under control, no matter how much you think the outcome depends on you and your good efforts.

> Fear not, for I am with you;
> be not dismayed, for I am your God;
> I will strengthen you, I will help you,
> I will uphold you with my righteous right hand.
>
> ISAIAH 41:10

►► *What causes your mind to race at night?*

►► *How can hope cover your worries and anxieties?*

How Is Life a Journey?

*O*ne of the ways I live hope is by looking at life like a journey. In addition to all the ups and downs that life's journey includes, it also implies that this point where you are at right now is not the end. There is still more to come. Even though you might feel like this is the end, it's not.

As believers in Christ, we can also hold to the promise that our journey is only a blink in the span of eternity. This is where we are getting our training wheels, a practice run for what's to come. This is not all there is. God has you in his hands and is making all that's happening in your life "work together for good" (Romans 8:28).

My task is to remind myself that where I am today, no matter what it looks like, is only a step on the way to where God is taking me.

> God paid a ransom to save you from
> the impossible road to heaven which your fathers
> tried to take, and the ransom he paid was not mere
> gold or silver as you very well know.
> 1 PETER 1:18 TLB

▸▸ *Why do so many believers live trapped in hopelessness?*

▸▸ *What would you call this chapter of life God has you in now?*

How Do You Greet Each Morning?

A new friend and I were talking about living life to the fullest, being adventurous and brave. In his raw, nonreligious way, he said, "When I get up in the morning, I look up and say, 'Okay, what do you have for me today? I'm ready to do anything and go anywhere.'" In a similar way, I love looking to God with open eyes and open hands, asking to be guided toward what he has for me.

Sometimes the best God-ordained moments can be missed when we're not looking for them. Romans 8:15–16 says, "You have received the Spirit of adoption as sons, by whom we cry, "Abba! Father!" The Spirit himself bears witness with our spirit that we are children of God." As a child of God, you can live hope by approaching each day with an expectancy directed straight at the source of all hope.

> Now we have received not the spirit of the world, but the Spirit who is from God, that we might understand the things freely given us by God.
>
> 1 Corinthians 2:12

▸▸ *What helps you fine-tune your attention toward God?*
▸▸ *How have you experienced the guidance of God?*

Looking to God with Expectancy

*A*re you looking to God to bring about new things in your life? If so, what are you doing about it? Some of you may feel stuck in your current job and would love God to bring you something new—are you applying for other jobs? Or maybe you're wanting to sit down and write the novel you've been dreaming about for years—how many words did you write yesterday? How much are you praying about your dreams? Or are you only complaining about them?

To live hope means to not just sit and wait for a dream to come true, but to do the one thing in front of you that will move you in a new direction. God is all about doing new things in and around us. Look to him with great expectancy today, but pray for wisdom to know what the next action step should be.

> Whoever sows sparingly will also reap sparingly, and whoever sows bountifully will also reap bountifully.
>
> 2 CORINTHIANS 9:6

▸▸ *What is one thing you can do today to sow your dream seeds?*

▸▸ *Whose permission are you waiting for before you finally go for it?*

Fighting against Cynicism

*D*o you ever battle cynicism? Cynicism often says, *Well, things have always been this way, so they'll never get any better.* It's a negativity that looks to our past painful experiences and assumes our future experiences will also be painful. That's not hope. Hope says that despite how our past has been, God is involved in writing a new story with our lives. He is all about making things new.

Author Sara Hagerty describes the battle between cynicism and hope: "I will not talk myself out of hope, hiding behind Scripture to support all my reasons for being 'wise' and 'measured' in my responses to the not-yets in my life. Because when I choose hope, when I choose to engage in that awkward intimacy of believing that He might say no while asking expectantly that He say yes, He gets the most beautiful part of me."[8]

Give God the most beautiful part of yourself by hoping with expectancy today.

> "Therefore I tell you, whatever you ask in prayer,
> believe that you have received it, and it will be yours."
>
> MARK 11:24

▸▸ *How do you talk yourself out of hope?*
▸▸ *How can you be both realistic and hopeful?*

Responding to God

*I*t's always interesting how differently people react at my concerts. There are some places I go where people sit there, as if
they're just biding time until I'm finished. There are other places
where I see people engaged, smiling, and nodding at what I say.
And then there are places where people are interacting, talking
back to me, laughing, and even shouting amens. I'm not doing
anything differently in these different contexts, but it's the way
people are choosing to respond that is different.

How you choose to respond to what God is doing in your
life shapes the person you are. It might not be the volume of
your response, but *how* you respond. I'm committed to being a
person of gratitude, continually saying thank you to God for all
he's done, all he's doing, and all he's going to do. I want to tell him
that I see what he's up to, even if it's just a glimpse. Gratitude is
my secret weapon against hopelessness.

> Give thanks in all circumstances; for this is
> the will of God in Christ Jesus for you.
> 1 THESSALONIANS 5:18

▶▶ *How are you responding to what God is doing?*
▶▶ *Why is gratitude so powerful?*

Why Is Authenticity Such a Commodity?

A lady came up to me in Florida and told me how much she loves hearing the *Live Hope Minute* on the radio. She and her daughters listen every morning on their way to school. I'm blown away that people hear this little feature that I create in my kitchen. She appreciates my authenticity, which is the best compliment I could get. But it makes me wonder why authenticity is such a commodity.

Most people, especially in those leadership positions, are afraid of showing too much of their humanity because it might put them in jeopardy of losing their jobs. So they create a culture of perfection that can't possibly exist, since we are all flawed humans who are desperately in need of a Savior. Can I encourage you to live hope today by choosing to be truly authentic with others? Let's admit how we are choosing to live hope, despite how challenging life can be.

> Therefore, confess your sins to one another and pray for
> one another, that you may be healed. The prayer of
> a righteous person has great power as it is working.
>
> JAMES 5:16

▸▸ *Whom can you be more authentic with?*
▸▸ *What is the value of practicing authenticity?*

How Timely Is God?

"God is never late, but always on time." This saying reminds me of all the movies I've seen where you know the superhero is about to show up, even though it seems as if the bad guy is going to win. It makes a good story, unless you're the person dangling from the top of the building waiting to be rescued!

If you're waiting on God, let me encourage you with the timelessness with which God seems to operate. Second Peter 3:8 says, "But do not overlook this one fact, beloved, that with the Lord one day is as a thousand years, and a thousand years as one day." You might have been waiting a long time for a loved one to come to the Lord, or for the healing of a sickness, or something else. Know that God is with you, he knows what you're going through, and he's at work behind the scenes in ways you cannot see.

To live hope, trust that God is not waiting for you to fall. He promises his presence, help, and love, no matter the circumstances.

> A thousand years are but as yesterday to you!
> They are like a single hour!
> PSALM 90:4 TLB

▸▸ *How can we trust God's plan when it doesn't look like ours?*

▸▸ *What promises of God can you hang on to while waiting?*

Been Moved Out of Your Comfort Zone

I had a friend who wanted to live his dreams, but it took getting fired from his job to move him in that direction. He had been working in a ministry for nearly twenty-five years but always struggled at being content with the positions he held. His dream was not more leadership, more stress, or more hours working; his dream was something that looked a bit more like self-employment, something that would afford him more flexibility of schedule to spend time with his family. God knew his heart, just as he knows your heart.

Sometimes we get caught in the surface stuff when God is working underneath, seeing into the depths of our heart, as my friend discovered when he was let go through the ministry's downsizing. Living hope goes beneath the surface to the depths of our hearts, seeking to eliminate the barriers to bring our wildest dreams to life.

> You have multiplied, O LORD my God,
> your wondrous deeds and your thoughts toward us;
> none can compare with you!
> I will proclaim and tell of them,
> yet they are more than can be told.
>
> PSALM 40:5

▸▸ *What would it look like for you to live from your heart?*
▸▸ *What barriers are preventing you from living that way?*

Hope = Grounded in Faith + Fueled by Love + Guided by Vision

Prisoners of Hope

*W*hile we are all sinners, we are in prison. Yet we aren't without hope because of the way out provided by our stronghold, Jesus Christ. The prophet Zechariah spoke to being a prisoner of hope: "Return to your stronghold, O prisoners of hope; today I declare that I will restore to you double" (Zechariah 9:12). Do you feel trapped by the prison of sin? Are you trapped in addiction or a mind-set that doesn't honor God?

Jesus is offering you rescue. Let him know what you're thinking, how you're struggling, and how you'd like him to help. And then find other people who can come alongside you and help you keep seeking Christ as your hope. You don't have to do it alone. In fact, many people will say you *can't* do it alone. To live hope, believe that rescue is near and the help you need will become available, as you keep your eyes and hands wide open.

> Shake yourself from the dust and arise;
> be seated, O Jerusalem;
> loose the bonds from your neck,
> O captive daughter of Zion.
>
> Isaiah 52:2

▸▸ *What would you like to be rescued from?*

▸▸ *What will you gain by asking others for help?*

Hope in Sinfulness?

*N*ewsweek reported that to accommodate people, many clergy have airbrushed sin out of their sermons. I argue that there is actually great hope found in sin. Instead of stopping at the part about how everyone is a sinner and how we need to stop sinning to get into heaven, looking at sin and its destruction allows us to see how a loving God doesn't want us to hurt ourselves or others.

Sin brings about destruction, creating separation. But God is all about restoration and making the broken whole again. He offers forgiveness for the sins you've committed, and he invites you to look at life with hope, seeing the value of not sinning as a way of honoring him and others. There's no room for shame in the gospel; there's only room for hope. Sin is not the end of the story—forgiveness and salvation are offered freely to all.

> I am completely discouraged—I lie in the dust. Revive me by your Word. I told you my plans and you replied. Now give me your instructions. Make me understand what you want; for then I shall see your miracles.
>
> Psalm 119:25–27 TLB

>> *What role have guilt and shame played in your relationship with God?*

>> *Where are you experiencing separation between you and others? You and God?*

Courage to Hope

*T*here are so many signs that our culture is growing in wickedness and destruction. Pundits and newscasters love to point out all that's wrong in our world, how what *might* happen could ruin everything. We must remain vigilant and aware, for these days are calling us to catch a godly vision for how things can be. It takes great courage to live hope.

Hope casts a vision for how our lives can reveal the beauty and glory of God. It also works to bring that vision to life. It stays focused, allowing our steps to be guided. God is asking us to help build his kingdom of love, which requires us to move into dark places where there doesn't appear to be much love or hope. Hang on to the vision, for God will guide you and equip you to do his hope-building work.

> "Be strong and courageous. Do not fear or be in dread of them, for it is the LORD your God who goes with you. He will not leave you or forsake you."
>
> DEUTERONOMY 31:6

▸▸ *What sort of vision might God be building in you?*

▸▸ *How does the love of God help you to be brave?*

What Music Are You Listening To?

"*H*ope is the ability to hear the music of the future, while faith is having the courage to dance to it."[9] Hope presses its ear to the train track to hear the oncoming train, even when it can't be seen. Hope listens to the birds outside the window announcing the coming spring. Hope listens for God by praying with expectancy and trusting he will answer. The music of the future resonates in your heart and tells you that everything is going to be okay, even when it doesn't appear that way.

When you have the courage to dance to the music of hope, you risk looking like a fool. You'll look like a person who doesn't belong to this world. And you'll look like a person whose house is built on solid rock, not sand. Count me in.

> Do not be conformed to this world, but be transformed by the renewal of your mind, that by testing you may discern what is the will of God, what is good and acceptable and perfect.
>
> ROMANS 12:2

▸▸ *How is hope enough to make you dance?*

▸▸ *How much certainty do you need before you have hope?*

Hope = Grounded in Faith + Fueled by Love + **Guided by Vision**

Hope for Heaven

*I*n *Mere Christianity*, C. S. Lewis writes about Christians looking forward to the eternal world, not as escapism or wishful thinking, but as something we're meant to do. But that doesn't mean we leave the present world simply as it is: "If you read history you'll find that the Christians who did most for the present world were just those who thought most of the next."[10] So, how can we live fueled by the hope of heaven, yet still maintain a proper perspective on our lives now?

God is inviting us to help him build his kingdom of love—everything we do should be viewed through that mission. To live with eternity in mind means seeing the meaninglessness of much of what we busy ourselves with, keeping our eyes focused on that which we all hunger for—the beauty and wholeness we will experience in heaven.

> "Who then is the faithful and wise manager,
> whom his master will set over his household,
> to give them their portion of food at the proper time?
> Blessed is that servant whom his master will find
> so doing when he comes. Truly, I say to you,
> he will set him over all his possessions."
>
> LUKE 12:42–44

▸▸ *How does heaven make life more valuable?*

▸▸ *What are some practical ways you could show the worth you place on this world?*

Hope = Grounded in Faith + Fueled by Love + **Guided by Vision**

Trusting God's Timing

*H*ope is found while we wait on God with patience and trust. I struggle with this, wishing God would do everything I want him to do, exactly when I think it's best. When I'm committed to living hope, I'm going to have faith in God, that he's at work and doing what I can't see. But when the days are quiet and the victories seem too far in between, I rest in the hope I claim to have—believing God's timing is best.

Holding too firmly to the way I want things to be different pulls me out of the present moment; I can easily miss what God is doing in front of me. I like to operate on my own schedule, but God is asking me to lay that down and simply abide with him—to simply rest in his arms while I wait.

> And going a little farther, he fell on the ground
> and prayed that, if it were possible, the hour might
> pass from him. And he said, "Abba, Father, all things
> are possible for you. Remove this cup from me.
> Yet not what I will, but what you will."
>
> MARK 14:35–36

▸▸ *What plans are tempting to pull you out of the present moment?*

▸▸ *How can you abide with God today?*

Bravery in the Midst of Pain

Richard has been struggling with some debilitating physical conditions that have left him unable to walk. He wrote, "Because of everything that is going on with me lately, the message of *I Live Hope* has become one that I am trying to embrace, not just concerning my health but in every aspect of my life. I am starting out a lot slower than I would like, but for me, if I am without hope, then I am without life."

He wrote further: "My hope is not grounded in the doctors, the medical treatments, or even my family, who have been a major source of encouragement and support. *I Live Hope* is grounded in Jesus Christ, His promises to never leave me nor forsake me, and the promise that the Holy Spirit would be with me no matter what I am facing."

> The LORD is my strength and my shield;
> in him my heart trusts, and I am helped;
> my heart exults,
> and with my song I give thanks to him.
>
> PSALM 28:7

▸▸ *What is your hope grounded in?*

▸▸ *How can you demonstrate to the world that you live hope?*

Escaping Isolation

*O*ne of the best lies the enemy uses against us is to tell us that life is better in isolation. Everyone knows that when you start dealing with people, your hands get messy; or nobody actually cares what you're going through, so it's best to just keep it to yourself. You can even be surrounded by people, yet still living in isolation, guarding your heart against additional pain and sadness you've already experienced. God says to get out and love people.

Ephesians 5:2 says, "And walk in love, as Christ loved us and gave himself up for us, a fragrant offering and sacrifice to God." Give your life to someone else by loving them. A big part of loving them is the willingness to share your heart with them, to share your personal story, trusting that God can use it to be an encouragement to them and will bring hope to yourself. Step out of the shadows and let God shine his light through you.

> "Even as the Son of Man came not to be served
> but to serve, and to give his life as a ransom for many."
> MATTHEW 20:28

▸▸ *How qualified do you have to feel to love people?*

▸▸ *What is the value of alone time? When can it be detrimental?*

Hope in Your Suffering

*M*any people are going through incredibly difficult circumstances. Perhaps even you. When I go through difficult circumstances, it's easy to say, "Why, God? Why am I going through this?" And to be honest, it's rare to get an answer in the moment. Usually, the answer comes a bit later when I meet someone going through something I've already been through. That's when hope shows up for that other person, through the compassion and understanding that was birthed in me during my difficult circumstances.

Second Corinthians 1:4 says that God "comes alongside us when we go through hard times, and before you know it, he brings us alongside someone else who is going through hard times so that we can be there for that person just as God was there for us" (MSG). Hope is found by trusting the presence and love of God amid what we're going through, and then giving it away to others when we see an opportunity.

> Comfort, comfort my people, says your God.
> Isaiah 40:1

▸▸ *Who do you know that could use some comforting or companionship?*

▸▸ *Why is it so easy to get stuck focusing on our own pain and troubles?*

Does Your Hope Have Courage?

*W*hen you're waiting on God, it takes courage to keep hoping. Some define *courage* as a strength, an inner fortitude, to keep going even when it's tough. But the root of the word is *cor*, which is the Latin word for heart. This implies that courage is more based in your heart than in your strength. Having courage is related to how and where your beliefs are pointing.

Deuteronomy 31:6 says, "Be strong and of good courage, do not fear nor be afraid of them; for the LORD your God, He is the One who goes with you. He will not leave you nor forsake you" (NKJV). Perhaps you're a fan of *The Lord of the Rings* and know this quote: "Take courage, Lord of the Mark; for better help you will not find."[11] Having courage, rooted in faith, keeps you hoping even when you can't imagine holding on for another minute.

> Wait for the LORD;
> be strong, and let your heart take courage;
> wait for the LORD!
>
> PSALM 27:14

▸▸ *Where do you look for strength and help when faced with difficult tasks?*

▸▸ *In what area of your life would you like to have more courage?*

APRIL

Hope says, *Yes, I believe, even though I don't feel like believing right now. But I trust that God is good and he is with me.*

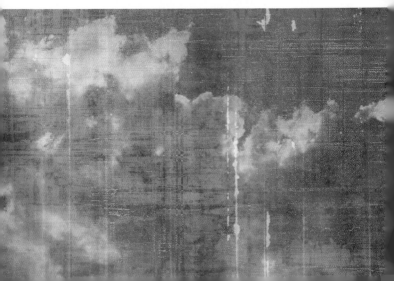

Hope in Context

I was reading an article about a man who does biblical archae-ology. He said, "God acted at a particular time, a particular place, and among a particular people. Thus, God's revelation to His people needs to be understood in a space-time continuum."[12] This makes me wonder if your hope has a context to it too.

To know how God is going to operate in the future, we can look to the past to see how God has already operated. I can have hope in God for his presence during my difficult times because I know God has been there for me in the past. I can put my hope in God for strength and help because he's been there for me in the past. Placing our faith in him, and waiting to see how he's going to show up, is one of the best ways to live hope.

> But let him ask in faith, with no doubting,
> for the one who doubts is like a wave of the sea
> that is driven and tossed by the wind.
>
> JAMES 1:6

▸▸ *How has God shown his faithfulness to you in the past?*

▸▸ *What is the best way to wait for God with hope?*

Hope = Grounded in Faith + Fueled by Love + Guided by Vision

Where Are You Finding Refuge?

*W*e had a huge rainstorm the other day in Nashville. I love going out on my patio when a big storm is going on and watching and listening to the incredible force of nature happening just a few feet away from the safety of my shelter. Do you feel like you're experiencing a gully-washer in your own life right now? Where do you find shelter during the storm?

Nahum 1:7 says, "The LORD is good, a refuge in times of trouble. He cares for those who trust in him" (NIV). God longs to be your shelter—the place you go when you need to escape from the downpours of life. To be honest, I've haven't ever experienced a storm that didn't end. The rain always subsides, the dark clouds move on, and the sun returns. I want to hold on to hope whether I can see the sun or not. I trust it's still there, even behind the darkest clouds and heaviest storms.

> For the LORD is good;
> his steadfast love endures forever,
> and his faithfulness to all generations.
>
> PSALM 100:5

▸▸ *How can you be a shelter to someone in need?*

▸▸ *How do you experience God's love and care during a storm?*

Can You Do What Scares You?

I'm honored to have this minute each day to deposit some hope into your life. Today I offer you my humanity. By that, I mean that writing this has been difficult for me. Coming up with one of these for every day was an incredibly daunting task that frightened me. What if I say something wrong? What if I say something about God that isn't true? The enemy often tries to paralyze me with questions like, *Who do you think you are?*

My point is this: we are all the same. We all have hopes and dreams that fuel us, but we also have things that scare us to death. But when I pray, "God, you've got to show up, because I've got nothing," He does, and I know again that hope is real. Fighting through the fear is something I need to continue to do. It's something we all can do.

> The LORD is on my side; I will not fear.
> What can man do to me?
>
> PSALM 118:6

▸▸ *What important task do you face today that tempts you to fear?*

▸▸ *To what extent does perfectionism hold you back from trying?*

Love and Boundaries

*J*esus set the bar high for how much we are supposed to love in John 15:13: "Greater love has no one than this, that someone lay down his life for his friends." I often think about Jesus, who, out of his great love, went to the cross for us. But I've struggled with boundaries. I'm willing to do so much for other people, regardless of what I get in return, but it's often to my own detriment. I think my zealous desire to lay down my life for others has hurt me at times, leaving me exhausted, bitter, resentful, and wondering, *When is someone going to lay down his life for me?*

I have to remember that God is taking care of me, but I also need to learn to take care of myself, loving myself as best I can, and then I'll be fully equipped to give away my life to others. My roots must be solid in God's firm foundation before I can focus on the fruit I want to give away.

> Beloved, let us love one another,
> for love is from God, and whoever loves
> has been born of God and knows God.
>
> 1 JOHN 4:7

▸▸ *How can you let go of resentment without denying your valid feelings?*

▸▸ *How does disappointment lead you to better personal boundaries?*

Waiting for the Hope Bus

*L*amentations 3:26 says, "It is good that one should hope and wait quietly" (NKJV). This makes me think about seeing people waiting at the bus stop. They are usually quiet, sitting or standing in one place. They are expectant that their bus will arrive at its expected time.

Have you ever met someone who is impatient? He keeps looking at his watch, trying to see if there's a bus coming in the distance through the oncoming traffic, wondering out loud, "Where is that bus?" I've been that person, even though sometimes I just want to say to the impatient person, "Relax! It's coming—just like it always does."

When we wait and hope quietly and with patience, we can stay present and keep our stomachs from getting tied up in knots.

> But for me it is good to be near God;
> I have made the Lord God my refuge,
> that I may tell of all your works.
>
> Psalm 73:28

▸▸ *While you're waiting, who are other people near you who are also waiting?*

▸▸ *How can you be a source of hope and encouragement to them?*

When You Don't Believe

*P*salm 42 starts off with this familiar phrase: "As the deer longs for streams of water, so I long for you, O God" (NLT). But this isn't a happy chapter. The person who wrote it is in major pain. It's a conversation between the side that hurts and the side that still wants to have faith. I have those kinds of conversations sometimes!

Then I come to Psalm 42:5, which says, "Why are you cast down, O my soul, and why are you in turmoil within me? Hope in God; for I shall again praise him." This is the essence of hope. Hope says, *Yes, I believe, even though I don't feel like believing right now. But I trust that God is good and he is with me; he is working all things for my good, so that I can indeed praise him again—hopefully soon.*

> O God, you are my God; earnestly I seek you;
>> my soul thirsts for you;
>> my flesh faints for you,
> as in a dry and weary land where there is no water.
>
> PSALM 63:1

▸▸ *What circumstances cause you to doubt God's goodness?*

▸▸ *What would be the benefit of choosing hope in those situations?*

Rest Your Mind

*W*orry is what causes my mind to race, my stomach to get into knots, and my soul to start giving into fear. Sometimes it is good for me to run through situations in my head, to be responsible and concerned. But sometimes it is good to let my mind rest, taking intentional time to not think about all that is spinning in my head.

Writer Sarah Young says that worry is largely a matter of thinking about life at the wrong time. That means there's a right and a wrong time to think about certain situations. When you're trying to fall asleep, for example, which is my favorite time to worry, probably isn't the best. I love thinking through things with a pen and paper. Expressing my thoughts, and then offering them up to God with a prayer, helps my mind to rest like it needs.

> "Therefore I tell you, do not be anxious about your life,
> what you will eat or what you will drink, nor about
> your body, what you will put on. Is not life more
> than food, and the body more than clothing? Look at the
> birds of the air: they neither sow nor reap nor gather into
> barns, and yet your heavenly Father feeds them.
> Are you not of more value than they?"
>
> MATTHEW 6:25–26

▸▸ *Do you have a wrong time to think about things? When might be better?*

▸▸ *How can you surrender worry without giving up responsible concern?*

Do You Need a Nap?

*D*o you love naps but never get one? What about your spiritual life? Are you tired and worn out? I love what Jesus said in Matthew 11:28: "Are you tired? Worn out? Burned out on religion? Come to me. Get away with me and you'll recover your life. I'll show you how to take a real rest" (MSG). He's obviously offering us an alternative to busyness and stress, and being overburdened by expectations.

How do we get away with Jesus and find this rest? It's as simple as shutting off all the noise, closing my eyes, and reminding myself what I believe about him—how he's taking care of me, and how he's a God of hope and not stress. I remind myself that there's nothing I need to do to earn his love and nothing I can do to escape it. I'm saturated with his love—nothing needed to prove or accomplish. That's a Jesus nap.

> On the last day of the feast, the great day,
> Jesus stood up and cried out, "If anyone thirsts,
> let him come to me and drink."
>
> JOHN 7:37

▸▸ *What makes you feel worn out in your spiritual life?*

▸▸ *Which promise of God offers you the best feeling of rest?*

Ready for a God Promotion?

*A*re you ready for what God has for you next? First Peter 5:6 says, "If you will humble yourselves under the mighty hand of God, in his good time he will lift you up" (TLB). What does "lift you up" mean? That he will *raise me up on eagle's wings*? That love will *lift me up where I belong*? Pardon the humorous song references, but I have always thought of that verse as meaning that when I'm humble, God will promote me.

I'm not sure if it means God will take me from this place of struggle into a new place of pleasure and bliss, or if it means that once I figure out this level of faith, then it's time to be challenged on the next level. But I know that hope says God is loving me best by turning me into his son. God is making me holy and perfect. That's the kind of promotion I can look forward to!

> One's pride will bring him low,
> but he who is lowly in spirit will obtain honor.
>
> PROVERBS 29:23

▸▸ *How is God refining you, making you more like Jesus?*

▸▸ *In what ways do you need to humble yourself?*

Do You Ever Feel Apathetic?

*I*t's impossible to keep track of everything going on in the world, much less have the correct opinion, or even know what is actual truth. It's a challenge to not become numb. It's a subtle but completely paralyzing one-two punch of apathy. Apathy is a lack of interest, concern, or emotion. It's a flat-lined, comatose state of living that feels like nothing.

Hope and apathy can't coexist. Hope believes things can always get better, but apathy says, *I don't care*. Hope tries to find ways to tear down walls and build bridges, while apathy doesn't even try. To live hope means we engage the world around us, to come alive to how God wants to break our heart and use that to build compassion for others. Though hope requires us to get our hands dirty, we keep choosing to look at the world through the lens of hope.

> Finally, be strong in the Lord and in the strength
> of his might. Put on the whole armor of God, that you
> may be able to stand against the schemes of the devil.
>
> EPHESIANS 6:10–12

▸▸ *What dilemma are you apathetic about?*

▸▸ *What need do you see in the world that breaks your heart?*

Hope through Compassion

*W*hat I see happening in our society is that we are constantly picking sides. Our side is the good guys, while the other side is the bad guys. Then we find the best way to fight the battle so that we win. This happens in sports, politics, and even religion.

It's not difficult to be consumed with constantly trying to identify what organizations or persons are different from us, opposed to us, or even dangerous. It might be easy to point and then run for cover, but how much more of an act of faith might it be to move toward those we oppose, seeking understanding and demonstrating compassion? This is not so we can drag them over to our side, but so we can see God in each of us more clearly.

Can you imagine someone saying to you, "How refreshing is it to meet a Christian who is actually loving and not judgmental and trying to get me to change"? When I find similarities between me and those I used to judge, I know that's when I'm living hope.

> The LORD is gracious and full of compassion,
> slow to anger, and great in mercy.
>
> PSALM 145:8

▸▸ *How will you love somebody who sees God's best differently than you?*

▸▸ *How has your love for others been (however slightly) entangled by an agenda?*

Are You on a Journey?

*A*re you boldly going after a dream that God has placed in your heart? If so, I want to encourage you and dump hope all over you. If you're anything like me, the road you're on can be challenging at times. The difficulty of the journey can be overwhelming. Even though the road is long and it can be difficult, you are not alone. God is carrying you. It's not all up to you.

God is aware of where you're at and what you're going through. He is with you. And don't forget that his love for you is the same amount of love he'll have for you when you get where you're going. And do me a favor—don't let other people's discouragement or small-mindedness discourage you from your path.

> "Write the vision;
>   make it plain on tablets,
> so that he may run who reads it.
> For the vision is yet for an appointed time;
>   it hastens of the end—it will not lie.
>   If it seems slow, wait for it;
>   it will surely come; it will not delay."
>
> HABAKKUK 2:2–3

▶▶ *How are the challenges of pursuing your dream making you more like Jesus?*

▶▶ *What part does God play in the pursuit of your goals?*

Hope = Grounded in Faith + Fueled by Love + Guided by Vision

The Most Powerful Force that Holds Us Back

The powerful force that holds us back from living a life of hope is fear—fear of the unknown, fear of what might happen. We prefer the comfort and stability of where we are at, even if it isn't exactly where we want to be. It's what's familiar, and it's what we know. Even if it's not completely fulfilling, it's better than being seen as a failure, or bringing pain and discomfort into our life.

I refuse to let fear have any place in my life. It pulls up in front of my house sometimes, engine rumbling; sometimes it even comes up and knocks on my door. But I'm not answering. When you're tempted to fear, stop and remind yourself of the faith you have in God—you are loved and cared for, that he is with you. The fear will melt away and hope will emerge.

> "Behold, I am with you and will keep you
> wherever you go, and will bring you back to this land. For
> I will not leave you until I have done
> what I have promised you."
>
> GENESIS 28:15

▸▸ *How does fear hold you back from a life of hope?*

▸▸ *How can you prepare to reject fear the next time it raises its head?*

Hope Is Found in Relationship

*J*esus told the Pharisees that the greatest commandment is "'Love the Lord your God with all your passion and prayer and intelligence.' This is the most important, the first on any list. But there is a second to set alongside it: 'Love others as well as you love yourself'" (Matthew 22:37–39 MSG). God wants us to be in relationship with him and with others.

You may have heard the phrase "No man is an island." Well, we sure try sometimes. It's important to be surrounded by people who are tuned into God, people who see things I miss, people who hear what I'm not listening for, people who understand what I can't comprehend. We need to be surrounded by people who pull us into a deeper place of realization that God is alive and longs to be trusted and loved, and people who remind us of hope, even when we're blind to the evidence of it surrounding us.

> Whoever walks with the wise becomes wise,
> but the companion of fools will suffer harm.
>
> PROVERBS 13:20

▸▸ *Who is someone you can thank for being a person of hope to you?*

▸▸ *What circumstances cause you to isolate?*

Hope = Grounded in Faith + **Fueled by Love** + Guided by Vision

How's Your Vision?

*L*egendary baseball guy Yogi Berra said that if you don't know where you're going then you'll end up somewhere else. Most of us don't know what we want or where we're going. We are so busy consuming what is advertised to us, as what will bring us joy, that we end up with a false desire for what we don't actually want. That's why it's important to have vision—to clearly define exactly where you want to go. That's when hope shows up.

Once you have clearly defined your objective, then you can more easily identify the steps it will take to get you there. Being unclear will only lead down a road that will take you someplace you don't want to go. God is on your side, working behind the scenes on your behalf, leading you down the path he wants you on. Romans 8:28 reminds us, "And we know that in all things God works for the good of those who love him, who have been called according to his purpose" (NIV). The best way to get someplace is to know where you are going.

> For you are my rock and my fortress;
> and for your name's sake you lead me and guide me.
>
> PSALM 31:3

▸▸ *How do you sense God leading down the path?*

▸▸ *What gets in the way of moving the direction you want to go?*

Delighting in the Lord

*P*salm 37:4 says, "Delight yourself in the LORD, and he will give you the desires of your heart." I can't run after the desires of my heart and expect to delight in the Lord; I can't run after my desires and expect God to delight in me. When I delight, or find joy and my identity, in God, that's when I find him in me. He awakens me to his desires inside my heart. That's what we need to wake up to.

God puts desires in our hearts to be the compass that guides us on the path he wants us to be on. If you're his, it's time to dive into your heart and uncover the desires that are hidden there. Are you waiting for someone to give you permission to start living the desires of your heart? Here's your chance. Today's the day to reclaim that fire of desire that has been smoldering in the background of your heart. What are you waiting for?

> Let me hear in the morning of your steadfast love,
> for in you I trust.
> Make me know the way I should go,
> for to you I lift up my soul.
>
> PSALM 143:8

>> *What buries the desires in our hearts that God has placed there?*

>> *How do we uncover them most effectively?*

What Do You Hope For?

*W*hen you think about hope, do you have expectations? Do you ever say you put your hope in God for your health to get better, or for your income to improve, or for your life to be more comfortable? I once asked my pastor what he placed his hope in God for, trying to see what realistic expectations I could have of God. He said, "I don't put my hope in God for anything. I simply put my hope in God."

What would it look like to simply say, "God, my hope is in you. I have no expectations about what you're going to do for me. I will simply trust you. I trust that you love me, you're caring for me, and you'll continue to make good out of all things, even if they don't look so good to me"?

My desire is to grow more and more in my understanding of how to place my hope in God without having any expectations about how he should be doing his job.

> And now, O Lord, for what do I wait?
> My hope is in you.
> PSALM 39:7

▸▸ *How is it possible for hope to have unrealistic expectations?*

▸▸ *What would it mean to solely have hope in God, not in what he does for you?*

Hope = **Grounded in Faith** + Fueled by Love + Guided by Vision

Follow the Money

*W*here does the money go when you put it in the offering plate? I try not to worry about that because I'm choosing to trust the leadership of my church to do the right thing with the money. But what about the person on the street corner asking for money? Should I follow her to find out what she spends it on?

Living hope means saying, "God, I'm going to do my part, and I'm going to give my portion, and I'm going to trust you to do with it exactly what you desire and what will bring you the most glory." I want to live being extremely generous in all aspects, but I also want to continually surrender my desire to know exactly what's going to happen because of my giving. That is how I can live hope.

> "In all things I have shown you that by working hard
> in this way we must help the weak and remember
> the words of the Lord Jesus, how he himself said,
> 'It is more blessed to give than to receive.'"
>
> ACTS 20:35

▸▸ *How does your generosity have strings attached?*
▸▸ *Is it irresponsible to give money away?*

Pointing out Mistakes

*I*t's difficult to show someone the hope of the gospel when you are disappointed or disgusted by something they're doing. I've not handled this very well in my past. At my worst, I can say I love another person but subtlety *make sure* they know that I don't approve of a certain area in his or her life that I think is wrong. This doesn't make the other person feel my love. It says, *I love you*, but …

I want to remove the *love buts* from my life. I want to risk loving someone too much or too recklessly. This is how God loves us. What value is my love if I only surround myself with people who are easy to love? When I live hope, I let go of my desire to change another person so that it'll be easier to love him or her. I want to love without expectations. I want to give to others without hoping to get something in return.

> Love one another with brotherly affection. Outdo one another in showing honor. Do not be slothful in zeal, be fervent in spirit, serve the Lord. Rejoice in hope, be patient in tribulation, be constant in prayer.
>
> ROMANS 12:10–12

▸▸ *In what context does pointing out others' shortcomings help?*

▸▸ *How would you want people to treat you if they disagreed with you?*

No Room for Negativity

*I*t's easy to let people in our lives tell us what we can or cannot do. Especially when well-intentioned people try to steer us toward comfort and away from what they think might be difficult for us. What results is people passing through life, doing only what is expected of them. But living hope means so much more than that.

Dawn put some excellent words to this, as she's on the hunt for a great job, one that lines up with her dreams and passions: "'Just Watch Me' is my new motto. I am no longer listening to the people who tell me I should not go for certain job types. … I am going for my dreams, my hopes, my aspirations. My body may not want to go along for the ride, but I am going for it! It has been really difficult to find full time work in my field, but I am not giving up hope!"

> May the God of endurance and encouragement grant you to live in such harmony with one another, in accord with Christ Jesus, that together you may with one voice glorify the God and Father of our Lord Jesus Christ.
>
> ROMANS 15:5–6

▸▸ *Which unhealthy voices have you listened to for too long?*

▸▸ *What would you be free to pursue if you eliminated negativity from your life?*

Hoping without End

*I*s there something you're hoping for, but it seems as if God is taking forever to answer? I know the feeling. There are some prayers I've been praying for all my life. I don't completely understand why God seems to answer some prayers quickly, while with others it seems as if he's taking his time.

I was happy to hear from Lorelei. She said, "As for hope, I've found throughout my life that as long as I keep going, God reveals to me why things happened the way they did and when they did. Things don't run on our time; they run on God's time." Isaiah 40:31 says: "But those who hope in the LORD will renew their strength. They will soar on wings like eagles; they will run and not grow weary, they will walk and not be faint."

If you're in a time of waiting, put your hope in God, and he will keep you strong.

> We are afflicted in every way, but not crushed; perplexed,
> but not driven to despair; persecuted,
> but not forsaken; struck down, but not destroyed;
> always carrying in the body the death of Jesus, so that the
> life of Jesus may also be manifested in our bodies.
>
> 2 CORINTHIANS 4:8–10

►► *How does God strengthen you while you wait?*
►► *Is there any benefit to giving up hope for something to happen?*

Hope = Grounded in Faith + Fueled by Love + Guided by Vision

Changing Seasons

The changing of the seasons is one of life's great constants—you can always count on spring coming after the winter, summer after spring, and winter coming after fall. Think about the life cycle of a tree for a moment—it blossoms in the spring, is green all summer long, it has beautiful reds and oranges in the fall, and then the leaves die and fall off to prepare for the barren winter, only to blossom again in the spring. There is hope in this cycle because whatever season you may currently be going through, there's another one on its way.

Ecclesiastes 3:1–4 assures us, "There is a time for everything, and a season for every activity under the heavens … a time to plant and a time to uproot … a time to weep and a time to laugh, a time to mourn and a time to dance" (NIV). If you're mourning now, your time to dance is coming soon, just like spring after a long winter.

> And let us not grow weary of doing good,
> for in due season we will reap, if we do not give up.
> GALATIANS 6:9

▸▸ *How is the life of Christ seen in the changing of seasons?*

▸▸ *What do you think is the purpose of the season you are currently in?*

Share in the Sufferings of Christ

*S*econd Corinthians 1:5 says, "For just as we share abundantly in the sufferings of Christ, so also our comfort abounds through Christ" (NIV). Many of you are going through sufferings that have nothing to do with you—you can't take your suffering personally, because we can never fully know at the time what God is putting us through. Trying to figure out the *why* only leads to frustration, and even self-centeredness.

Hope arrives when we suddenly come to a place where we can see what we haven't been able to see. We can clearly see how God has strengthened us, how he has refined us, made us more loving, more compassionate, more like his Son. With that kind of perspective, we can look forward to sharing in the sufferings of Christ and experiencing his loving comfort.

Indeed, I count everything as loss because of the
surpassing worth of knowing Christ Jesus my Lord.
For his sake I have suffered the loss of all things and count
them as rubbish, in order that I may gain Christ.

PHILIPPIANS 3:8

▸▸ *How does the suffering of Christ allow you to endure your own trials?*

▸▸ *How are you sharing in the sufferings of Christ?*

Restoring Relationships

I've been spending a lot of time with a buddy who just got out of prison. It's been an amazing experience to watch a grown man dive into freedom for the first time in several years. But I'm fascinated by how he is reconnecting with people from his past over the phone. He's not the same person he used to be; God has changed him. In the process, God is restoring relationships that have been fractured or even nonexistent for years.

Is there someone in your life you need to reconnect with? Someone you love and you can't remember why you stopped talking? God is in the business of making all things new, which includes the broken relationships from your past. The pain you've been carrying around for too long is about to be lifted from your shoulders. Step out in hope and make that call.

> "You're blessed when you can show people
> how to cooperate instead of compete or fight.
> That's when you discover who you really are,
> and your place in God's family."
> MATTHEW 5:9 MSG

▸▸ *What would you gain by restoring a broken relationship?*

▸▸ *How can you still love and forgive someone who has no interest in reconciliation?*

Children Represent Hope

*W*e have a playground just outside our church. I love walking out of church on a nice, sunny day and seeing the kids running around, swinging, sliding, and yelling. They're not trying to figure out where to eat lunch; they're not wondering why someone ignored them in the lobby. They are simply present and full of joy.

These kids represent hope. Not only are they the future of our church, with their children most likely one day playing on that same playground; these children represent the promise of what's to come. And Jesus says it's good for us to be like them: "I tell you the truth, unless you change and become like little children, you will never enter the kingdom of heaven" (Matthew 18:3 NIV). I'm thankful for the children at my church and the legacy they represent. But mostly, I'm thankful for the reminder that hope is available for me.

Anybody want to hit the swings?

> Brothers, do not be children in your thinking.
> Be infants in evil, but in your thinking be mature.
>
> 1 Corinthians 14:20

▸▸ *What would be the benefit of having childlike faith?*

▸▸ *How do you, like these kids, represent hope to others?*

No More Head Shaking

S ometimes I shake my head at some of the crazy things people do. I'm sure I've done some things that have made people shake their heads at me! But I wonder if all this head shaking keeps us from the kind of relationships God wants us to have. Do you think God shakes his head at us? I don't. He loves us with an incredible passion that is not superseded by our behavior.

When we show unconditional love to another person, we show a love that says, *I don't need to know why you did that, or even what happened, or whose fault it was.* It's a love that says, *I'm not going anywhere. I'm going to walk through this with you, no matter what, because love is greater than any of our mistakes.* Love triumphs over sin every time.

Don't let sin in another person's life keep them from knowing the unbelievable, unconditional, all-consuming love of God. God's love changes us, not our shame or our guilt. When we see God's love changing us, that's when hope becomes real.

> Above all, keep loving one another earnestly,
> since love covers a multitude of sins.
>
> 1 PETER 4:8

>> *Do you need to know a person's motives before you love them?*

>> *How has God's love covered all your mistakes and wrong intentions?*

Where Do You Make Your Deposits?

*W*hat does it mean to place your hope in God? Think about it like a bank. When we work a job, we receive a paycheck and then put our check in the bank because we believe that is the safest place for it. Similarly, when we place our hope in God, we believe that's the best way for us to live. Putting our hope in God is the best place we can put it. We are placing our lives in God's hands, trusting he's going to take care of us, no matter what.

Placing our hope in God says that this life is not up to us. We're going to do our best with what we've been given, but our life is in bigger, better hands. That's when hope can truly blossom.

> Blessed is the man who trusts in the LORD,
> whose trust is the LORD.
> He is like a tree planted by water,
> that sends out its roots by the stream,
> and does not fear when heat comes,
> for its leaves remain green,
> and is not anxious in the year of drought,
> for it does not cease to bear fruit.
>
> JEREMIAH 17:7–8

▸▸ *How could you place more hope in God than you already have?*

▸▸ *Why does putting your life in God's hands feel like relinquishing responsibility?*

Hope = **Grounded in Faith** + Fueled by Love + Guided by Vision

Hope in Your Church

I grew up in the church, which I'm incredibly thankful for. Even though there are plenty of things one can find wrong with any church, church might be the very *best* place for a person to see hope.

Hope is visible when people rally around a family with a new baby, bringing food to their house. It is visible when people gather around and pray for a person who has an illness. I see hope when the pastor reveals the truth of the Scripture in a way I've never seen. Hope is seen when my church reaches out to another church in our city, helping to fill kids' backpacks for school, feeding them lunch during the summer.

It's easy to live in my bubble or throw stones from my glass house and criticize the imperfections I see all around me. But the church helps me see how awesome and hope-filled life can be when we seek to serve others.

> As each has received a gift, use it to serve one another,
> as good stewards of God's varied grace.
>
> 1 PETER 4:10

▸▸ *In what ways could you help increase the hope output of your church?*

▸▸ *How do you notice hope revealing itself when you serve others?*

Hope = Grounded in Faith + Fueled by Love + **Guided by Vision**

Are You a Fan of Superhero Movies?

*A*re you one of the millions of people who enjoy movies about superheroes? I sure am. What is so compelling about these stories is that there's usually some kind of conflict brought on by a bad guy, while somebody innocent is in trouble. And just when it seems too late, our hero shows up and saves the day, and everybody cheers.

These stories are so popular because this theme exists in our lives, even if not to such cartoonish extremes. To all of us innocent ones who are caught in conflict, waiting for our rescue, to all who hope in the Lord, Psalm 31:24 gives us our direction: "Be brave. Be strong. Don't give up. Expect GOD to get here soon" (MSG). With hope, your story is going to have a great ending.

> Strengthen the weak hands,
> and make firm the feeble knees.
> Say to those who have an anxious heart,
> "Be strong; fear not!
> Behold, your God
> will come with vengeance,
> with the recompense of God.
> He will come and save you."
>
> ISAIAH 35:3–4

▸▸ *How can you be part of God's rescue of someone you know?*

▸▸ *How could you help someone be brave and strong while they're awaiting rescue?*

Hope = **Grounded in Faith** + Fueled by Love + Guided by Vision

Whistling While You Work

*A*re you one of those people who walk through the day whistling or humming a tune? Some people always have a song in their heart and aren't even aware of how it spills out through a melody in the air. Grandpa Kenny was like that. He was a whistler. I think of him whenever I hear Bing Crosby whistling in "White Christmas." A person of hope is a person who is continually singing a melody of joy, a melody of gratitude.

The poet Emily Dickinson mentioned that hope has feathers and is perched in the soul. Do you have hope perched in your soul? It's hard to be depressed, frustrated, or afraid when you're whistling a happy tune. I think I can hear you whistling now!

> Let the word of Christ dwell in you richly,
> teaching and admonishing one another in all wisdom,
> singing psalms and hymns and spiritual songs,
> with thankfulness in your hearts to God.
>
> COLOSSIANS 3:16

▸▸ *What song do people around you hear you singing?*

▸▸ *What causes your song of hope to stop?*

MAY

It might feel like the world is ending,
but God is in the middle of whatever it is you're
going through. Keep placing your hope in him,
and he will continually renew your strength.

Are You at a Crossroads?

*M*any of you are facing a major decision; some of you can't even see all the options in front of you. I know the feeling all too well. It can be paralyzing, can't it? At times like this, I have to remind myself that I am solely placing my hope in God, reminding myself of what that means. It is helpful to remember verses like Proverbs 3:5–6, which says, "Trust in the LORD with all your heart, do not depend on your own understanding. Seek his will in all you do, and he will show you which path to take" (NLT).

Life is so full of questions that don't have any answers and situations that have many options. It's impossible to always know the exact step to take. But when I seek God for help, I know he hears me. It is that connection with my Maker that helps me to continue moving forward.

> Let us then with confidence draw near to
> the throne of grace, that we may receive mercy
> and find grace to help in time of need.
> HEBREWS 4:16

▸▸ *What Scripture verses do you turn to when you feel helpless or hopeless?*

▸▸ *How does God's help reveal itself to you?*

Rejoicing in This Day

I love Psalm 118:24, which says, "This is the day that the LORD has made; let us rejoice and be glad in it." This verse is a great way to begin the day with a giant dose of hope. There is great purpose for each day. God has given us another day to live and breathe, and it's best if we spend our time during the day rejoicing and being glad in all that God has made and is doing in our lives.

Maybe that sounds a little religious to you—me using the word *rejoicing*. The word *rejoice* means to feel or show great joy or delight. Approaching the day with an attitude of joy and gratitude is a great way to live hope. But it's also a powerful way to go through the rest of the day as well. No matter what happens, no matter what may come my way, whether good or bad, I will choose to be glad and rejoice in God.

Rejoice in the Lord always; again I will say, rejoice.

PHILIPPIANS 4:4

▸▸ *Is it possible to be glad when things aren't going so well?*

▸▸ *Can you still honor your feelings and emotions while choosing to rejoice?*

Why Is Faith Confusing?

*S*ometimes the concept is faith can be confusing. It's like a supernatural filling-in-of-all-the-blanks. It's the go-to answer when there's a tough question, like, why do bad things happen to good people? They say that we might never have the answer while here on earth, but we just should *have faith* that God knows what he's doing.

Sometimes, I'd really like to know what God *is* doing, because faith doesn't always fill in the blanks. Faith is a huge component of hope. If I want to live hope, I need to be grounded in faith. It's a faith that holds fast to God, rather than to my circumstances. Then when the hard times come—which we all know they will—I'm grounded like a house that is built on a solid foundation.

> Now faith is the assurance of things hoped for,
> the conviction of things not seen. For by it
> the people of old received their commendation.
> By faith we understand that the universe was created
> by the word of God, so that what is seen
> was not made out of things that are visible.
> HEBREWS 11:1–3

▸▸ *What would make faith easier for you?*
▸▸ *Would faith have any value if all your questions were answered?*

A Friend in Need

I have a friend who is going through a difficult time with a personal situation in his family. My heart breaks for him and for the incredible load he has carried around with him every day. Yet he has to keep showing up to work as if nothing out of the normal is going on. I don't know how he does it.

Hope tells me that I can still hold out that God might show up in my friend's life and do a miracle. But until God shows up, I want to show up for my friend and be the hope he needs. When I do that, or someone does that for me, God shows up—maybe not by fixing the horrible circumstances, but by letting me know that I'm not alone. How do you live hope for the people you care about?

> For God is not unjust so as to overlook
> your work and the love that you have shown for
> his name in serving the saints, as you still do.
>
> HEBREWS 6:10

▸▸ *How has God shown up for you through other people?*

▸▸ *How could you show up for someone today?*

Filled with Possibility

I meet people all the time who are discouraged, feeling as if their best days are behind them. These are people who have resigned themselves to live without passion or enthusiasm; they are people who have tried to go after their goals or dreams, only to be met with frustration and roadblocks.

A life lived with hope can't help but look ahead with great joy and optimism, even when the road ahead is difficult. Hope says the future holds great possibility. American inventor Ken Hakuta said, "People will try to tell you that all the great opportunities have been snapped up. In reality, the world changes every second, blowing new opportunities in all directions, including yours."[13] Hope says, *Don't give up. God is blowing new opportunities in your direction right now.*

> Look carefully then how you walk, not as unwise
> but as wise, making the best use of the time,
> because the days are evil.
>
> Ephesians 5:15–16

▸▸ *What is an opportunity you hope God sends your way?*

▸▸ *Is there anything you can do to take the first step toward it?*

Nothing to Worry About

*I*t's easy to worry. But even when I'm tempted to worry, it doesn't mean I let it have its way with me! A pastor in Minnesota said, "Hope means that your past is forgiven and your future is secure." That just about covers it, doesn't it? All that's left is for me to be completely present, to keep my eyes open to what God is doing, and not worry about what happened in the past or what might happen in the future.

To live hope means we keep our eyes open to the people God is placing in front of us, whether we're at home, at work, or in line at the grocery store. Chances are, you can find someone worrying about something, and a simple word of hope might be all they need to get through the day.

> From the end of the earth I call to you
> when my heart is faint.
> Lead me to the rock
> that is higher than I,
> for you have been my refuge,
> a strong tower against the enemy.
>
> PSALM 61:2–3

▸▸ *What part have you allowed worry to play in your life?*

▸▸ *How can you strive to be more present?*

In a Barren Place

*B*ritish writer Frank Topping writes a beautiful prayer: "Here I wait in quiet hope, that you will come, to water my barren fields, to make blossom the flower and fruit, that wither in the merciless heat. Do not forsake me. Amen." Do you feel like your fields are barren? Is your fruit withering in the merciless heat? I am convinced that God is working to make it all right, to bring fruit and life into the places where it seems the most hopeless.

Psalm 33:20 says, "We wait in hope for the LORD; he is our help and our shield" (NIV). But how can you wait in hope? Remind yourself that God is your help and rescuer, that his love is so great that he won't leave you in a barren place, that even while you wait he's making you more mature. And keep your eyes fixed on him, for his life-giving power is closer than you think.

> For God alone my soul waits in silence;
> from him comes my salvation.
> He alone is my rock and my salvation,
> my fortress; I shall not be greatly shaken.
>
> PSALM 62:1–2

▸▸ *Why does waiting feel so helpless and empty?*

▸▸ *How can you wait in hope?*

Life's Bus Stop

A big part of hope is looking ahead—seeing somewhere you aren't right now, and looking forward with anticipation. Some believers live with great hope for what heaven is going to be like. Looking ahead with vision is an important part of living hope, but not if it takes you out of the present moment.

Imagine if you spent your life waiting at a bus stop. You know the bus is coming, but you're not sure when. So you wait, and you miss out on life because you're waiting, focused on what's ahead. However, waiting with hope is an active waiting. It looks into the eyes of other people waiting alongside and showers them with love. It finds out their stories and asks what they're hoping for. My hope is based in the truth that something good is ahead, but I can experience my deepest joy only when I'm fully present in the moment.

> But they who wait for the LORD shall renew their strength;
> they shall mount up with wings like eagles;
> they shall run and not be weary;
> they shall walk and not faint.
>
> ISAIAH 40:31

▸▸ *How can you do some active waiting today?*

▸▸ *Can you still praise God while you're waiting for your long-delayed bus?*

Trying to Figure Out the Future

*W*hen I think about waiting on the Lord, I can't help but think about how impatient I can be—like when I'm waiting for a package from Amazon to show up or a text to be returned. If I'm going to say that I am waiting with hope, then I have to be rooted in faith—that God is in control of my world, that he loves and cares for me, and that he will bring about his plans in his perfect time.

There's no room for impatience living with faith in God. Still, I'm tempted to try to figure out what might happen in the future. But God is asking me to trust him, to loosen my grip on the future, and to wait with great hope for what he's going to do.

> Be still before the LORD and wait patiently for him. …
> Refrain from anger, and forsake wrath!
> Fret not yourself; it tends only to evil.
> For the evildoers shall be cut off,
> but those who wait for the Lord shall inherit the land.
>
> PSALM 37:7–9

▸▸ *What does it mean for you to be still before the Lord?*

▸▸ *How much of your life do you think God is in control of?*

How Are You Waiting?

A big part of being a believer in Christ is the idea of waiting—for what's ahead and for God to work, all the while trusting that God is already at work, that he's not sleeping or waiting for a prescribed time to begin his redemption. This great combination of the now and the not yet is filled with hope and allows me to wait on God with patience and trust.

Psalm 130:5 says, "I wait for the LORD, my whole being waits, and in his word I put my hope" (NIV). When our faith wavers, we often get ahead of ourselves and try to figure out what is going to happen. But waiting in hope places confident trust in God, in his promises and his love. He's got you, and he's doing a good work in you.

> I waited patiently for the LORD;
> he inclined to me and heard my cry.
> He drew me up from the pit of destruction,
> out of the miry bog,
> and set my feet upon a rock,
> making my steps secure.
>
> PSALM 40:1–2

▸▸ *What is the most difficult part about waiting?*

▸▸ *What would it mean for you to have confident trust in God?*

Hope = Grounded in Faith + Fueled by Love + Guided by Vision

Overflowing

*T*he apostle Paul has some great advice for how to wait with hope. In Romans 8:25, he writes, "But if we hope for what we do not yet have, we wait for it patiently" (NIV). Perhaps your hope is for something you don't yet have, something you desire, something you've been praying for God to do, but he hasn't yet. If you hope, then do it patiently. Hope has no room for anxiety or worry or fear.

In fact, a few chapters later, in Romans 15:13, Paul continues, "May the God of hope fill you with all joy and peace as you trust in him, so that you may overflow with hope by the power of the Holy Spirit" (NIV). How do you overflow with hope? By trusting him. Trust that God knows what's going on in your life and that he is offering you joy and peace as you trust in him.

> "Peace I leave with you; my peace I give to you.
> Not as the world gives do I give to you. Let not your
> hearts be troubled, neither let them be afraid."
>
> JOHN 14:27

▸▸ *Is it possible to have too much hope? Explain.*

▸▸ *How can you let God fill you with hope?*

Fighting for Hope

*F*or many, hope is a concept that is easy to grasp; while for others, it might be a bit more difficult to understand. This is for you who feel as if hope is just out of reach. Hope is something worth fighting for, and it's a serious fight. Everything in our culture wants to get you to put your hope in something it has to offer, something that will surely fade away the moment the next trend makes its appearance on the social scene.

But God's grand story is one of redemption. He's redeeming us, his people, and drawing us into a deeper, more intimate love relationship with him. This is not just something written in the Bible, but something that God is still doing today. This gives me hope because though today things might feel a bit bleak, God is redeeming the world, this situation, and me. He's making all things right. I fight against hopelessness when I remember these truths.

> Surely there is a future,
> and your hope will not be cut off.
>
> PROVERBS 23:18

▸▸ *What is something society is tempting you to put your hope in?*

▸▸ *How can you fight for hope today?*

Purifying Your Hope

*I*n *The Healing Path*, Dan Allender writes about how God often traps us between our desire and our demands in order to satisfy our deepest hungers with himself. He will not lessen our hunger, nor will he feed us when his bread is viewed as our rightful claim. He will be no person's butler, only our God.

We must wrestle with our refusal to keep traveling between desire and satisfaction, where God neither answers our prayer for healing nor clearly illumines a path away from fear. God allows us to wait, not to punish us, not because he has forgotten us, but because our waiting is the crucible he uses to purify our hope.

Is God purifying your hope by making you wait? It might feel like the world is ending, but God is in the middle of whatever it is you're going through. Keep placing your hope in him, and he will continually renew your strength.

> Trust in the LORD, and do good;
> dwell in the land and befriend faithfulness.
> Delight yourself in the LORD,
> and he will give you the desires of your heart.
>
> PSALM 37:3–4

▸▸ *How is it possible to grow more content with your hunger?*

▸▸ *How can you allow waiting on God to strengthen you instead of frustrating you?*

Hope = **Grounded in Faith** + Fueled by Love + Guided by Vision

Creeping Hopelessness

*S*ometimes the temptation to feel hopeless creeps in and tries to take root in my soul, no matter how much I try to be hopeful. Does this ever happen to you? Someone once said that hope commonly requires reestablishing a sense of connection and belonging. This connection can occur when you believe there is some benevolent disposition toward yourself somewhere in the universe, conveyed by a caring person. I can't help but think about the caring doctors and nurses I've met over the years, and how they live hope this way.

It seems as if it's the easiest to feel hopeless when I'm not doing anything. That's when I know it's time to get out and do something productive—in particular, I need to find a way to connect with someone else, getting outside of myself and showing God to the world through my love and benevolence. It's hard to show God to others when I'm so focused on myself. That's why I need to take my eyes off myself and set them on the world around me.

> Let no one seek his own good,
> but the good of his neighbor.
> 1 CORINTHIANS 10:24

▸▸ *What do you turn to when you feel helpless?*

▸▸ *How much is hopelessness rooted in selfishness?*

What Is Your Hope Built On?

*W*endy from Nebraska sent me the lyrics from her favorite hymn, "My Hope Is Built on Nothing Less." She said, "As I read and sing through these verses, I stand firm in knowing exactly where my hope is placed." The hymn, written by Edward Mote and inspired by Jesus' Sermon on the Mount found in Matthew 7 and Luke 6, proclaims that our hope is built on nothing less than Jesus' blood and righteousness.

People try to build their hope on all kinds of things—their bank account, career, reputation, relationships, or appearance—all of which will pass away. But not Jesus. When we build our hope on him, we have the assurance that no matter what may happen, we will stand firm. This is not because of anything we've done, but simply because of who he is.

> Be sober-minded; be watchful. Your adversary the devil
> prowls around like a roaring lion, seeking someone
> to devour. Resist him, firm in your faith.
>
> 1 PETER 5:8–9

▸▸ *How does Jesus help you stand firm against difficult circumstances?*

▸▸ *What are some things you place differing amounts of hope in?*

How Does Faith Differ from Hope?

*I*t's easy to use the words *faith* and *hope* interchangeably, even if they are incorrect. Faith is a trust and belief in God; as Christians, we place our complete trust in God. But hope takes it a step further, anticipating something good to happen. Because I have faith in God, I can live with great hope, knowing that he loves me and is working all things for my good (Romans 8:28).

Can I have hope without faith? I don't believe so. My hope has to be rooted in something or else I'm just making a wish. But can I have faith without hope? Sadly, many people do. They have faith in God but don't have any godly anticipation. Even if a believer is looking forward to one day being in heaven with Jesus, there is still so much more to hope for now. And you can find it today by looking with God-focused eyes on the world around you.

> For through the Spirit, by faith,
> we ourselves eagerly wait for the hope of righteousness.
>
> GALATIANS 5:5

▸▸ *How would you describe the difference between faith and hope?*

▸▸ *Does hope make your faith stronger or the other way around? Explain.*

Hope for Our Future

*M*any people's favorite verse in the Bible is Jeremiah 29:11, which boldly asserts, "'For I know the plans I have for you,' declares the LORD, 'plans to prosper you and not to harm you, to give you hope and a future'" (NIV). We love this verse because it tells us that everything is going to be okay. In context, Jeremiah 29 is speaking to the nation of Israel, and reminding them of the promises God has made to them.

We like to take this verse for ourselves, believing that God's got it all figured out, so we don't have to worry about anything. But the true hope of Jeremiah 29 is not that God knows the plans that he has for each individual, but that he knows the plans he has for all people. God is inviting us to take our eyes off ourselves and to think about all of us being in this together. For all of us as his children, our future is secure in him.

> "For my thoughts are not your thoughts,
> neither are your ways my ways, declares the LORD.
> For as the heavens are higher than the earth,
> so are my ways higher than your ways
> and my thoughts than your thoughts."
>
> ISAIAH 55:8–9

▸▸ *What do you like about Jeremiah 29:11?*

▸▸ *Why have we made Christianity so individualistic?*

Hope = **Grounded in Faith** + Fueled by Love + Guided by Vision

Close Neighbors

G. K. Chesterton, an English writer and Christian apologist, captures how hope and hopelessness are close neighbors: "To love means loving the unlovable. To forgive means pardoning the unpardonable. Faith means believing the unbelievable. Hope means hoping when everything seems hopeless."[14]

It's easy to love those who love us back, and it's easy to forgive small offenses. Having faith in something believable doesn't have much worth. And those who hope probably have experienced a strong sense of hopelessness. This is why hope is so important to me. I know what it's like to feel hopeless, to see the darkness of clouds and wonder if they're ever going to blow away. Even though it might be raining for weeks, and the sun never seems to peek through the clouds, hope trusts that the sun is still there and will come out again. It always does.

> But rejoice insofar as you share Christ's sufferings, that
> you may also rejoice and be glad
> when his glory is revealed.
>
> 1 PETER 4:13

▸▸ *What part of your desire for hope comes out of a place of knowing hopelessness?*

▸▸ *How does hope in the dark make your hope stronger when the sun comes out?*

It's Okay to Ask God

I love how the Psalms are refreshingly honest. It's as if one minute the psalmist is saying, "God, are you even real? Do you even care?" And then in the next minute, he is saying, "Thank you, God, for loving me and being with me." There is plenty of room for questions in God's economy.

In Psalm 39:7, there is a desperate plea as the writer looks around and sees the darkness and trouble of the world. He writes, "And now, O Lord, for what do I wait?" He's asking, "Come on, God. Where am I supposed to put my hope?" And then he answers his own question with five simple words: "My hope is in you."

Sometimes I have to ask gut-wrenchingly honest questions of God before I'm able to land back on the truth of what the Scriptures reveal about him. Through my questions and my honesty, hope shows up in the beauty of the truth.

> But for you, O LORD, do I wait;
> it is you, O Lord my God, who will answer.
>
> PSALM 38:15

▸▸ *What truths do you need to be reminded of?*

▸▸ *Where else do you look for answers to your questions about God?*

Where Do You Turn?

I lived many years feeling as if there was something wrong with me because I didn't always feel hope. If you've had these thoughts, let me encourage you that you are not alone and God is not surprised. But where do you turn when you feel hopeless?

Dinah e-mailed me about where she turns when she needs hope: "When I am weak and feel like giving up, I read about Paul, how he asked three times to have the thorn in his side removed, and God responded: *My grace is sufficient for thee.* Jesus always makes a way for me to know he loves me and gives me extra strength for the journey. I have learned so much about hope and love from all that Jesus did here on earth, what he does from the throne, and what he will one day do face to face."

> I sought the LORD, and he answered me
> and delivered me from all my fears.
> Those who look to him are radiant,
> and their faces shall never be ashamed.
>
> PSALM 34:4–5

▸▸ *Where do you turn when your hope tank is empty?*

▸▸ *How do you demonstrate the hope you have to others when they feel hopeless?*

Why Is Love the Greatest?

I'm sure you've heard the love chapter read at a wedding or two. First Corinthians 13:13 says, "So now faith, hope, and love abide, these three; but the greatest of these is love." Why is love the greatest? There are all kinds of theological explanations of this verse, but let's think about heaven.

When we get to heaven, we aren't going to have any need for faith or hope; heaven will be the fruition of all we've been hoping for. But you know what will remain? Love. When Paul wrote the word *greatest*, he could have written that "the one which will stand the test of time of all time and into eternity is love." Our hope today is to keep us focused on what's ahead. And, oddly enough, what's ahead is a time when hope will no longer be needed.

> My prayer for you is that you will overflow more and more with love for others, and at the same time keep on growing in spiritual knowledge and insight, for I want you always to see clearly the difference between right and wrong, and to be inwardly clean, no one being able to criticize you from now until our Lord returns.
>
> PHILIPPIANS 1:9–10 TLB

▸▸ *How does hope help us get to eternity?*

▸▸ *How can you bring the love of heaven into your day today?*

Hope = Grounded in Faith + Fueled by Love + Guided by Vision

Waiting and Watching

*E*ugene Peterson, in his book *A Long Obedience in the Same Direction*, wrote: "Hoping does not mean doing nothing. It is not fatalistic resignation. It means going about our assigned tasks, confident that God will provide the meaning and the conclusions. It is not compelled to work away at keeping up appearances with a bogus spirituality. It is the opposite of desperate and panicky manipulations, of scurrying and worrying. And hoping is not dreaming. It is not spinning an illusion or fantasy to protect us from our boredom or our pain. It means a confident, alert expectation that God will do what he said he will do. It is imagination put in the harness of faith. It is a willingness to let God do it his way and in his time. It is the opposite of making plans that we demand that God put into effect, telling him both how and when to do it. That is not hoping in God but bullying God. My life's on the line before God, my Lord, waiting and watching till morning."[15]

> "For you say, I am rich, I have prospered,
> and I need nothing, not realizing that you
> are wretched, pitiable, poor, blind, and naked."
> REVELATION 3:17

▸▸ *Why is hope sometimes viewed as a crutch?*

▸▸ *How can you let faith harness your imagination and turn it into hope?*

Hope = Grounded in Faith + Fueled by Love + Guided by Vision

Hope in a Tree

*J*ob tells God that he's tired. He's feeling the pain of loss and death. But then he sees hope—in a tree, of all places: "For there is hope for a tree, if it be cut down, that it will sprout again, and that its shoots will not cease. Though its root grow old in the earth, and its stump die in the soil, yet at the scent of water it will bud and put out branches like a young plant" (Job 14:7–9).

You may feel like a tree that's been cut down. You may feel as if your stump is dying in the soil. But just like Job writes, all it takes is a scent of water and you will bud again and put out branches like a young plant. Don't give up hope quite yet; the rain and the water will come, and you will have your hope restored as you see the tiny buds on your branches once again.

> There shall come forth a shoot from the stump of Jesse,
> and a branch from his roots shall bear fruit.
>
> Isaiah 11:1

▸▸ *What part in reviving your deadness can you play?*

▸▸ *What would be a tiny glimpse of hope you could be looking for?*

What the Doctor Ordered

I asked a friend, who is a doctor, what part hope plays in the treatment of his patients, especially those near the end of their lives. I expected him to say something like, "Well, we do what we can and hope for the best." But instead he said, "Sometimes my job is to realign what people are hoping for." I was intrigued.

He continued, "You can't always honestly tell people to put their hope in getting healed, but you can help them hope that they get to live their final days comfortably. Or that they get to spend time with the people who mean the most to them—family and friends. You can help them to hope in something more tangible, something that can actually be obtained rather than wished for."

The truth is the same for all of us. We can't control what happens, but we can control who we choose to be and how we're going to respond to whatever happens to us.

> When the cares of my heart are many,
> your consolations cheer my soul.
>
> PSALM 94:19

▸▸ *Do you think there is such a thing as "reasonable" hope? Explain.*

▸▸ *In what ways do your hopes need to be realigned?*

Confidence to Speak Boldly

*D*o you have a fear of speaking in front of people? It has been estimated that 75 percent of people experience some degree of anxiety or nervousness when speaking in public. There's even a term for speech anxiety—*glossophobia*. Interestingly enough, one of the heroes of the Old Testament didn't consider himself worthy of speaking in public. Moses had a speech impediment—he stuttered. It was also difficult for Paul to speak with boldness.

We find hope in something Paul wrote in 2 Corinthians 3:12, referring to the struggle Moses had with his speech: "Therefore having such a hope, we use great boldness in our speech" (NASB). We have the hope that God calls us and qualifies us, giving us the confidence we need to not be afraid. We can speak the truth of the gospel in plain, easy-to-understand language, without reservations.

> I am acting with great boldness toward you;
> I have great pride in you; I am filled with comfort.
> In all our affliction, I am overflowing with joy.
>
> 2 CORINTHIANS 7:4

▸▸ *How does hope give you confidence?*

▸▸ *What steps of boldness would you take if you had more confidence?*

Hope in Unexpected Places

*I*t was Jake's first summer as a counselor at Camp Carol Joy Holling in Ashland, Nebraska. I met Jake and the other counselors one summer as they were preparing for campers to arrive for the week. We talked about hope and where they saw it in the culture, and how it has shown up in their own lives.

Jake said, "It could be a hundred degrees out and you're just dead tired, but one look at a camper and you are ready to go." Who knew hope could come in the smallest things, like a little camper. The hope these counselors see and then encourage in their campers is something akin to possibility—it's an anticipation, it's an I-can't-wait-to-see-what's-going-to-happen-this-week longing.

I live hope by constantly saying to God, "I can't wait to see what you have for me." And hopefully there will be s'mores involved.

> For you did not receive the spirit of slavery to fall back
> into fear, but you have received the Spirit of adoption
> as sons, by whom we cry, "Abba! Father!"
>
> ROMANS 8:15

▸▸ *How can you approach each day with anticipation?*
▸▸ *How would this change your perspective toward life?*

Hope for Everyone?

*T*here's a horrible disease that runs rampant through humanity—some call it judgmentalism, while others call it conditional love. But it reveals itself when we pick and choose who deserves our love—who receives grace and mercy from us. First John 3:16 and 18 reminds us, "This is how we know what love is: Jesus Christ laid down his life for us. And we ought to lay down our lives for our brothers and sisters. ... Dear children, let us not love with words or speech but with actions and in truth" (NIV).

Let's take a lesson from Jesus on the issue of love: he didn't die on the cross for just some of us; he died on the cross for all of us. His love looks beyond our sin and beyond our good works, and he loves us completely. Let us live out that hope with outrageous love to those God puts in our lives.

> "The LORD appeared to him from far away.
> I have loved you with an everlasting love;
> therefore I have continued my faithfulness to you."
>
> JEREMIAH 31:3

▸▸ *Where have you drawn lines in the past about who you'd choose to love?*

▸▸ *What makes you difficult to be loved by others?*

What Role Does the Bible Play in Hope?

I'm guessing you have a Bible. Most people do. But how often do you crack it open? If you're not big on Bible reading, I get that. It can be confusing and difficult to know how to apply the Bible to your life. But the Bible is the grand story of God's love for you and me, an incredibly profound telling of God's interaction with his people and creation. Pastor Charles A. Allen said, "On every page of the Bible there are words of God that give us reason to hope."[16]

Second Peter 1:4 says, "And because of his glory and excellence, he has given us great and precious promises. These are the promises that enable you to share his divine nature and escape the world's corruption caused by human desires" (NLT). You can know God and his promises simply by reading the Bible. These promises will be a great source of hope for your soul.

> For the word of God is living and active, sharper than any two-edged sword, piercing to the division of soul and of spirit, of joints and of marrow, and discerning the thoughts and intentions of the heart.
>
> HEBREWS 4:12

>> *What's a key verse for you to remember during your hope journey?*

>> *How is the Bible a story of hope?*

Keep Your Eye on the Ball

I'm a big baseball fan (especially the Minnesota Twins!). I love watching it—and playing it, as well. If you've ever played baseball, one of the key pointers that you'll be told is to "keep your eye on the ball." It's amazing how that one simple tip can make a world of difference when hitting and fielding. If I take my eyes off the ball I find myself swinging into thin air—usually met by catcalls from my teammates in the dugout. Watch the ball all the way in and one has a much better chance of hitting it.

First Peter 1:13 encourages us to keep our eyes on the ball—to keep our eyes set on Jesus. "Therefore, with minds that are alert and fully sober, set your hope on the grace to be brought to you when Jesus Christ is revealed at his coming" (NIV). Keep your eyes on Jesus, your hope focused on him. I'm cheering you on from the dugout.

> Stand therefore, having fastened on the belt of truth,
> and having put on the breastplate of righteousness,
> and, as shoes for your feet, having put on the
> readiness given by the gospel of peace.
> EPHESIANS 6:14–15

▸▸ *In what ways can you keep your eye on the ball?*

▸▸ *What are the things that tempt you to lose focus?*

The Birth of Hope

*I*f you're on a journey to understand hope, then you know how difficult it is to look ahead and know exactly what to trust God for. We were never meant to see the future; faith is always blind. But one of the best ways to live hope today is to see how God has worked throughout history, not just biblical history, but in your history. How have you seen God show up throughout your life? Do the character and actions of God allow you to trust him more or less?

Anne Graham Lotz said, "If God can bring blessing from the broken body of Jesus and glory from something that's as obscene as the cross, He can bring blessing from my problems and my pain and my unanswered prayer. I just have to trust Him." I have to believe that hope emerges from trust.

> Such is the confidence that we have through Christ toward God. Not that we are sufficient in ourselves to claim anything as coming from us, but our sufficiency is from God, who has made us sufficient.
>
> 2 CORINTHIANS 3:4–6

▸▸ *Where have you seen blessings emerge from your pain?*

▸▸ *How can you let trust be the birthing ground for hope?*

Living in the House of God

*T*here are some interesting references in Scripture to houses and homes, who oversees the house, what kind of foundation we build ours on, and so on. Images of houses are used frequently because we can relate to the idea of living in a house and the dynamics that go along with that. In Hebrews 3:5, Moses is mentioned as being "faithful as a servant in all God's house, bearing witness to what would be spoken by God in the future" (NIV). It then says that Jesus was "faithful as the Son over God's house" (3:6 NIV).

Here's the clincher—it says that "we are his house." We live in God, and additionally God lives in us. As God's house, "we hold firmly to our confidence and the hope in which we glory" (Hebrews 3:6 NIV). As God's house, we approach God with boldness and confidence, secure in the incredible love and care he has for us. As we do that, we are truly living hope.

> But in these last days he has spoken to us by his Son,
> whom he appointed the heir of all things,
> through whom also he created the world.
>
> HEBREWS 1:2

▶▶ *What does it mean for Jesus to be faithful as a Son over your life?*

▶▶ *How are you holding on to courage and the hope of the glory of God?*

Hope = **Grounded in Faith** + Fueled by Love + Guided by Vision

JUNE

As we let God's truth fill us up and define who we are, we will have greater endurance to run the race set before us.

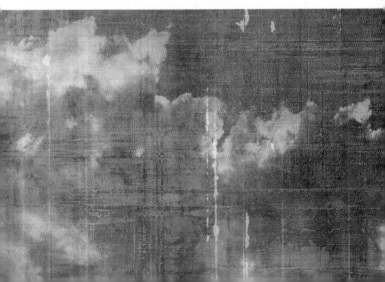

Let God Worry

*T*here's a difference between worry and concern. Being concerned allows one to think productively and figure out if there's anything a person can do about it. But worry tends to get our stomachs in a bind, our minds on overdrive, leaving us feeling helpless and frustrated. It is focused on something in the future, forgetting that God is in control of our lives.

In Matthew 6:33–34 Jesus reminds us, "But seek first His kingdom and His righteousness, and all these things will be added to you. So do not worry about tomorrow; for tomorrow will care for itself. Each day has enough trouble of its own" (NASB). You have permission to stop worrying, even if just for today. Rest in the hope that God is with you and taking care of you. William Law, a Church of England priest, put it well when he said, "Pray, and let God worry."

> "And which of you by being anxious can add
> a single hour to his span of life? If then you are
> not able to do as small a thing as that,
> why are you anxious about the rest?"
>
> LUKE 12:25–26

▸▸ *What is the foundation of your worry?*
▸▸ *How can you hand over your worries to God?*

How Can You Hold On?

*T*here's no question that life can be hard at times. The trials and the difficulties we encounter can be truly overwhelming. There are days when you wonder when you are going to get a break from the struggle. Do you find it difficult to live hope when you're trying to simply keep your head above water?

Hope may be the very rescue you are looking for. Romans 8:25 says, "But if we hope for what we don't see, we wait for it with patience." A big part of patience is faith. We wait with patience because we have faith in God's promises. And as we wait, our hope grows.

Hold on and wait with hope, because all that you are hoping for is coming. This hope will fill you and carry you through these difficult days.

> It will be said on that day,
> "Behold, this is our God; we have waited for him,
> that he might save us.
> This is the LORD; we have waited for him;
> let us be glad and rejoice in his salvation."
>
> ISAIAH 25:9

▸▸ *What do you hold on to while you're waiting?*

▸▸ *What does impatience stem from?*

Has Hope Passed You By?

*I*f you feel as if hope is out of your grasp because of what you've done in the past, what you're doing today, or what you're planning for tomorrow, God is still passionately loving you. Pastor Barbara Crafton said, "It's never too late. You can't screw up so badly that God can't find something worth building in the wreckage, that life can't assert its return when it is time."[17] Do you believe that, or do you think you're the exception to the rule—that somehow God's grace and mercy are probably good enough for everyone else, but not for you?

I have two things to say: First, you're not that special—you qualify for God's grace just like everyone else. And second, you're more special than you realize—your life's story, full of nuance and mystery, will be a blessing to others and a grand testimony to the unbelievable, unconditional love of God—if you let it.

And God is able to make all grace abound to you,
so that having all sufficiency in all things at all times, you
may abound in every good work.

2 CORINTHIANS 9:8

▸▸ *What basis do you have for thinking God can't love you?*

▸▸ *How can you let your life be a testimony of God's love?*

How Much Does God Love You?

*D*o you think about how much God loves you? This is an important question for a couple of reasons: First, your view of God as all-loving has the power to transform your heart. God's love can turn a person from fearful and selfish into a loving, kind, peaceful person. Second, I'm convinced we will love other people with the same amount of love we have received. If you're not loving others with an unconditional love, you may want to take a step back and remind yourself how much you are loved.

John 3:16 describes God's love for the world: "He gave his only Son, that whoever believes in him should not perish but have eternal life." God wants to live forever in relationship with us and the rest of God's family. How much does God love you? This may be the most important question you ever answer.

> Your steadfast love, O LORD, extends to the heavens,
> your faithfulness to the clouds. …
> How precious is your steadfast love, O God!
> The children of mankind take refuge in
> the shadow of your wings.
>
> PSALM 36:5, 7

▸▸ *How has the continually, ever-increasing revealing of God's love changed your life?*

▸▸ *How does God's love pull you deeper into relationship with him?*

How Is It Going to Turn Out?

*H*ow's it going to end? This is usually what I wonder as I'm enjoying a great story on screen or on the page. I love getting hooked in, enjoying the ride so much that I don't want to story to end. Try telling a friend about a great movie you just saw, and she will quickly jump in and say, "Don't ruin the ending!"

God's great story of love and redemption was written before time began and will continue even beyond our comprehension of time. And this is a good story—one that we get to play a part in. Do you ever wonder how it's all going to turn out? Billy Graham once said, "I've read the last page of the Bible. It's all going to turn out all right." His reminder of the hope we have in God is good to hear, especially when some days feel dark. Don't forget that God already knows what's going to happen; he promises a good ending.

And this is the promise that he made to us—eternal life.

1 JOHN 2:25

▸▸ *If your life were a book, where in the story would you be?*

▸▸ *What would you like someone to know after reading your story?*

The Motivation of Hope

*H*ope is a powerful force that can motivate us to do great things. I believe that hope has more power over us than fear that threatens to paralyze us. Dr. Scott Todd, of Compassion International, said, "Hope is made up of three key things. First, it has a clear vision of the better future. Second, it has at least one path to get there. And third, hope has guts. It has that internal courage and will to give that path a try. Wishful thinking or optimism doesn't lead to change, but hope ignites the muscles of action. When those three things come together, that kind of hope can change the world. So, I don't believe hope is just a nice, soft idea. Hope is one of the toughest motivators around."[18]

Has God given you a vision to accomplish? Hang on to hope with everything you have, trusting that God's presence and power are with you and are surely working through you.

> For it is God who works in you,
> both to will and to work for his good pleasure.
> PHILIPPIANS 2:13

▸▸ *Can you clarify your vision of a better future?*
▸▸ *How is hope a motivator for you?*

Hope = Grounded in Faith + Fueled by Love + **Guided by Vision**

Thinking Big

*H*ave you ever spent time dreaming about something big you might like to accomplish in the future? For some of you, it might be cleaning out the closet in the hallway; for others, it might be writing a book or learning to play the piano. Why don't more of us take time to think about what we really want to do— projects we want to tackle, places we want to go, relationships we want to restore? Is it because we don't have a full vision of our true worth?

Hope says that every human life is extremely valuable. That includes you and me. A German writer named Walter Anderson said, "Believe in something big. Your life is worth a noble motive." Have you identified a noble motive? You might say, "I'm working to build the kingdom of God." Well, how do you specifically want to do that?

You are worth spending time working on something big. What are you waiting for?

> "Remember not the former things,
> nor consider the things of old."
>
> ISAIAH 43:18

▸▸ *How would understanding your true worth help you to have more courage?*

▸▸ *What is something big you could start working on?*

Dream On

*M*ost people I know are so focused on what is right in front of them that the thought of prioritizing their dreams seems like a self-indulgent luxury. But dreaming plays a large part in living a life of hope.

Former NASA astronaut Pamela Melroy said, "In your life's journey, there will be excitement and fulfillment, boredom and routine, and even the occasional train wreck. ... But when you have picked a dream that is bigger than you personally, that truly reflects the ideals that you cherish, and that can positively affect others, then you will always have another reason for carrying on."

Dreaming doesn't have to be pie-in-the-sky wishing; it can be as simple as working to bring focus to all your thoughts, talents, passions, and faith. God wants to help you uncover how you might live hope through the pursuit of your dreams, bringing meaning and significance to all your days.

> Commit your work to the LORD,
> and your plans will be established.
>
> PROVERBS 16:3

▸▸ *How can you benefit from going after a dream, however big or small?*

▸▸ *Is there an emotional toll in not going after your dreams?*

Hope = Grounded in Faith + Fueled by Love + **Guided by Vision**

Living Life Too Small

*T*here's nothing wrong with living a modest, quiet life. But how does the love of God and the power of hope fuel you to live beyond the boundaries of what's easy and comfortable? Business philosopher Jim Rohn said, "Let others lead small lives, but not you. Let others argue over small things, but not you. Let others cry over small hurts, but not you. Let others leave their future in someone else's hands, but not you."

Many people live the life that others expect them to live. You belong to God, and he's empowering you to bring life, love, and hope to the world around you. But that may require you to adopt a vision for your life that's bigger than you currently have. What would it look like for you set aside fear, comfort, and false security?

> "You did not choose me, but I chose you and
> appointed you that you should go and bear fruit and
> that your fruit should abide, so that whatever you ask
> the Father in my name, he may give it to you."
>
> JOHN 15:16

▸▸ *Why is it such a challenge to live big?*

▸▸ *Why do we value comfort so much?*

Dreaming Too Big

I have lived most of my life going after my dreams. Along the way, however, several well-intentioned people have tried to convince me to dream "more reasonably"—to set my sights on what might be easier or make more sense. Instead, I have determined to keep my eyes focused on God, trusting him to lead me. Hope has played a big part in keeping me directed. Hope says, *God, you are with me, and you can do anything.* And I've seen some amazing things happen as a result!

Jesus said in Matthew 19:26, "With man this is impossible, but with God all things are possible." Yes, *all* things—not just reasonable things. You are not alone, wherever you are and whatever you are going through. And when you go after your dreams, trust that God is with you, and dive into the hope he's placed in your heart to clarify your focus and direction.

> "Have I not commanded you?
> Be strong and courageous. Do not be frightened,
> and do not be dismayed, for the LORD your God
> is with you wherever you go."
>
> JOSHUA 1:9

▸▸ *How can you uncover what God has planted deep inside your heart?*

▸▸ *Why doesn't the impossible happen sometimes?*

Incredibly Unique

A big part of hope is understanding how incredibly deep you are loved by God—not just in a I-*have*-to-love-you kind of way, but in a I-think-you're-amazingly-awesome kind of way. God has made each of us unique for a particular reason. The sad part of life is that many of us live our lives just like everyone else. We sacrifice our uniqueness to fit in, to toe the line, to make other people happy.

Poet and playwright E. E. Cummings said, "To be nobody but yourself in a world which is doing its best, night and day, to make you everybody but yourself means to fight the hardest battle which any human being can fight; and never stop fighting." As you dive into hope, cherish the gifts, talents, and abilities that make you unique, trusting that God wants to tell his story to the world through what makes you so special.

> "I knew you before you were formed within your mother's womb; before you were born I sanctified you and appointed you as my spokesman to the world."
>
> JEREMIAH 1:5 TLB

▸▸ *What are three things that make you unique?*

▸▸ *Why is it so easy to think there's nothing special about ourselves?*

Under the Weight of Heaviness

*P*oetry is a great way to see things in a new light. Great writing usually paints word pictures that you can only see in your mind. Sarah Young uses a beautiful picture of God longing for us to place our hope in him: "Hope in Me, and you will be protected from depression and self-pity. Hope is like a golden cord connecting you to heaven. The more you cling to this cord, the more I bear the weight of your burdens; thus, you are lightened. Heaviness is not of My kingdom. Cling to hope, and My rays of Light will reach you through the darkness."[19]

Are you living in darkness, under the weight of a heavy burden? There is hope within reach. As you reach out to God, he will make your burdens light. Let the lifting of the heaviness from your shoulders allow you to reach out to others who need hope.

> "Come to me, all who labor and are heavy laden,
> and I will give you rest. Take my yoke upon you,
> and learn from me, for I am gentle and lowly in heart,
> and you will find rest for your souls. For my yoke is easy,
> and my burden is light."
>
> MATTHEW 11:28–30

▸▸ *How does reaching out to God help lighten your load?*

▸▸ *What is the yoke that Jesus is asking us to take upon ourselves?*

Hope in Your Workplace

*A*s you live hope, it will infiltrate everything you do and every place you go—even work. People who say they like their jobs have a few reasons: many say they simply enjoy what they do, while others say they feel valued, or they're making a significant contribution through what they do. If you are in a job you're not enjoying, then find out how to express your unique gifts in a way that will bring value to those around you.

Author Al Sacharov wrote, "The key is to trust your heart to move where your unique talents can flourish. This old world will really spin when work becomes a joyous expression of the soul."[20] This might sound like a daunting or nearly impossible task, but hang on to hope that as you seek to live out of your heart and your God-given uniqueness, he will indeed direct and guide you.

> For we are his workmanship, created in Christ Jesus
> for good works, which God prepared beforehand,
> that we should walk in them.
>
> EPHESIANS 2:10

▸▸ *Why do we get trapped into thinking we have no options in how we live?*

▸▸ *What is one way you can move toward living more from your heart?*

What Are You Leaning On?

*D*o you feel as if life is a bit like a long and exhausting climb up a mountain? While on a long trek through the unknown, it's always a relief to find a sturdy rock to sit down on and take a rest—take your shoes off, rub your feet, eat a little snack. Hope says that when life gets difficult, we have a place to rest, a rock to lean on.

Proverbs 3:5–6 reminds us, "Trust in and rely confidently on the Lord with all your heart and do not rely on your own insight or understanding. In all your ways know and acknowledge and recognize Him, and He will make your paths straight and smooth [removing obstacles that block your way]" (AMP). These verses tell me I can rest in God, I can put my hope in God.

As I do this, God is going to direct my way up the mountain. It's not a random path designed to wear me out, but an intentional path created and directed by God. Live with hope, leaning on God.

> "Behold, God is my salvation;
> I will trust, and will not be afraid;
> for the Lord God is my strength and my song,
> and he has become my salvation."
>
> Isaiah 12:2

▶▶ *How can you rest in God today?*

▶▶ *Why do you still feel confused at times, even when you're seeking God?*

Hope = Grounded in Faith + Fueled by Love + Guided by Vision

How's Your Vision?

A large part of hope is having a vision—something we are looking toward. As Christians, we are told what we can look toward and place our hope in. Second Corinthians 4:18 says, "We fix our eyes not on what is seen, but on what is unseen. For what is seen is temporary, but what is unseen is eternal" (NIV). Our life of faith is directed toward what we physically can't see.

In the awesome person of Jesus, we have something tangible to look toward—God as an actual human being we can read about and know. Hebrews 12:2 says that we are to look "to Jesus, the founder and perfecter of our faith, who for the joy that was set before him endured the cross, despising the shame, and is seated at the right hand of the throne of God."

If you find it difficult to know where to focus, then turn your eyes toward Jesus. Learn about him and how he lived his life. Study who he was and how he was different from all others.

> And walk in love, as Christ loved us and gave himself
> up for us, a fragrant offering and sacrifice to God.
>
> Ephesians 5:2

▸▸ *What is the value of studying the life of Jesus?*

▸▸ *What is something unseen that we should specifically focus on?*

In the Valley of Trouble

*I*nspirational author of many books, Catherine Marshall said that God can turn a valley of trouble into a door of hope. I thought the "valley of trouble" was intriguing, so I looked it up. It turns out it's an actual place mentioned in Joshua chapter seven. Near Jericho, there is a valley called Achor, where a man and his family were stoned for immoral theft of items that were commanded to be destroyed.

The term *valley of trouble* appears in Isaiah 65:10 too, but Hosea 2:15 says, "There I will give her her vineyards and make the Valley of Achor [troubling] a door of hope. And there she shall answer as in the days of her youth." This is a great message of hope if you feel like you ended up camped out in the valley of trouble. This is the very place where hope is born.

> Even though I walk through the valley
> of the shadow of death,
> I will fear no evil,
> for you are with me;
> your rod and your staff,
> they comfort me.
>
> PSALM 23:4

▸▸ *How can hope emerge from the valley of trouble you are in?*

▸▸ *What would the door of hope look like today?*

Hope = Grounded in Faith + Fueled by Love + Guided by Vision

Growing Hope

*L*iving the Christian life can sometimes feel upside down to what makes sense to the natural mind. For instance, to live we have to die, and to get what we want we need to give away what we have. When someone says he or she wants to grow in hope, that is a difficult request indeed.

Hope comes as a result of being thankful for our sufferings, knowing they are building in us something that will last. Paul said, "We know how troubles can develop passionate patience in us, and how that patience in turn forges the tempered steel of virtue, keeping us alert for whatever God will do next" (Romans 5:3–4 MSG). Having this alert expectancy is what it means to live hope. God will see you through whatever it is you're going through, and the hope that remains will carry you through whatever is next.

> Count it all joy, my brothers, when you meet trials
> of various kinds, for you know that the testing
> of your faith produces steadfastness.
>
> JAMES 1:2–3

▸▸ *How can you increase your level of alert expectancy?*

▸▸ *Does "God seeing you through" mean a victory or simply an end?*

Jack-in-the-Box God

I've lived most of my life telling God everything I want and don't want, and then getting resentful when God doesn't do for me what I think he should. In a lot of ways, I've been living as if God was somehow obligated to me. I don't want to live that way any longer. Rather, I want to say, "God, how about you do what *you* want!" It's important to surrender our expectations and live with expectancy of what God will do.

Popular Women of Faith speaker Thelma Wells said, "God does not always heal us instantly the way we think. He is not a jack-in-the-box God. But God is walking with me through this." Hope says, *God is in this. Even when I cannot see him or how he's working, I trust that I am never alone.* Even better than that, he is at work, doing something for our good, because of our love for him and his love for us.

> For the moment all discipline seems
> painful rather than pleasant, but later it yields
> the peaceful fruit of righteousness
> to those who have been trained by it.
>
> HEBREWS 12:11

▸▸ *In what area of your life have you grown resentful or disappointed with God?*

▸▸ *How do you surrender your desires and submit to God's?*

Running with Endurance

*H*ave you ever made it through something you never thought you would? For me, running is a great analogy for life. When I go for a run, I often determine that I'm going to run for thirty minutes. But then when I hit the fifteen-minute mark, I'm done. My mind starts trying to negotiate with itself: *Perhaps I could just do twenty minutes, or I could slow down so it's not so tiring.* My endurance is being tested. Just to experiment, sometimes I'll speed up.

Romans 15:4 talks about how Scripture is written for our instruction: "That through endurance and through the encouragement of the Scriptures we might have hope." God knows that we are in a long race and continually offers us hope through the pages of the Bible. As we let God's truth fill us up and define who we are, we will have greater endurance to run the race set before us.

> My soul longs for your salvation;
> I hope in your word.
> My eyes long for your promise;
> I ask, "When will you comfort me?"
> For I have become like a wineskin in the smoke,
> yet I have not forgotten your statutes.
>
> PSALM 119:81–83

▸▸ *Why is it difficult to use the Bible as a source of hope?*

▸▸ *What is one verse you can choose as your key verse of hope?*

Is God Ever Surprised?

*Y*ou might be feeling like you've been sideswiped recently. Something happened and you can't believe it—and you can't fathom how you're going to get through it. It helps to remember that God is not surprised by anything we go through in life. He never says, "How did that happen?" God knows. God cares. And he's not surprised.

Pastor Rick Warren has gone through some dark days with the death of his son. Maybe you've lost a child and the pain feels too much to bear. It's in situations like these where what we believe about God and hope become so important. Warren said that God's grace gave him the most hope. He knew that God's grace would give him strength; he knew that nothing would be a surprise to God.

God's grace is all over you, no matter what you're going through.

> Three times I pleaded with the Lord about this,
> that it should leave me. But he said to me,
> "My grace is sufficient for you, for my power is made
> perfect in weakness." Therefore I will boast all the
> more gladly of my weaknesses, so that the power
> of Christ may rest upon me.
>
> 2 CORINTHIANS 12:8–9

▸▸ *What does it mean for you to have God's grace all over you?*

▸▸ *How can you share that same grace with others going through trials?*

Hope = Grounded in Faith + **Fueled by Love** + Guided by Vision

What Makes You Dance around the Room?

A magnet on my fridge says, "Dance like no one is watching. Love as though you've never been hurt before. And sing as though no one can hear you." It puts words on a freedom and a joy that I long to know on a daily basis. Hope has this same kind of effect. God is singing over us a song of love, a song of grace, a song of faithfulness, and a song of relationship that he's wanting with us. And he's inviting us to dance. Sometimes God even uses music we've never heard to reach places in our hearts that have never been reached.

I find joy in the future hope that God is offering to me through his song. It is going to be good, because the musician is the world's greatest. He is making all things new. God is doing a work that we cannot see but trust that it is happening. That's something worth dancing about!

> The LORD your God is in your midst,
> a mighty one who will save;
> he will rejoice over you with gladness;
> he will quiet you by his love;
> he will exult over you with loud singing.
>
> ZEPHANIAH 3:17

▸▸ *How can you better listen to God's song over you?*
▸▸ *Why is it hard to believe that God is rejoicing over us?*

Giving Love Away

*H*ope chooses to let love be the fuel that propels us. We choose to love every person God puts in our path, maybe not in the exact way, but in a way that speaks love and life to them. This requires us to be aware how people are acting, how they are feeling, and learning to approach them with joy and sensitivity, without any agenda besides love.

One of the biggest barriers to living this kind of outrageous love is that many people don't understand how deeply they are loved. I'm convinced we will love others with the amount of love we believe we have received. The truth is, you are loved way more than you can even fathom, warts and all. Once you realize this, you won't help but want to tell others they are loved. Hope says, *Love is my fuel that allows me to continually give to others because of all I've been given.*

> "A new commandment I give to you, that you love
> one another: just as I have loved you, you also are to
> love one another. By this all people will know that
> you are my disciples, if you have love for one another."
>
> JOHN 13:34–35

▸▸ *Are we still loving if the other person doesn't feel loved?*

▸▸ *How can you increase the amount that you believe you are loved?*

When You're Hopeless

G. K. Chesterton is referred to as the "prince of paradox." *Time* magazine, in a review of a Chesterton biography, observed of his writing style: "Whenever possible Chesterton made his points with popular sayings, proverbs, allegories—first carefully turning them inside out."[21] When he wrote about hope, Chesterton said, "Hope means hoping when things are hopeless, or it is no virtue at all."[22]

This is like how the Bible talks about love. What value does your love have if you only love those who love you? It's truly love when you love someone who doesn't love you. Chesterton is saying that when you're feeling hopeless, that's when true hope is born. If you only have hope when things are going great, that's not hope at all.

> Uphold me according to your promise, that I may live,
> and let me not be put to shame in my hope!
>
> PSALM 119:116

▸▸ *Have can you muster up hope when you feel hopeless?*

▸▸ *What value does your hope have when things are going well?*

Is Hope Based in Having Good Things Happen?

I need to let go of the notion that good things must happen in order for me to have hope. To have value, my hope should be in place regardless of what happens to me or the world around me. Eugene Peterson, in *A Long Obedience in the Same Direction*, writes: "Every day I put hope on the line. I don't know one thing about the future. I don't know what the next hour will hold. There may be sickness, personal, or world catastrophe. Before this day is over I may have to deal with death, pain, loss, rejection. I don't know what the future holds for me, for those whom I love, for my nation, for this world. Still, despite my ignorance and surrounded by tinny optimists and cowardly pessimists, I say that God will accomplish his will and cheerfully persist in living in the hope that nothing separates me from Christ's love."[23]

> "I give them eternal life, and they will never perish,
> and no one will snatch them out of my hand. My Father,
> who has given them to me, is greater than all, and no one
> is able to snatch them out of the Father's hand."
>
> JOHN 10:28–29

▸▸ *Is your hope strengthened when things go your way?*
▸▸ *What is the best way to increase your level of hope?*

Hope = Grounded in Faith + Fueled by Love + Guided by Vision

Craving Wisdom

I'm thankful that my dad instilled in me, from an early age, a love for the book of Proverbs. We talked about them, and he prayed for me to desire wisdom. Proverbs is filled with wise sayings, uniquely delivering deep truths in tasty morsels. For instance, Proverbs 24:13 says, "Eat honey, my son, for it is good; honey from the comb is sweet to your taste" (NIV). Kind of makes you hungry, doesn't it?

And then verse 14 continues: "Know also that wisdom is like honey for you: If you find it, there is a future hope for you, and your hope will not be cut off" (NIV). Wisdom is like honey. If you seek God's wisdom, the promise is that hope will come alive and it won't ever end. If you're wondering how to live hope, then open Proverbs and seek the wisdom that its sticky pages offer.

> Do not forsake her, and she will keep you;
> love her, and she will guard you.
> The beginning of wisdom is this: Get wisdom,
> and whatever you get, get insight.
>
> PROVERBS 4:6–7

▸▸ *How is wisdom a source of hope?*

▸▸ *If hope is sticky, why do you feel hopeless sometimes?*

When You Want to Give Up

*A*re you going through something breathtakingly difficult right now? And you're tempted to give up? There are days when I certainly feel like giving up. Sometimes it's because I don't feel like I'm up for the challenge in front me, but most days it's usually because I'm tired, lonely, or sometimes even bored. Sometimes just going to bed and getting some sleep is what helps me the most.

Little Orphan Annie said (and my sister often reminds me), "The sun will come out tomorrow." And with that sun comes another opportunity to live hope, to wake up and say, *Even though I can't see through the clouds, I know the sun is behind them. If I hold on, the clouds will float away.*

Hope believes that the best is yet to come, even if we can't fathom our circumstances getting any better. Don't give up—you will be so grateful you didn't.

> But we have this treasure in jars of clay, to show
> that the surpassing power belongs to God and not to us.
> We are afflicted in every way, but not crushed;
> perplexed, but not driven to despair.
>
> 2 Corinthians 4:7–8

▸▸ *When you want to give up, how can you remind yourself things will get better?*

▸▸ *Make a list of what to do or people to call to help you get through crisis times.*

Not Having Enough

*S*ometimes it feels as if life is all about hunting and gathering, going out and collecting all we can to bring home and enjoy. But perhaps you know the feeling, when it seems as if more is going out than coming in. Do you worry about not having enough? Hope is characterized by expectancy—a grateful, joyful, patient looking ahead to what God has in store.

Romans 5:5 says, "In alert expectancy such as this, we're never left feeling shortchanged. Quite the contrary—we can't round up enough containers to hold everything God generously pours into our lives through the Holy Spirit" (MSG). If you ever feel like you don't have enough or the bottom of the barrel is about to fall out, stop for a minute and thank God for all he's done in your life, all he's doing, and for all he is going to do. Let hope fill you up.

> It is my eager expectation and hope that
> I will not be at all ashamed, but that with full courage
> now as always Christ will be honored in my body,
> whether by life or by death.
>
> PHILIPPIANS 1:20

▸▸ *What makes you feel as if you don't have enough?*

▸▸ *What role does gratitude play in your hope journey?*

Loving without Expectation

*J*esus had two commands for us: love God and love others. The first one is a lot easier to do; loving other people can be very difficult. Jesus even said, in Luke 6:35, "Love your enemies, do good to them, lend to them without expecting to get anything back." To live hope, we have to be fueled by love, no matter what—without conditions—just like God loves us.

If you're trying to love people and keep on getting worn out, don't give up. Make sure you're first filling yourself up with God's love. Continually bombard yourself with the truth that God loves you so much more than you can comprehend. If you don't completely believe it for yourself, you'll not only be focused on all you think is wrong with yourself, but you'll continually find what is wrong with other people too. Let's live hope and let love fuel every step of the way.

> "You have heard that it was said, '
> You shall love your neighbor and hate your enemy.'
> But I say to you, Love your enemies and
> pray for those who persecute you,
> so that you may be sons of your Father
> who is in heaven."
>
> MATTHEW 5:43–45

▸▸ *How do you know God loves you?*

▸▸ *What are practical ways to love people who don't like you?*

Hope = Grounded in Faith + **Fueled by Love** + Guided by Vision

Is Anyone Listening?

*W*e live in a noisy world. When do we get a moment of silence? I jump in the car and turn on the radio. I get home and turn on some music. I'm on the phone. It's rarely quiet. Do you wonder if you can hear what's going on in your heart? It takes a lot of focus and concerted effort to stop what you're doing and really listen.

Hope says that God listens. He hears us. He hears our prayers, our cries. Psalm 10:17 says, "LORD, you know the hopes of the helpless. Surely you will hear their cries and comfort them" (NLT). God knows what's going on with you; he hears you. To live hope, it's your job to find someone else and be a good listener to them. Represent God to someone else by turning off the radio or the television, set down your cell phone, then look him straight in the eye and really listen.

> For the eyes of the Lord are on the righteous,
> and his ears are open to their prayer.
>
> 1 PETER 3:12

▸▸ *Who is someone who could use a listening ear?*

▸▸ *What qualifications do you need to be a good listener?*

Is the End Near?

*H*ope looks ahead, believing this is not the end—no matter what is happening. When Jesus was crucified and buried, it would have been easy to think that it was over. It must have felt hopeless. But it wasn't that Jesus was finished; it was the curse of sin that was finished. And the greatest miracle was just about to happen with Jesus emerging from the tomb.

This same kind of miraculous resurrection is what we're going to receive as well. This truth allows us to look at any situation with hope. You might feel as if you're at the end, and it looks as if the stone is being rolled in front of the tomb. But because of Christ, there is always room for hope. Hang on to hope for yourself and for those around you. Even death can't hold us down.

> Indeed, I count everything as loss because of the
> surpassing worth of knowing Christ Jesus my Lord. …
> That I may know him and the power of his resurrection,
> and may share his sufferings, becoming like him
> in his death, that by any means possible I may attain
> the resurrection from the dead.
>
> PHILIPPIANS 3:8, 10–11

▸▸ *What ends when we die?*

▸▸ *How does the idea of your personal resurrection give you hope today?*

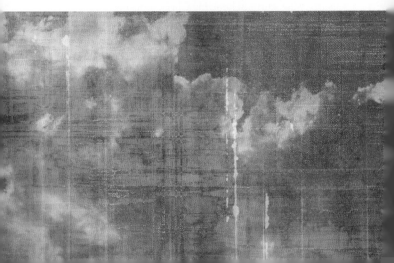

JULY

The enemy wants you to think you're the only one who has ever gone through what you're going through. Hope says you're not alone and your resurrection day is coming.

Waiting for a Harvest

S ummer is the time of year marked by vacations, camp, and staying up late. For farmers, spring is a time of planting and fall is a time of harvest. With summer right in the middle of the two, there's something unique about this season that requires waiting.

Is this where you are in your life? You've planted the right seeds, but it seems difficult to tell whether or not the seeds have caught root and are growing. Hope trusts that some of them are. It's impossible to know exactly which seeds are growing and which have not caught root, but hope carries a strong element of patience and trust. Whatever you are waiting for, you can trust that the rain and the hot days are causing those seeds to grow. In God's time, you will reap a harvest.

"Your threshing shall last to the time of the grape harvest,
and the grape harvest shall last to the time for sowing.
And you shall eat your bread to the full
and dwell in your land securely."

LEVITICUS 26:5

▸▸ *How can you wait for harvest without having expectations of time and size?*

▸▸ *How do you know which seeds to plant to reap your harvest?*

Eating at the Buffet

I don't like buffets, all-you-can-eat extravaganzas. I get overwhelmed by all the choices, but I also get overwhelmed by the freedom to choose how much I'm going to eat. When you order off the menu, the portion size is controlled; with a buffet, it's all up to you and your willpower.

Lamentations 3:24 says, "'The LORD is my portion,' says my soul, 'therefore I have hope in him.'" Another translation says, "GOD's loyal love couldn't have run out, his merciful love couldn't have dried up. They're created new every morning. How great your faithfulness! I'm sticking with God (I say it over and over). He's all I've got left" (vv. 22–24 MSG). The Lord is sufficient. He's enough to get me through today, whatever may come.

You might be going through something difficult. Put your hope in God and trust that he is with you, carrying you through. Let the Lord be your portion—his love is a never-ending buffet.

> My flesh and my heart may fail,
> but God is the strength of my heart
> |and my portion forever.
>
> PSALM 73:26

▸▸ *How can you let God be your portion?*

▸▸ *What can lead you to believe that God isn't going to be enough for you?*

Why Is Hope Such a Big Deal?

*S*omeone recently asked me, "Why is hope such a big deal for you?" The truth is that I was raised in the church, for which I'm grateful; but it gave me a lot of pat answers for life. It was a kind of escapism. More than anything now, I want my faith to be real. As I've journeyed along these paths, I've seen my love expand, my hope come alive, and my faith deepen. It's been a rediscovering, an awakening, a new perspective. It's a simplified back-to-the-basics, cut-to-the-chase kind of faith.

Hope is about living the clear-cut gospel of Jesus Christ. It is a hope that says the grave cannot hold me down, a hope that believes that anything is possible with God. It is a hope that continually sees the incredible worth and value of every single person I meet. Living hope means living with God's eyes and seeking to love the world with his love. I'd love to have you join me on this journey.

> For you, O Lord, are my hope,
> my trust, O Lord, from my youth.
>
> PSALM 71:5

▸▸ *How would you give a simple take on the gospel message?*

▸▸ *Why is hope important to you?*

Hope = Grounded in Faith + Fueled by Love + Guided by Vision

Set Free for What?

Galatians 5:1 says, "It is for freedom that Christ has set us free. Stand firm, then, and do not let yourselves be burdened again by a yoke of slavery" (NIV). Paul isn't talking about a freedom to run crazy and reckless and do whatever one pleases, but a freedom for something more important. Paul said it all comes down to this: "Faith expressing itself through love" (v. 6 NIV).

God knows that when we do whatever we want, we leave a trail of destruction. We get so focused on ourselves that we neglect the people right next to us who are looking for hope. If we were still under the chains of religious requirements, we could insist that others should be so as well. But we're not. We are so loved and so free that we can extend that same unconditional love and hope to anyone we meet.

> Live as people who are free, not using your freedom
> as a cover-up for evil, but living as servants of God.
>
> 1 PETER 2:16

▸▸ *If we're truly free, why do we still monitor behavior?*

▸▸ *Are there risks to showing unconditional love?*

Part of a Bigger Story

*H*ope trusts that life has great meaning and purpose, that we are not just stray satellites floating aimlessly through space. Part of this belief is because I'm unabashedly Christian and hold to the hope that is only found in the resurrection of Jesus Christ. But to live hope, you don't have to subscribe to everything I believe (I won't subscribe to everything you believe either!).

Being a part of God's body means that we each have unique roles to play in the grand story God is writing with us here on earth. We are each playing a purposeful role, not just living some random existence. When I see my life as part of a story that is bigger than what I feel, and whatever happens to me is part of something bigger than myself, that's when I find meaning and purpose—not in myself, but outside of myself. That sounds like hope to me!

> For just as the body is one and has many members,
> and all the members of the body, though many,
> are one body, so it is with Christ.
>
> 1 Corinthians 12:12

▸▸ *How can you see that your life is part of a bigger story?*

▸▸ *How do you find meaning outside of yourself?*

Hold on Loosely

*A*nyone who has set a goal knows that we can't always control what the outcome of our efforts are going to be. Setting goals requires a bit of flexibility. But more than anything, being a go-getter requires us to continually surrender our expectations of how we think things should turn out, or else we're going to simply get clogged up with disappointment.

God has taught me to have an agenda but hold on to it loosely with how I think it should play out. This is how I want to live hope, as well. I want to place my hope in God before I place my hope in anything I want to achieve. I want to keep my hands open to receive whatever it is God has for me, even if it doesn't look anything like I had hoped it would. So how can you best hold on to hope? With open hands.

> But as for me, I will look to the LORD;
> I will wait for the God of my salvation;
> my God will hear me.
>
> MICAH 7:7

>> *How do you commit to something while holding loosely to how it should turn out?*

>> *In what way is living open-handedly a temptation to passivity?*

Hope and Disappointment

*W*hen thinking about the correlation between hope and disappointment, I found a quote from Martin Luther King Jr.: "We must accept finite disappointment, but never lose infinite hope." Chances are, you are familiar with disappointment. It can be painful, can't it? These words remind me that disappointment ends, but hope has a timelessness to it.

When you choose to live hope, you are saying that you are not going to be held down, held back, or held up by your past. You're looking forward and to God for the good he has in store for you. Jesus addressed this when he said, "I have told you these things, so that in me you may have peace. In this world you will have trouble. But take heart! I have overcome the world" (John 16:33 NIV). With this kind of focus, the world won't be able to steal our infinite hope.

> For everyone who has been born of God overcomes
> the world. And this is the victory that has
> overcome the world—our faith.
>
> 1 JOHN 5:4

▸▸ *How is the object of our focus that which keeps hope infinite?*

▸▸ *How can you let disappointment only be temporary in your life?*

Hope = **Grounded in Faith** + Fueled by Love + Guided by Vision

Praying for Hope

*T*here are days when hope seems far away. It's during these days that's it is important to remember what you believe. Perhaps you could write your own prayer for hope—like this:

Dear God, today is one of those days where hope seems far away. I want to remember you are always with me, always loving me, always taking care of me, regardless of how I feel. God, please wake me up to hope so I can be open to whatever you have for me. Help me to live hope so I can love myself and other people openly, without judgment. Help me to live in the present moment and see it as the true gift you're giving me. I believe you are a God of hope and you sent your Son, Jesus, so I could know hope. And just as you rolled the stone away from in front of the tomb, you will also roll away the stone that's in front of me right now. Amen.

"I seek out my sheep, and I will rescue them
from all places where they have been scattered
on a day of clouds and thick darkness."

Ezekiel 34:12

▸▸ *How would you write a prayer of hope?*

▸▸ *Why is it so easy to have days when we forget what we believe?*

Hope = **Grounded in Faith** + Fueled by Love + Guided by Vision

Does Fear Steal Your Hope?

*F*ear is a powerful force that threatens me and my strong belief in the power of hope. Fear tries to make me think the worst about a situation. It tries to control my mind by eliminating the option for anything good to happen. But what is hope's response to fear?

Jesus said, "Peace I leave with you, My peace I give to you; not as the world gives do I give to you. Let not your heart be troubled, neither let it be afraid" (John 14:27 NKJV). He knows we are tempted to feel fear. But he gives us a way out—his gift of peace.

Hope believes that I can have peace in any situation—a peace that surpasses all understanding. Even when it doesn't look like it should make sense, you can show how you live hope by claiming the peace of Christ as your own, refusing to let fear have any place in your life.

> Now may the Lord of peace himself give you peace at all times in every way. The Lord be with you all.
>
> 2 Thessalonians 3:16

>> *In what areas do you allow fear to control your thinking and behavior?*

>> *How does hope help you defeat fear?*

Earning God's Love

*W*e believe that there is nothing we can do to earn God's love. But if someone watched the way we lived our lives, would they see something differently? I have lived most of my life trying to be good and doing nice acts for others. There's nothing wrong with doing good for others. But doing good works to get God's favor, or approval, or his love, is a waste of time. It has already fully and completely been given.

My job is to simply grow in understanding of what it means to live being loved—being the beloved. Out of being fully loved, I can then love others and do good things for them, without the entanglement or expectations of getting anything in return. Hope is based in knowing we're unconditionally loved by God, then learning how to give it away to others—that's how we live hope.

> For by grace you have been saved through faith.
> And this is not your own doing; it is the gift of God,
> not a result of works, so that no one may boast.
>
> EPHESIANS 2:8–9

▸▸ *What's the difference between trying to please God and trying to earn his love?*

▸▸ *If you can't change the love God has for you, what are you free to do?*

Impatience

*W*hat makes you impatient? For me, traffic is a big challenge—not just normal traffic, but the kind that I get stuck in when I really need to be somewhere at a specific time. I also struggle with e-mails that take forever to be returned.

Impatience feels a lot like fear; it imagines the worst. Impatience can't fathom being inconvenienced. It always wants its own way. In contrast, hope has a strong element of patience to it. Hope says, *It's all going to work out. I can't do anything about the things out of my control, so why should I worry?*

If you find yourself being impatient, stop and ask yourself where your hope is placed. Is it in my circumstances, or is it in God who is with me, loving me and protecting me? Take a deep breath and let hope fill you with peace and patience while you wait.

> We wait in hope for the LORD;
> he is our help and our shield.
>
> PSALM 33:20

▸▸ *How is impatience related to selfishness?*

▸▸ *How does hope allow you to have patience?*

Making Your Own Map

Whenever I travel, I pull up a map and see where I want to go and the best way to get there. Then I follow the directions. I would never think about making my own map because it would be two dots and a squiggly line between them.

When I think about the road of life, it's easy to want to follow my own map—to follow my own directions. It sounds a lot like, "God, here are my plans. Would you please bless them?" But Proverbs 16:9 says, "A man's mind plans his way [as he journeys through life], but the Lord directs his steps and establishes them" (AMP). To live a life of hope, I should say, "God, here's where I'd like to go—would you please direct my steps? Lead me where you want me to go." And then trust he will.

> O Lord, I know it is not within the power
> of man to map his life and plan his course—
> so you correct me, Lord; but please be gentle.
> Don't do it in your anger, for I would die.
> JEREMIAH 10:23–24 TLB

▸▸ *How does hope direct your steps?*

▸▸ *Do you wait for God's direction before moving, or do you let God direct you as you move?*

Crossing Your Fingers

I heard someone say the other day, "I sure hope that works out for you." And I thought about how they were defining hope. It was a kind of fingers-crossed, eye-wink, I'm-rooting-for-you kind of use. It said, *I'm not sure what's going to actually happen, but I hope you get what you want.*

Samuel Rutherford, a Scottish Presbyterian minister from the 1600s, said, "Our hope is not hung upon such an untwisted thread as, 'I imagine so,' or 'It is likely.' … Our salvation is fastened with God's own hand, and with Christ's own strength, to the strong stake of God's unchangeable nature."[24]

The word *hope* is based on something bigger than mere wishing. It's planted firmly in the fact that God loves us so much and is continually working everything out for our good and his glory, even if it isn't exactly what we're hoping for.

> And we know that for those who love God
> all things work together for good, for those
> who are called according to his purpose.
>
> ROMANS 8:28

▸▸ *How has a fingers-crossed type of hope served you?*

▸▸ *How does true hope go beyond just wishing?*

Hope Emerging from the Cross

*H*ope is such a powerful force, yet it's difficult for most people to know exactly what hope is. That's one of the main reasons I'm writing this book—so that we can grow in our understanding of what hope really is.

If we look to Jesus, he gives us a great way to know hope. Hebrews 12:3 tells us, "Consider Him who endured such hostility from sinners against Himself, lest you become weary and discouraged in your souls" (NKJV). Not only did Jesus experience horrible abuse, but he proved that pain and even death are not the end of the story. There's always hope.

You may be going through something incredibly difficult and painful. You can have hope, knowing that Jesus recognizes exactly what you're going through, because he went through it too. The enemy wants you to think you're the only one who has ever gone through what you're going through. But Jesus says you're not alone and that your resurrection day is coming.

> "I know you are enduring patiently and bearing up
> for my name's sake, and you have not grown weary."
>
> REVELATION 2:3

▸▸ *How does Jesus give you hope?*

▸▸ *Why do people feel alone in struggles that so many people share?*

Out of Clay

*D*id you ever take an art class where you had to mold something out of a lump of clay? How long did you stare at the lump of unformed clay before you jumped in and tried to make something out of it?

If this piece of clay is a metaphor for life, it can seem like a lot of people live their lives staring at the clay, wondering if it's ever going to turn into anything usable. Some people even wait for God to shape it into something he wants it to look like. I want to catch a vision for what my life can look like, and, with God's help, jump in feet first. Hope sees things as they can be, not just as they are.

If life is like a lump of clay, dive in with both hands and let hope show you what a beautiful piece of art you can create.

> "Can I not do with you as this potter has done?
> declares the LORD. Behold, like the clay
> in the potter's hand, so are you in my hand."
>
> JEREMIAH 18:6

▸▸ *How does hope shape the way you see life?*

▸▸ *How could you, like clay, let the Potter shape you?*

Look to the Source

*I*f you were to stop random people on the street and ask them where they are looking to find hope, some would say God; some may say they find hope in their children; and others may say they find hope in the arts, politics, or maybe even their church. British Baptist preacher Charles Spurgeon said, "Do not look to your hope, but to Christ, the source of your hope."[25]

His comment reminds me a bit of the sun. It would be like we sat around and talked about how warm it is outside, or how bright it is, but we never actually talked about the sun itself. Spurgeon was saying that if you're to talk about the effects of the sun, then you better talk about the sun itself. Likewise, if we're talking about hope, we need to talk about the source of hope—Jesus. Then everyone will be able to feel his affects. Look to the Son of God to find the true source of your hope.

> You are my hiding place and my shield;
> I hope in your word.
>
> PSALM 119:114

▸▸ *Where do you think most people place their hope?*

▸▸ *In what way is Jesus your source of hope?*

Hope through Prayer

*L*iving hope means we are living the gospel in daily life. This means we don't have to worry about anything, since one of the results of hope is a feeling of peace, a feeling that everything is as it should be. Is this something you'd like to have a bit more of in your life?

The apostle Paul has a great way for us to experience this type of peace and hope. In Philippians 4:6–7, he writes, "Be anxious for nothing, but in everything by prayer and supplication, with thanksgiving, let your requests be made known to God; and the peace of God, which surpasses all understanding, will guard your hearts and minds through Christ Jesus" (NKJV).

Direct your longing for hope toward God, and bombard him with gratitude for all he's done. Ask for what you want, and trust that he is listening and working on your behalf.

> And he told them a parable to the effect that they
> ought always to pray and not lose heart.
>
> LUKE 18:1

▸▸ *What are the roots of worry in your life?*

▸▸ *How does hope help you have more peace in your life?*

Grounded in Faith

*D*oes it take faith to have hope? It sometimes seems like people who don't have a particular faith can still talk about having hope in something. But, as a Christian, the hope we have is rooted in our faith in Christ and his promises. To be a person of hope, then, it's imperative to have your hope grounded in faith. Faith provides the foundation from which you can live your life.

Thomas Manton, an English Puritan clergyman, said that we have hope and confidence when we reflect upon the Father's love, the Son's merit, and the Spirit's power, in prayer. If you're looking for hope, you can know for certain that God loves you, that Christ paid the price for your sins, and that God is actually living inside of you. You are in direct partnership with God to build his kingdom here on earth. That's hope!

> But Scripture has locked up everything under the control of sin, so that what was promised, being given through faith in Jesus Christ, might be given to those who believe.
>
> GALATIANS 3:22 NIV

▸▸ *How do you define hope?*

▸▸ *What role does faith play in your life of hope?*

Anchor Your Soul

*G*od is all about hope; he's all about making promises to his people and keeping them. As followers of God, we are continuing the story written throughout time. It's a story of a people putting their hope in him, trusting his promises. Hebrews 6:18–19 tells of God confirming his promise to Abraham: "So that, by two unchangeable things, in which it is impossible for God to lie, we who have fled to take hold of the hope offered to us may be greatly encouraged. We have this hope as an anchor for the soul, firm and secure" (NIV).

My job is to let that hope be what I anchor my soul to, instead of anchoring it to all the temporary stuff life offers. If you let it, your hope in God will be an anchor for your soul. It's solid, trustworthy, and dependable.

> Blessed is he whose help is the God of Jacob,
> whose hope is in the LORD his God,
> who made heaven and earth,
> the sea, and all that is in them,
> who keeps faith forever.
>
> PSALM 146:5–6

▸▸ *How is hope an anchor for your soul?*

▸▸ *What are other anchors for your soul?*

In the Face of Opposition

$\mathcal{V}$aclav Havel was considered by some to be one of the most important intellectuals of the twentieth century. After the fall of communism in 1989, Havel served as the first democratically elected president of Czechoslovakia. He was considered a Communist dissident, meaning he spoke out against the government. He used his power as a playwright and poet to speak truth to his audience, slowly trying to wake people up to what was actually going on around them.

He was also a man of hope. He said, "Hope is not the conviction that something will turn out well but the certainty that something makes sense, regardless of how it turns out." The truth is that hope rests beyond the misunderstood present moment. When I put my hope in God, I'm certain that what happens will make sense, even if I can't see it at the time.

> Jesus answered him, "What I am doing you do not understand now, but afterward you will understand."
>
> JOHN 13:7

▸▸ *What is an experience where you later understood why something happened?*

▸▸ *How would you have handled that situation differently knowing what you know now?*

Hope = **Grounded in Faith** + Fueled by Love + Guided by Vision

Let Hope Shape Your Future

*W*hen I was a young, I was entranced by Robert Schuller's *Hour of Power* television broadcast from Garden Grove, California. The sun was always shining, so there was something magical about the setting. But he was also committed to helping people live better lives by placing their faith in God. I remember Dr. Schuller saying that we should let our hopes, and not our hurts, shape our future.

I can carry around my hurts, my resentments, and my frustrations, letting them shape how I view everybody and every circumstance I go through. Some call this a "victim mentality," those who believe everything bad that happens to them is always someone else's fault. But if hope is shaping my future, I surrender those hurts, fears, and bitterness, trusting that God loves me and he is redeeming my past and turning it into something beautiful. That lens of hope allows me to live with a grateful expectancy of good things to come.

> And I am sure of this, that he who began a good work in you will bring it to completion at the day of Jesus Christ.
>
> PHILIPPIANS 1:6

▸▸ *Who helped focus your attention toward God when you were young?*

▸▸ *How do you let hope shape your future?*

Are Your Efforts Making a Difference?

*A*re you somebody who likes to serve others? Do you find joy in doing things for other people? If so, know that you're awesome. But I also imagine that from time to time you feel discouraged, and that maybe you feel as if what you're doing isn't making that much of a difference. I'm with you! At times, I struggle with feeling as if my efforts to make a difference in the world will have little impact.

But hope believes that even the *smallest* efforts to serve other people will make a long-term difference. I don't have to worry about how much difference my efforts make; God will take care of that. Having hope that God is in the middle of everything I'm doing, weaving in his love and grace and hope, allows me to be brave and to keep on going.

> "In the same way, let your light shine before others,
> so that they may see your good works and
> give glory to your Father who is in heaven."
>
> MATTHEW 5:16

➤➤ *What holds you back from serving others?*

➤➤ *How might hope help release you from that fear?*

Talking about Yourself

I have a difficult time promoting some of what I do, mostly because I don't want to come across as self-serving or arrogant. But there's a difference between bragging about yourself and believing you have something valuable. Wendy reminded me, "Listen to the message God has put in your heart to share with others. Listen, and you will hear it too. Be brave!"

What has God put in your heart? God is speaking to you, guiding you toward purpose. As you tell your story and express what's in your heart, using your unique style to share your gifts and talents, people will see God, not you simply talking about yourself. Listen to the message of hope God wants to share through you.

> But you have received the Holy Spirit, and he lives
> within you, in your hearts, so that you don't need anyone
> to teach you what is right. For he teaches you all things,
> and he is the Truth, and no liar; and so, just as he has said,
> you must live in Christ, never to depart from him.
>
> 1 JOHN 2:27 TLB

▸▸ *Why do we struggle trusting the validity of the message in our hearts?*

▸▸ *How can we test whether the message is from God?*

Feeling Unqualified

*D*o you ever feel as if there might be something you want to do—or something you're *supposed* to do—but for some reason, you don't feel good enough? I know that feeling well. I feel it before I get on stage to sing or speak. I have also felt it while working on a big project. I lose sight of my experience, strength, and wisdom, assuming I can't do it. I keep pushing myself through the doubt, mostly by praying, but also by staying on task, despite my feelings.

Living hope means trusting that the all-powerful God of the universe is with me, strengthening me and helping me to be brave. Philippians 4:13 says, "I can do all things through him who strengthens me." It's Christ who makes me brave.

> Walk in a manner worthy of the Lord, fully pleasing to him: bearing fruit in every good work and increasing in the knowledge of God; being strengthened with all power, according to his glorious might, for all endurance and patience with joy.
>
> Colossians 1:10–11

▸▸ *How does relying on Christ's power and creativity help you be brave?*

▸▸ *In what other ways could you become qualified for the task in your heart?*

Hope in Jesus

*W*ho do you believe Jesus was? Was Jesus a good man, maybe a good teacher, or a prophet? Or the Son of God? I'm a Christian, believing hope is ultimately found in the resurrection of Jesus, but to live hope you don't have to subscribe to everything I believe. When I look at Jesus, he shows me a better way to live than a life that is focused on getting more, consuming more, and using people to get my way. He shows me how dying for others is the best way to live. He shows me that death is not the end, that the way to true hope is only through him.

If you've been on the fence about who you think Jesus is, I'd encourage you to think about him more. If you're hungry for hope, go to the source—he'll meet you there with a cup of cool water that will never end.

> "Whoever drinks of the water that I will give him will never be thirsty again. The water that I will give him will become in him a spring of water welling up to eternal life."
>
> JOHN 4:14

▸▸ *How does the life of Jesus give you a vision for how to live?*
▸▸ *What aspect of Jesus is the most difficult to understand?*

Being Brave

*T*he concept of being brave is something I am fascinated with and have written a lot about in music and word. Why is it such a big deal to me? It is because being brave is one of the best ways to live out what we truly believe.

One of the most repeated phrases in the Bible is "fear not" or "don't be afraid"; obviously, God thinks it's important for us to not live lives of fear. When I believe that I'm held securely in the hands of God, filled with his unconditional love, then I'm free to be brave.

What would you do if you let go of fear, let go of what might happen, let go of what people might think about you? What would you be freed up to do? Trusting God's continual presence and power, you are now enabled to live Joshua 1:9, being "strong and courageous, for … God is with you wherever you go."

> The LORD is my light and my salvation;
> whom shall I fear?
> The LORD is the stronghold of my life;
> of whom shall I be afraid?
>
> PSALM 27:1

▸▸ *In what area of life would you like to be braver?*

▸▸ *What do you risk losing by being brave?*

Belonging

*T*here's something beautiful about belonging, about feeling comfortable and accepted, about being someplace where everyone knows your name. I love that there are places and people with whom I belong. Do you feel as if you belong with God? Isaiah 43:1 reminds us, "But now thus says the LORD, he who created you, O Jacob, he who formed you, O Israel: 'Fear not, for I have redeemed you; I have called you by name, you are mine.'"

The fact that we belong to God is an incredible thought, one that can give us courage. Knowing I belong to God means I'm completely loved and accepted, which frees me up to be brave, strong, and confident. And as I courageously lean into the lives of the people around me, treating them as if they're part of the insiders' club run by the God of the universe, I see hope show up in great measure.

> "I will give you the treasures of darkness
> and the hoards in secret places,
> that you may know that it is I, the LORD,
> the God of Israel, who call you by your name."
>
> ISAIAH 45:3

▸▸ *How does a sense of belonging lead you to hope?*

▸▸ *What makes you feel as if you don't belong?*

Brave to Serve

*D*o you think being a Christian holds you back from being brave? There appears to be something in Christianity that says we must die to ourselves, that we must think about others before ourselves, and that somehow this flies in the face of being brave. It's almost as if you decided to do something brave, people might think that you're being arrogant or self-focused. I've had those feelings—I hope I'm not the only one.

I'd like to encourage you to be brave going after what God has placed deep within your heart. Don't do it to find your identity or to get people to like you; rather, do it in a way that serves others. Live from your heart in a way that reveals the goodness of God, waking people up to how loved and cherished they are by their Creator. Be brave for God's purposes. You will be living hope, no matter what other people say about you.

> I can do all things through him
> who strengthens me.
>
> PHILIPPIANS 4:13

▸▸ *How can you be brave today?*

▸▸ *How does living hope help you to be brave?*

The Role of Feelings

*L*ife is difficult. I can't fathom some of the circumstances people live with. To say that our feelings have no place in a life of hope comes across callous and cold. But I have seen people live lives with extraordinary peace, grace, and hope when everything was completely upside down. It's a great testimony when they choose to place all their hope in Christ, regardless of circumstances.

Psalm 42:5 says, "Why are you in despair, O my soul? And why have you become disturbed within me? Hope in God, for I shall again praise Him for the help of His presence" (NASB). If you are going through something challenging, I pray that God meets you with mercy and peace. As you turn your focus and your feelings to God's promise to never leave you, your days will become infused with hope.

> For you have need of endurance, so that when you have
> done the will of God you may receive what is promised.
> For,
> "Yet a little while,
> and the coming one will come and will not delay."
> HEBREWS 10:36–37

▸▸ *How can feelings challenge your idea of hope?*

▸▸ *What's the best way to not let your feelings decide your attitude toward life?*

Being Fully Present

*O*ne of my goals is to be more present in each situation. When I'm having a conversation with someone, I don't want to be thinking about what I'm going to do next, or even what I'm supposed to say. It's a commitment to be all in, to be fully engaged. This is not only because the other person deserves it, but because I deserve to fully experience all that God has for me in this moment.

When I spend time worrying about what might or might not happen in the future, I'm pulling myself out of the present. I also miss out on the value of the present when I dwell on the past— the what-ifs and the what-might've-beens. As believers, we're not seeking to empty our minds, but to be more fully mindful of what God is doing in the moment, rather than wasting time speculating about the past or the future. Hope allows us to be fully present, knowing that God's got the future in his hands.

> Be kind to one another, tenderhearted,
> forgiving one another, as God in Christ forgave you.
> EPHESIANS 4:32

▸▸ *What prevents you from being fully present?*

▸▸ *How could you become more present in your relationships?*

Faith Like a Child's

*D*o you worry? I sometimes worry and like to think about what is ahead to make sure things go as planned. But I believe worry might be the biggest obstacle to my life of hope. But Jesus came to save us from worry and fear about what might happen in the future. He told us to have faith like a child. What does this mean? A child is present, in the moment. We cannot pay attention to the present if we're worried about the future.

When I place my hope in God instead of worrying about the future, I acknowledge that God holds my future, allowing my faith to take over. Christian writer Elane O'Rourke said, "Hope is the confident anticipation of good. Hope increasingly permeates our lives as our character comes to resemble Christ's."[26] Place your confidence in God, live as a child, and watch hope flourish.

> "What is the price of five sparrows? A couple of pennies?
> Not much more than that. Yet God does not forget
> a single one of them. And he knows the number of hairs
> on your head! Never fear, you are far more valuable
> to him than a whole flock of sparrows."
>
> LUKE 12:6–7 TLB

▸▸ *What aspect of Christ's character most closely resembles hope?*

▸▸ *What threatens your ability to be like a child?*

AUGUST

Listen with ears of hope as God
is holding you close, singing a song
about how incredibly loved you are.

Doing Good Deeds

S omeone once said that the best way to not feel hopeless is to get up and do something. We shouldn't wait for good things to happen; we should go out and make good things happen. This is practical encouragement on how to live hope.

It's true that when I climb out of my cocoon and do something for someone else, I receive a reward. That reward is not only a good feeling but a reward of hope. Let me add a warning to the quote above. Matthew 6:1 reminds us, "Don't do your good deeds publicly, to be admired by others, for you will lose the reward" (NLT). Go on a mission of hope, and make some good things happen. But resist the urge to post it on Facebook. And wait to see what happens.

> "For they loved the glory that comes from man
> more than the glory that comes from God."
> JOHN 12:43

▸▸ *What's the benefit of announcing our good deeds to others?*

▸▸ *What's a simple activity you could tackle when you start to feel hopeless?*

Approval of Others

*I*t's fulfilling to hear when people are moved by something I sang or wrote. So I have a bit of a hard time with Galatians 1:10, which asks, "For am I now seeking the approval of man, or of God? Or am I trying to please man? If I were still trying to please man, I would not be a servant of Christ." Paul was a bold, outspoken man. But something happened when he converted to Christianity—his focus changed from trying to win the approval of others to seeking to please only God.

There's a freedom that comes from seeking to bring pleasure to God and not worrying about what everyone else thinks. When I focus on God alone, it allows my actions and my creativity to be God-centric rather than me-centric. I pray that we can keep that focus in everything we do.

> But just as we have been approved by God to
> be entrusted with the gospel, so we speak,
> not to please man, but to please God
> who tests our hearts.
>
> 1 THESSALONIANS 2:4

▸▸ *How are you tempted to seek approval from others?*

▸▸ *How does God's approval lessen your need for approval from others?*

Joy and Peace

*S*ome days it's tough to get out of bed. Sometimes it's difficult to be bold and courageous in all aspects of life. It's easy to feel as if the tank is empty—I'm certainly not overflowing with hope. I love what Paul writes in Romans 15:13—it's like he's praying over us: "May the God of hope fill you with all joy and peace in believing, so that by the power of the Holy Spirit you may abound in hope."

God can infuse your life with joy and peace as you believe, and as a result, your hope will overflow. If you're facing a mountain you need to climb, even if it is just getting out of bed, ask God to fill you with joy and peace. Trust that God's power within you will make hope overflow. Being brave and taking that first step of faith will set you down the path of hope.

> Now may our Lord Jesus Christ himself, and God
> our Father, who loved us and gave us eternal comfort and
> good hope through grace, comfort your hearts
> and establish them in every good work and word.
>
> 2 Thessalonians 2:16–17

▸▸ *What does it feel like to have your hope overflowing?*

▸▸ *What can you do to make your hope overflow?*

Making Progress

*M*y dad sent me a story about Pablo Casals, who was the preeminent cellist of the first half of the twentieth century and one of the best cello players of all time. When he was still playing his cello in the middle of his tenth decade of life, a young reporter asked, "Mr. Casals, you are ninety-five years old and the greatest cellist who ever lived. Why do you still practice six hours a day?"

Mr. Casals answered, "Because I think I'm making progress."

Hope believes you are making progress too. Even if it seems like you're only making tiny steps of progress, take note of them. Look back and see that you are not where you used to be. Don't give up, for while you're not where you used to be, you are not yet where you're going to be. That's how to live with hope.

> "Yet the righteous holds to his way,
> and he who has clean hands grows stronger and stronger."
>
> Job 17:9

▸▸ *How does noticing small steps of progress help you keep going?*

▸▸ *In what ways does your perfectionism threaten your progress?*

Free to Be Brave

*A*uthor Sarah Bessey wrote, "Everyone likes to talk about being fearless, about owning your truth, about standing up and being counted. We sing songs in church about being brave, we hang prints up in our homes about courage, we talk about brave people or follow them on social media until we somehow make ourselves believe that we ourselves are somehow brave.

"I think we like to talk a lot about being brave because the actual doing of it is so … terrifying. And tiring. And ordinary.

"It's my belief that true fearlessness comes from living loved. When we find our worth and our value in Christ, then, as the psalmist wrote, what can man do to us? I don't think we can be a people-pleaser or an approval-addict *and* be brave with our lives."[27]

We find great hope by being loved by God; then we're free to be brave.

> The steps of a man are established by the LORD,
>   when he delights in his way;
>   though he fall, he shall not be cast headlong,
>   for the LORD upholds his hand.
>
> PSALM 37:23–24

▸▸ *How does the love of God empower you to be fearless?*

▸▸ *Does being a people-pleaser hold you back from somethings you'd like to do?*

Enduring Patiently

*I*n Oswald Chambers' incredible biography called *Abandoned to God*, he tells about how, at times, it can be difficult waiting for God. You might be in the middle of something and it seems like it'd be a great time for God to answer your prayers. A large part of hope is waiting—and waiting patiently.

Chambers writes, "If our hopes seem to be experiencing disappointment right now, it simply means that they are being purified. Every hope or dream of the human mind will be fulfilled if it is noble and of God. But one of the greatest stresses in life is the stress of waiting for God. He brings fulfillment, 'because you have kept My command to persevere…' which is a reference to Revelation 3:10. Continue to persevere in your faith."[28]

Believe that not only is God with you in the middle of your mess, but he is working behind the scenes in ways you cannot see.

> Blessed is the man who remains steadfast under trial,
> for when he has stood the test he will receive the crown
> of life, which God has promised to those who love him.
>
> JAMES 1:12

▶▶ *How is your hope being purified?*

▶▶ *What helps you to be patient while you wait?*

Suffering Produces Hope

*M*y friend Bruce spent some time in a rehab facility after having both of his hips replaced. During his time of pain, suffering, and waiting, he wrote this: "'Suffering produces perseverance; perseverance produces character; and character produces hope; and hope does not disappoint us' (Romans 5:3–4). [This is] a favorite passage of mine that I quote often. You want hope? Here is a path to follow. [It is] not for the faint of heart, but the assurance of what this process produces is a temporal *and* eternal hope. Don't miss that point in this passage. Stop *hanging on* and instead *grab hold*! There's a big difference."

As a patient in rehab, your job is to trust that if you do what the therapist tells you, you will get better. You put your hope in someone who knows better. Let's trust that whatever we're going through, God is making us more like his Son.

Now hope does not disappoint,
because the love of God has been poured out
in our hearts by the Holy Spirit who was given to us.
ROMANS 5:5 NKJV

▸▸ *What is your experience with having your suffering turn into hope?*

▸▸ *In what way have you been fighting against God's rehab plan?*

Hope = Grounded in Faith + Fueled by Love + **Guided by Vision**

Unique Problems

*A*uthor Karen Casey writes these words of hope for those struggling with addiction: "Some of us have had little or no hope for many years. It's no wonder we initially doubt that our lives can change. We're certain our struggles are different from the struggles that [other people have]. But we listen to their stories anyway. And slowly we learn that our paths are similar. Our problems are not unique, after all. Having hope … is a decision. Other men and women have made this decision. We can too. In time we will also understand that hope makes it possible for us to expect more positive outcomes to our problems."[29]

Thinking you're the only one to go through what you're experiencing can be paralyzing. We need people we can share our stories with. We share ours and we listen to theirs. In the process, we find out that our problems are not unique. That's when hope shows up.

> To the weak I became weak, that I might win the weak.
> I have become all things to all people,
> that by all means I might save some.
>
> 1 Corinthians 9:22

▸▸ *How difficult would it be to find someone who is going through a similar situation?*

▸▸ *How could you grow from finding common ground with them?*

Love Is the Destination

*W*here is your life's journey leading you? Some people think of a destination as the goal, but I'm wondering if Jesus intends for us to trust that love is the goal? Richard Rohr said, "Love is the source and goal, faith is the slow process of getting there, and hope is the willingness to move forward without resolution and closure. And these are indeed, 'the three things that last.' People who have these gifts—faith, hope, and love—are indestructible."[30]

The idea that you have to get somewhere is taken out of the picture; you may already be where you're going—if you're being led by God's love. That must be what Jesus was talking about when he said that the kingdom of God is within (see Luke 17:21). Let God move you forward, even without resolution and closure, trusting in the hope, love, and the faith he will provide.

> To them God willed to make known what are
> the riches of the glory of this mystery among the Gentiles:
> which is Christ in you, the hope of glory.
>
> Colossians 1:27

▸▸ *What is your need for closure holding you back from?*

▸▸ *Is there any peace knowing you may have already reached life's destination?*

Hope = Grounded in Faith + **Fueled by Love** + Guided by Vision

Hope of Lazarus

Jesus received a message that one of his friends was seriously sick—it didn't look good for Lazarus. Instead of rushing to his side, however, Jesus waited for several days before going to see him. And when he got there, Lazarus had already been dead for four days. It seems like Jesus might have shown up just a little too late. Do you ever feel that way?

Jesus was heartbroken and was crying with his friends over the death of Lazarus. But then Jesus shouted out his friend's name—"Lazarus"—and miraculously, his friend came back to life.

There are times I'm certain I know exactly when God should make his appearance and what he should do when he gets here. But I'm not God. Hope believes that God knows better than I what he should or shouldn't do, and when. When you hold on to hope that God is in charge, even when it looks as if he's not, that's when you're truly living hope.

> A man's heart plans his way,
> but the LORD directs his steps.
> PROVERBS 16:9 NKJV

▸▸ *How are you feeling like God is showing up a little too late?*

▸▸ *Does trusting God mean letting go of your plans and ideas?*

God's Plans for You

*O*ne of my favorite verses in the Bible is Jeremiah 29:11: "'For I know the plans I have for you,' declares the LORD, 'plans to prosper you and not to harm you, plans to give you hope and a future'" (NIV). It's such a hope-inducing verse because it sounds as id God has all kinds of great things in store for us, which he does. But the problem is in thinking I know what those great things are.

The interesting word in this verse is *hope*. The more I study hope, the more I believe that hope is a gift given to all, but particularly to those who know hopelessness. God's plans for you to know hope may mean you live through some difficult circumstances. But God has you in his hands. He's with you and is getting you through whatever you're going through. Trust God and his plans for you. It's going to turn out good.

> It is good that one should wait quietly
> for the salvation of the LORD.
>
> LAMENTATIONS 3:26

▸▸ *Why do we so quickly dismiss hard times as not being in God's plan?*

▸▸ *Which life circumstances help to mature and strengthen you the most?*

Hope in the Dark

*S*teven Curtis Chapman's music has continually given me hope and encouragement for almost thirty years. One of the most profound things Steven ever went through was the death of his young daughter, Maria, through a horrible accident. During the dark valley he and his family walked through, Steven struggled deeply. He said he would choose to recite the Psalms to himself and sing songs like "Blessed Be the Name" just to hear his own voice declare those truths over himself and his family.

Steven said, "God, I'm going to trust You, that You are with us in this. That is really what helped save my heart, my life and my faith. I could either run into the dark, [filled with] questions and despair, or run to the one hope that I have that God is with us."[31] It's in the days that followed the accident that the idea of creating a worship album started to blossom.

If you're in a dark time, you can find hope through worshiping God.

> Therefore let us be grateful for receiving a kingdom
> that cannot be shaken, and thus let us offer to God
> acceptable worship, with reverence and awe,
> for our God is a consuming fire.
>
> HEBREWS 12:28–29

▸▸ *How would you define worship?*

▸▸ *How does worshiping God give birth to hope?*

When You Can't See the End

Reginald Heber pastored an Anglican church in England. Between 1811 and 1821, he wrote fifty-seven hymns, which he longed to see published, but the Anglicans hadn't yet adopted the singing of hymns in worship. So Heber packed away his hymns and sailed as a missionary to India, where he labored with intensity for a few short years before passing away at age forty-two. His hymns were published after his death. One is famous to this day: "Holy, Holy, Holy."

Do you have something you're working on that you hope to see come to fruition, but you're not quite sure how it's going to all turn out? There is great hope in working on something that you might never see to the end, trusting that God is involved, even if you can't see it.

> These all died in faith, not having received
> the things promised, but having seen them and greeted
> them from afar, and having acknowledged that they
> were strangers and exiles on the earth.
>
> HEBREWS 11:13

▸▸ *What's the point of working on something if you can't see it to fruition?*

▸▸ *What would you want to tell Reginald Heber about his love for hymn writing?*

"Counting" on Hope

*H*ave you ever read the classic book *The Count of Monte Cristo*? It is a story of hope that is based on a man who has everything going for him until he is wrongly imprisoned for treason. It appears Edmond Dantes will be sent off to prison to die, but he escapes and assumes a new identity as the Count of Monte Cristo. He spends his days upending the status quo and seeking to bring justice to those who wronged him. Some say it's a story about revenge, but actually it's about hope.

At the end, Dantes entreats his readers to live and be happy, understanding that human wisdom essentially contains just two things—waiting and hoping. In sustaining hope, Dantes creates a better reality for his friends and for himself. Let hope keep you afloat, especially when it seems like there's no reason for it.

> If we are faithless, he remains faithful—
> for he cannot deny himself.
>
> 2 TIMOTHY 2:13

▸▸ *When has hope kept you afloat?*

▸▸ *Why is it so easy to be tempted to give up hope?*

Push out into the Deep

*F*rom a boat, Jesus spoke to a crowd that was trying to get closer to him. When he finished teaching, he said to Simon, "Push out into deep water and let your nets out for a catch." Simon had all kinds of excuses about how they had been trying to fish all night, but with no luck. Then he finally said, "But if you say so, I'll let out the nets " (Luke 5:4–5 MSG). And the nets couldn't hold all the fish they caught.

This was an illustration not just about fishing, but about fishing for people. Jesus wanted to teach about hope. Simon had excuses, but then he did what Jesus suggested. Is God trying to tell you a story of hope, but you've got excuses why it won't happen? Once you get done with all the reasons why hope isn't real, push out into the deep and let out your nets. Wait and see what God does.

> Now to him who is able to do far more abundantly
> than all that we ask or think,
> according to the power at work within us.
>
> Ephesians 3:20

➤➤ *How is God asking you to push out into deep water?*

➤➤ *What kind of "catch" would you like to make?*

Time for a Feast

*J*esus came so that we may know life, and life more abundantly. Throughout much of his teaching, he explained what that life is all about. In John 6:35, Jesus said, "I am the Bread of Life. The person who aligns with me hungers no more and thirsts no more, ever" (MSG). If you are hungry, then study what Jesus said and did, especially in Matthew, Mark, Luke, and John. From the Gospels, it is clear he came to show us the way to live our lives and point us to his Father. But more importantly, he came to help us live continually feeding on the Bread of Life.

> "I am the bread of life. Your fathers ate the manna
> in the wilderness, and they died. This is the bread
> that comes down from heaven, so that one may
> eat of it and not die. I am the living bread that came
> down from heaven. If anyone eats of this bread,
> he will live forever. And the bread that I will give
> for the life of the world is my flesh."
>
> JOHN 6:48–51

▸▸ *How does Jesus fill you with hope?*

▸▸ *How do you feed on the Bread of Life?*

Which Body Part Are You?

*P*aul writes to the Corinthians: "I want you to think about how all this makes you more significant, not less. A body isn't just a single part blown up into something huge. It's all the different-but-similar parts arranged and functioning together. … If the body was all eye, how could it hear? If all ear, how could it smell? As it is, we see that God has carefully placed each part of the body right where he wanted it" (1 Corinthians 12:14, 17–18 MSG).

God has carefully placed you right where he wants *you*. I find great hope in knowing that I play a specific part in the body of Christ. I don't have to compare myself with others, as we all have different roles to play. But as I grow in understanding of how unique I've been made, and for what particular purposes, I can easier see the beauty and unity of the body of Christ.

> Therefore, having put away falsehood,
> let each one of you speak the truth with his neighbor,
> for we are members one of another.
>
> Ephesians 4:25

▸▸ *How do you discover the specific part you are made to play in the body of Christ?*

▸▸ *What part of the body would people closest to you say you are?*

Will the Floodwaters Subside?

*N*oah answered God's call to build a giant boat, even while everyone around him was convinced he was completely crazy. When the day finally came for everyone to get on board, there wasn't even a drop of rain. But then the storm came and killed everything that moved. "Then God turned his attention to Noah and all the wild animals and farm animals with him on the ship. God caused the wind to blow and the floodwaters began to go down" (Genesis 8:1 MSG).

Are you in the middle of what feels like a horrible storm? Remember how God sent a rainbow as a sign of his covenant with Noah to never again destroy the earth. Keep your hope-filled eyes on the horizon, for there will be a rainbow appearing for you one day soon.

> "I have set My rainbow in the cloud, and it shall
> be a sign of a covenant between Me and the earth.
> When I bring a cloud over the earth, the rainbow will
> be seen in the cloud; then I will remember My covenant,
> which is between Me and you and every living creature
> of all flesh, and the waters will never again
> become a flood to destroy all flesh."
>
> GENESIS 9:13–15 NKJV

▸▸ *What made Noah so special that God would choose him for this assignment?*

▸▸ *How can you trust God for the rainbow, even in the midst of your storm?*

Hope = **Grounded in Faith** + Fueled by Love + Guided by Vision

Sing Songs to Your Children

*M*any parents will sing a lullaby to their children while putting them to bed. It's a vocal reassurance of the parent's love for the child that is intended to bring about calm and peaceful rest. I can't help but feel the same, when I read in Zephaniah 3:17: "The LORD your God is in your midst, a mighty one who will save; he will rejoice over you with gladness, he will quiet you with his love; he will exult over you with loud singing."

Just as a parent singing a song of love and calm over her child, so God is wanting us to know that we are loved, being rejoiced in, and being sung over. Instead of thinking of God as an angry parent who puts his kids in bed and then slams the door, listen with ears of hope as God is holding you close, singing a song about how incredibly loved you are.

> "These things I have spoken to you,
> that my joy may be in you, and that your joy may be full."
>
> JOHN 15:11

▸▸ *What song of hope is God singing over you?*

▸▸ *How can you better hear this song of love?*

Waiting and Waiting

*D*o have certain prayers you've been praying for an awfully long time, and you can't help but wonder if God is still listening? There are days when it probably feels like it'd be easier to give up, to quit praying, to quit hoping. And honestly, it would be easier for the moment. But giving up on hope can lead to cynicism and despair.

When I signed up for this life of faith, I put my trust in Jesus as my savior, knowing that God's ways were not like mine. Deuteronomy 31:6 reminds us, "Be strong and courageous. Do not be afraid or terrified, for the LORD your God goes with you; he will never leave you nor forsake you" (NIV). To keep praying with hope and expectation requires effort and perseverance, as well as courage and patience. Don't give up, for one thing is certain: God wants you to know his love is more extravagant and all-encompassing than you could ever understand.

> "Fear not, little flock, for it is your Father's
> good pleasure to give you the kingdom."
>
> LUKE 12:32

▸▸ *Where does giving up on hope lead you?*

▸▸ *How does God's love allow you to stay strong and have patience?*

Good Things God Has Prepared

*P*aul writes in 1 Corinthians 2:9, "Eye has not seen, nor ear heard, nor have entered into the heart of man the things which God has prepared for those who love Him" (NKJV). This is a promise that God has good things planned for us—we can't fathom what's in store. We are going to go through some good times but also some difficult times. What we can't necessarily comprehend is what God is going to do to us and through us as we go through the circumstances of life.

Verse 10 adds, "But God has revealed them to us by His Spirit" (NKJV). We can know a bit of the character of God by the spirit that lives within us. And that God is offering us gifts of life and a promise of salvation, even in whatever we're going through. That's how we live hope, even when being challenged by the difficulties of life.

> Oh, how abundant is your goodness,
> which you have stored up for those who fear you
> and worked for those who take refuge in you,
> in the sight of the children of mankind!
>
> PSALM 31:19

▸▸ *Why is it easier to focus on our hard times instead of on God's gifts?*

▸▸ *What gifts from God can you thank him for today?*

Former Things Pass Away

*T*he book of Revelation is fascinating and extremely hope-filled. Revelation 21:4 says, "And God will wipe away every tear from their eyes; there shall be no more death, nor sorrow, nor crying. There shall be no more pain, for the former things have passed away" (NKJV). This sounds like a pretty good deal, doesn't it?

I'm sure you sometimes feel like you've had your fill of sorrow, crying, or pain—I have. This talks about a time when God's dwelling place will be among his people. Verse 3 says, "They will be his people, and God himself will be with them as their God." While we have hope that God is with us now in spirit and in truth, there is still yet to come a *better* day when we will see him and be made like him.

> He will swallow up death forever;
> and the Lord GOD will wipe away tears from all faces,
> and the reproach of his people he will take
> away from all the earth,
> for the LORD has spoken.
> ISAIAH 25:8

➤➤ *Which "former things" are you happy to get behind you?*
➤➤ *How does hope for eternity keep you going?*

Getting Enough Rest

*W*hen I'm on the road doing concerts or speaking, I am often in a different hotel room each night. While these different rooms all tend to look alike after a while, getting a good night's sleep is difficult with all the strange noises and air conditioners clunking on and off throughout the night. I am convinced it is God who strengthens me, helping me to accomplish what I need.

Psalm 3:2–5 is filled with hope: "Many are saying of me, 'God will not deliver him.' But you, Lord, are a shield around me, my glory, the One who lifts my head high. I call out to the Lord, and he answers me from his holy mountain. I lie down and sleep; I wake again, because the Lord sustains me" (NIV). If you're tired and weak, in need of rest, then ask God to sustain you. He will lift your head and help you accomplish what you need to do.

> "You keep him in perfect peace
> whose mind is stayed on you,
> because he trusts in you."
>
> Isaiah 26:3

▸▸ *How do you rely on God's strength when you have none of your own?*

▸▸ *What are the physical benefits of trusting God?*

Stuck in Traffic

*A*s I was running errands, I got frustrated because I got trapped behind all the slow drivers. I had to laugh at myself because I really didn't have anywhere I needed to be. *Why am I getting so impatient?* I asked myself. It was because I was held back. Other people seemed to be getting where they needed to go, but for some reason I was in the slow lane.

Do you ever express your frustration to God? I do. Then I find a great hope-filled verse like 1 Peter 5:6, which says, "Humble yourselves, therefore, under God's mighty hand, that he may lift you up in due time" (NIV). How much stress do you take on because things aren't going the way you think? To live hope means placing my faith in the truth that God's got me—even if I'm in the slow lane. Maybe it's so I can enjoy the ride more!

> "For everyone who exalts himself will be humbled,
> but the one who humbles himself will be exalted."
>
> LUKE 18:14

▸▸ *How do you humble yourself and still remember the value God says you have?*

▸▸ *How do you know if God has you in the correct lane?*

Lavished in Love

*H*ow is choosing to live a life of hope impacting your life? I hear the word *hope* mentioned all around me. An interesting statement about hope I heard the other day was this: "Hope teaches us that some things come at us that we do not anticipate, which makes life better than we expected it could be." I think they are talking about blessings, right?

I couldn't help but think about how God seems to love to surprise us with unexpected blessings, like a phone call or e-mail out of the blue that helps restore hope after a difficult day. Whatever it is, the more we are looking for God's blessings, the easier it is to see them, especially the unexpected ones. Hope believes that God is at work and is continually lavishing his love upon his children.

> See what great love the Father has lavished on us,
> that we should be called children of God!
> And that is what we are!
>
> 1 JOHN 3:1 NIV

▸▸ *How do God's surprise blessings help you to keep living hope?*

▸▸ *In what way do unexpected challenges make your life better?*

A Better Concept of Happiness

*W*hen John Calvin wrote his commentary on Psalm 128, he pointed out that we must develop better and deeper concepts of happiness than those held by the world, which makes a happy life consist in "ease, honors, and great wealth." Jesus said in John 16:33, "I have told you these things, so that in me you may have peace. In this world you will have trouble. But take heart! I have overcome the world" (NIV).

There are great joys to experience in this world; I'll be the first to say that I enjoy life. But happiness is rooted in something deeper than just good things happening or circumstances going the way we want. The older I get, the more I want a peaceful life. Basing my joy and happiness in the fact that God is offering a life filled with peace brings a deeper joy, or happiness, than anything else in this life.

> You, dear children, are from God and have
> overcome them, because the one who is in you
> is greater than the one who is in the world.
>
> 1 JOHN 4:4 NIV

▸▸ *What brings you the most happiness?*
▸▸ *How does God make a way for that to come to life?*

Do People Notice Your Hope?

*H*ow does hope affect your life? What happens when you live hope? Do people look at you differently? Do you look at people differently? Have you changed from being a glass-half-empty person to being a glass-half-full person? Are you more optimistic? Do circumstances have less bearing on your emotional health? I'm a person of hope, but I still seem to feel many different emotions. Hope doesn't cause us not to experience any other emotions.

But hope helps me remember that there's a bigger story at work than my feelings. It's a story that is being written by the God of the universe, who uniquely created me for a specific purpose. My story is not done being written yet, and it won't end even when my time on earth is through. I find great hope in that.

> The Lord is my light and my salvation—
> whom shall I fear?
> The Lord is the stronghold of my life—
> of whom shall I be afraid?
>
> Psalm 27:1 NIV

▸▸ *What happens externally when you live hope?*

▸▸ *How have you been missing out on showing hope to those around you?*

Hope = Grounded in Faith + Fueled by Love + **Guided by Vision**

Solving the World's Hunger Problem

*E*ugene Peterson writes about how experts on the world-hunger problem say there is presently enough food for everyone: "We don't have a production problem. We have the agricultural capability to produce enough food. We have the transportation technology to distribute the food. But we have a greed problem: if I don't grab mine while I can, I might not be happy. The hunger problem is not going to be solved by government or by industry but in church, among Christians."[32]

Think about how to live hope to the world around you. There is great need in the world, but it's going to take people like you and me choosing to live by a different paradigm, one that says it's important for all humans to know God's love and to know the reality of hope for themselves. It is indeed more of a blessing to give than to receive.

> And we urge you, brothers and sisters, warn those who
> are idle and disruptive, encourage the disheartened,
> help the weak, be patient with everyone.
>
> 1 THESSALONIANS 5:14 NIV

▸▸ *What need in the world has God broken your heart for?*

▸▸ *How can you live hope to the world through helping others?*

Having a Vision

*C*asting a vision for a brighter future is an important element of hope. By contrast, focusing on how the world is falling apart and singing songs of doom and gloom doesn't paint yourself as much of a person of hope, does it?

Being a person of faith, believing that God is making all things new, carries over into how we view the world. Hope says God is in the middle of this, he's not finished doing his work, and he wants us to be a part of it. Even when it seems as if there's no room for hope, God is right there beside you, saying, "Just watch me, trust me, and hold on because I've got you."

Catch a vision not only for your own life but for how God can work in amazing, miraculous ways. Then sing a song of hope for all the world to hear.

> Where there is no vision, the people perish;
> but happy is he who keeps the teaching.
> PROVERBS 29:18 MEV

▸▸ *Is there a vision for the future that you've given up on?*
▸▸ *How would you sing your song of hope?*

Where Is Your GPS Taking You?

*R*ecently, while driving through a city—relying solely on my phone's GPS—I realized I actually had no idea what city I was in. My GPS didn't announce, "Now driving through Cleveland or Akron or Cincinnati," or wherever I was. This is kind of how life can be sometimes.

We can get so focused on where we're going that we lose the ability to see where we are. I needed to be focused on where I needed to go, but something was missing on that trip because I didn't know where I was. I don't want my hope to be so focused on what's ahead that I miss out on where I'm at or where hope is showing up for me today. Hope doesn't just say that things are going to be good someday in the future; hope says, *God is in this today, and with me all the way.*

> Behold, what I have seen to be good and fitting is
> to eat and drink and find enjoyment in all the toil with
> which one toils under the sun the few days of his life
> that God has given him, for this is his lot.
>
> ECCLESIASTES 5:18

▸▸ *How has your focus on the future kept you out of the present moment?*

▸▸ *How are you finding joy in what you have been given?*

God Delights in You

*H*ave you stopped today to think about just how much God loves you? It's remarkable. The God of the universe, who uniquely created you, unlike anybody else on the planet throughout all of time, takes great pleasure in who you are. He simply digs the fact that you exist.

Psalm 147:11 says "The LORD delights in those who fear him, who put their hope in his unfailing love" (NIV). *Delight* isn't a word we use too often, but it's a great word because it goes beyond the concept of love. It says, *Not only do I love you unconditionally, but I really, really like you.* When someone takes this kind of pleasure in you, you can't help but breathe a little easier, walk a little taller, and see the world with even greater hope.

> Never again shall you be called "The God-forsaken Land"
> or the "Land That God Forgot." Your new name will be
> "The Land of God's Delight" and "The Bride," for the Lord
> delights in you and will claim you as his own.
>
> ISAIAH 62:4 TLB

▸▸ *Why do you think God digs you?*

▸▸ *What prevents you from fully believing God's unbelievable delight in you?*

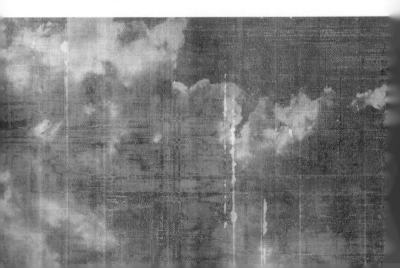

SEPTEMBER

A big part of living hope is having a vision
for who we are and what we are to do.
The vision keeps compelling us forward,
especially when feelings of hopelessness creep in.

Feeling Alone

*L*oneliness is a powerful feeling I know well. Sometimes I'm bored or tired, and at other times I want to know I'm not a stray balloon someone let go of, and I'm floating in some random airspace no one knows about. It can feel that way sometimes. During these times, I make a phone call or get out of the house and interact with others.

I remind myself of a truth that my hope is rooted in—that one of the most important names Jesus was called was Emmanuel, which means "God with us." And Jesus comes right out and declares, "And be sure of this: I am with you always, even to the end of the age" (Matthew 28:20 NLT). He is always with us, even when we don't feel it. His presence surrounds us and his Spirit fills us. When I remember that, I am blessed rather than bummed.

> And the Lord said to Paul one night in a vision,
> "Do not be afraid, but go on speaking and do not be silent,
> for I am with you, and no one will attack you to harm you,
> for I have many in this city who are my people."
>
> ACTS 18:9–10

▸▸ *What circumstances make you feel alone?*

▸▸ *What do you do that helps you feel not so lonely?*

Ravaging Effects of Disease

*S*ue-Ellen has an amazing story of hope. In 2000, she moved to Texas to marry the love of her life. Just two years later, her husband became ill, progressively deteriorating from complications of Alzheimer's disease and diabetes.

She said, "Over the years, as his health has continued to decline, I was only able to find my strength by reaching out to God … We became patient and caregiver, both learning to trust in God's grace, mercy, and hope. Each time I reached out, God answered my prayers … by having two of my three children move to our state with our grandchildren. Our oldest son lives with us and stands with me in carrying some of the weight I couldn't possibly carry alone. But it's God who is always and forever our hope."

> "Even to your old age I am he,
> and to gray hairs I will carry you.
> I have made, and I will bear;
> I will carry and will save."
>
> Isaiah 46:4

▸▸ *How can you lean on God's grace and mercy more fully?*

▸▸ *Is there anyone in your life who could use your help to find hope?*

Encouraging Courage

*L*eafing through the pages of a magazine recently, I came across an ad for Scope, the mouthwash. The tagline was what caught my attention: "Courage encouraged." The ad was saying that when you have fresh breath, you're more apt to be courageous around others. It makes sense, since bad breath can make people cower from others until they find a breath mint! How does hope encourage courage?

Hope believes that God has me firmly held in his hands. I trust him with my life. "With God all things are possible" (Matthew 19:26). I don't have to worry about anything. I can be brave and courageous, whatever the situation. While swishing some mouthwash around in your mouth might possibly make you more courageous around others, try swimming in the great truth of God's presence and faithfulness. Start dreaming about how you can be courageous!

> And the Angel of the LORD appeared to him
> and said to him, "The LORD is with you, O brave man."
> JUDGES 6:12 AMP

▸▸ *How does hope makes you courageous?*

▸▸ *Is there a correlation between a lack of faith and a lack of courage?*

Directing Your Desire to Be Accepted

*I*t's not a bad thing to want to be accepted, right? Acceptance feels great. Like being an early draft pick for the good team, or being chosen for a cool opportunity. Thankfully, acceptance from God trumps all others.

A pastor and friend of mine, Pete Wilson, wrote a book called *Empty Promises*. In that book, he beautifully wrote, "Yes, you are made to do great things, and it's wonderful to work hard. It's a blessing to use your gifts and talents. But your worth, your value, is not based on your achievements. Letting anything other than Christ define you will grind you down. You will always be on a treadmill of achievement, always be haunted by the thought that you're not doing enough. Scripture teaches that you are to root your identity not in what you have accomplished, but what has been accomplished for you."[33]

Do you believe you're accepted, that you're enough because you're the beloved child of the King? That's when hope comes in and fills all the empty spaces.

> But to all who did receive him, who believed in his name, he gave the right to become children of God.
>
> John 1:12

▸▸ *How do your accomplishments tempt to define you?*

▸▸ *How can you allow your concept of identity to be found in God's truth?*

Hope = **Grounded in Faith** + Fueled by Love + Guided by Vision

The Way to Contentment

Friday Night Lights for Fathers and Sons is a practical book to help dads coach their sons in the pressing issues of what it means to be a godly man. One of my favorite parts is called "Take the Trophy Away from Entitlement" about beating entitlement with contentment, something I believe is so important when living a life of hope. Author Mark LaMaster writes, "So whether it be our prized possessions or temporary fame that we feel improves our self-worth, we have it all wrong in God's eyes. God wants us to be content with what we have because we have fully committed to Him and His ways. I am not saying that we should not have nice things or not strive to be great at what God has gifted us to be great at. I am saying that I believe God wants us to seek Him first—before we worry about our net worth, our possessions, or our status."

When you feel your contentment slipping away, think about what, other than God, you may be seeking first.

> "Do not work for the food that perishes, but for the food that endures to eternal life, which the Son of Man will give to you. For on him God the Father has set his seal."
>
> JOHN 6:27

▸▸ *How does contentment need to be increased in your life?*
▸▸ *What holds you back from feeling content?*

Hope = Grounded in Faith + Fueled by Love + Guided by Vision

Holding On

*I*t's interesting to see how hope is talked about in the Old Testament versus the New Testament. Micah, whose name means "Who is like Yahweh," was considered one of the twelve minor prophets. There is great encouragement toward hope in his writings.

Micah 7:7 says, "But as for me, I watch in hope for the LORD, I wait for God my Savior; my God will hear me" (NIV). Another translation says, "But me, I'm not giving up. I'm sticking around to see what God will do. I'm waiting for God to make things right. I'm counting on God to listen to me" (MSG).

Hope doesn't give up, even when it appears that the end is near. Rather, hope sticks around to see what God will do. No matter what you're going through today, the words of the prophet Micah can speak great hope to you.

> Therefore the LORD waits to be gracious to you,
> and therefore he exalts himself to show mercy to you.
> For the LORD is a God of justice;
> blessed are all those who wait for him.
>
> ISAIAH 30:18

▸▸ *How much of your hope is based in curiosity about what might happen?*

▸▸ *What are other ways to find hope in the Old Testament?*

Do Your Mistakes
Hold You Back?

*P*rison ministry is one of the coolest parts of my life here in Nashville. One of my friends on the inside wrote honestly about some of his mistakes: "I cannot change what I am or what I have done; however, I can change how I react to what I have done and how I react to what has been done to me. I can tell that every cruel word that was spoken to me, every cruel prank that was ever pulled on me, every abusive act that I experienced went into making me what I am today. Only by facing up to our past, owning up to it, and confessing it to our Maker can we begin to feel better about what we have done."

You are not defined by what you have done or by what has been done to you. Hope is still a real possibility for you and will appear as you choose to look ahead rather than remaining stuck by looking back.

> "For behold, I create new heavens
> and a new earth,
> and the former things shall not be remembered
> or come into mind."
>
> ISAIAH 65:17

➤➤ *Why do we blame ourselves for things that were done to us?*

➤➤ *How does hope look at your past?*

A Ballplayer's Journey to Hope

*W*e have a minor league baseball team in Nashville, and I love going to their games. Cy Young winner Barry Zito was a pitcher here with the Sounds, just before he retired. I read an article where he described his journey to hope: "Sometimes you have to go through difficulty and physical trials to really get broken down. In 2011, I got broken down physically as well as mentally. In August of that year, I committed my life to God. I realized I'd been relying on my own strength for so long. So this was about finding a strength outside of myself. The way I was raised, that's a concept I never would have given any credence."[34]

Barry has a tattoo on the inside of his right arm of a golden calf, which signifies idolatry—how he was putting things before God. Now that he's retired, Zito can work on his passion, which is music.

> He gives power to the faint,
> and to him who has no might he increases strength.
>
> ISAIAH 40:29

▸▸ *How have you been relying on your own strength?*

▸▸ *How does hope give you strength?*

Hope = Grounded in Faith + Fueled by Love + Guided by Vision

Finding the Target

A friend expressed something vulnerable, an area of defeat he's been struggling with. He told me his story, exhaled, then sat back, waiting for me to make my judgment. But instead of criticizing him, I chose to say something like, "Is that the kind of person you want to be?"

It is easy to not have a vision for what kind of person we want to be, so we end up wandering around, trying to stay out of trouble, not making much of an impact on the lives of those around us. Hope, guided by vision, seeks God for how our lives should look. This isn't necessarily about a job, but about what kind of person we are committed to being in whatever situation we find ourselves. This godly vision can be the target we keep aiming our hope arrows toward.

> "When the Spirit of truth comes, he will guide you
> into all the truth, for he will not speak on his own
> authority, but whatever he hears he will speak,
> and he will declare to you the things that are to come."
>
> JOHN 16:13

▸▸ *Why do we focus so much on what we want to do, rather than what we want to be?*

▸▸ *How are you not living like the person you want to be?*

Persevere with Certainty

*O*swald Chambers wrote about the essence of hope:

Perseverance is more than endurance. It is endurance combined with absolute assurance and certainty that what we are looking for is going to happen. It means more than just hanging on, which may be only exposing our fear of letting go and falling. It is our supreme effort of refusing to believe that our hero is going to be conquered. Our greatest fear is not that we will be damned, but that somehow Jesus Christ will be defeated. Also, our fear is that the very things our Lord stood for—love, justice, forgiveness, and kindness among men—will not win out in the end and will represent an unattainable goal for us. Then there is the call to spiritual perseverance—to work deliberately, knowing with certainty that God will never be defeated.[35]

You will persevere on your journey toward hope. Stay strong and focused on all you know to be true.

Listen, all Judah and inhabitants of Jerusalem
and King Jehoshaphat: Thus says the LORD to you,
"Do not be afraid and do not be dismayed at this
great horde, for the battle is not yours but God's."

2 CHRONICLES 20:15

▸▸ *Why does it seem like love and kindness aren't winning?*

▸▸ *What certainties does your hope hold on to?*

Follow the Compass in Your Heart

*J*ohn Eldredge, in *The Journey of Desire*, said, "Christianity is not an invitation to become a moral person, it is not a program for getting us in line. Christianity begins with an invitation to desire." Maybe you are thirsty today. Maybe you are tired and worn out. Maybe you're tired of the nagging desire inside of you that keeps saying, "Things should be better than this."

Let me encourage you: You are right. That feeling you have, the sense that there's got to be something more, is the voice of God inside of you. He's calling out to you to come to him as the only true source of living water. Life might appear easier if you settle for the way things are. But I refuse to settle. Hope never settles. Rather, I want to be continually reaching, seeking, growing, learning, and following the compass of my godly desires.

> What then shall we say to these things?
> If God is for us, who can be against us?
>
> ROMANS 8:31

➤➤ *In what ways have you let your godly desires take a back seat?*

➤➤ *How can you allow your desires to guide you toward God?*

A Mission Verse

*D*o you have a verse that serves as an anchor of hope for how you want to live your life? I hang on to 2 Corinthians 4:5–6, which says, "Remember, our Message is not about ourselves; we're proclaiming Jesus Christ, the Master. All we are is messengers, errand runners from Jesus for you. It started when God said, 'Light up the darkness!' and our lives filled up with light as we saw and understood God in the face of Christ, all bright and beautiful" (MSG).

I appreciate the simplicity and the profundity of these verses, powerfully declaring my mission and where it came from. Do you think it would do you any good to pick a life verse? A large part of living hope is having a vision for who we are and what we are to do. The vision keeps compelling us forward, especially when feelings of hopelessness creep in.

For the Son of God, Jesus Christ,
whom we proclaimed among you, Silvanus and Timothy
and I, was not Yes and No, but in him it is always Yes.

2 CORINTHIANS 1:19

▸▸ *What is your mission verse, and how does it point you toward hope?*

▸▸ *How is Christ continually saying yes over you?*

Hope = Grounded in Faith + Fueled by Love + Guided by Vision

Loving Yourself

*D*o you struggle with only being able to see all you think is wrong with yourself? Do you focus on the bad rather than the good? I've spent plenty of time focusing on all I think is wrong with myself, somehow believing that God will love how horribly I view myself, showing I have a twisted proof of humility.

You are unbelievably, unconditionally loved by God. Hope looks at life with God's eyes. It sees the beauty in nature and in every single human being. And you know what? That includes *you*. So stop dwelling on all you think is wrong with you—things you're certain God is disgusted with. If you're not able to see yourself with the eyes of hope, ask God to let you see how he looks at you. Trust that he's able to see you better than the best mirror can show yourself!

> Therefore, if anyone is in Christ, he is a new creation.
> The old has passed away; behold, the new has come.
>
> 2 CORINTHIANS 5:17

▸▸ *Why we do think there's a sort of nobility to being so aware of our flaws?*

▸▸ *How could loving yourself unconditionally free you from fear and worry?*

Headlights On

*W*ith your headlights on, you are able to drive down a pitch-black road and not crash into the ditch because you can see where you're going. Headlights help us see in the dark places. In John 8:12, Jesus said, "I am the light of the world. He who follows Me shall not walk in darkness, but have the light of life" (NKJV).

When we follow Jesus, he shines the way for us. With the headlights on our cars, we can't see a mile ahead of us, but we can hopefully see about 160 feet in front of us. In my experience, sometimes God only allows us to see one step ahead. But somehow, that's enough.

Bishop Desmond Tutu said, "Hope is being able to see that there is light despite all of the darkness." If you're walking in the dark, then let the hope of Christ be the light that lets you take one more step.

> In him was life, and the life was the light of men.
> The light shines in the darkness,
> and the darkness has not overcome it.
>
> JOHN 1:4–5

>> *How does hope light your path?*
>> *Why do you think God only lets us see one step in front of us?*

Hope = **Grounded in Faith** + Fueled by Love + Guided by Vision

An Honest Answer

A doctor and pastor talked about the power of hope. Both agreed that a confident patient stands a better chance of getting better than someone filled with fear and worry. I wondered whether I'd want a doctor to give me a prognosis with an honest answer or a hope-filled answer.

It is my goal to be a hope-filled realist. This life is difficult and horrible things happen to wonderful people all the time. But I hang on to the hope that somehow God is in the middle of all of this, unfolding his plan, for us and for the building of his kingdom. I certainly don't understand how he's doing that, and I certainly wish he'd do some things differently. But hope says, *I don't know—I can't know, but I'm going to trust him—not that bad things won't happen, but that God is making something good out of all this mess.*

> For the righteous will never be moved;
> he will be remembered forever.
> He is not afraid of bad news;
> his heart is firm, trusting in the LORD.
>
> PSALM 112:6–7

▸▸ *How can you trust God when things look bleak?*

▸▸ *How does hope walk the fine line between faith and realism?*

A Cup of Hope

*S*tarbucks is a popular place. And I think I've come up with a couple reasons why. We find meaning being a part of something popular. It's easy to feel so segmented and individualized in society that we love to do what makes us feel connected to others. I also think there's something about coffee that makes us feel more alive (it's probably the caffeine). Why stumble through life dragging our feet?

The power of hope can do the same. Hope keeps my feet moving when I can't see the path in front of me. It keeps my heart beating when the end feels near. Next time you share a cup of coffee with a friend, why not share a bit of hope as well.

> No temptation has overtaken you that is
> not common to man. God is faithful, and he will not
> let you be tempted beyond your ability, but with the
> temptation he will also provide the way of escape,
> that you may be able to endure it.
>
> 1 CORINTHIANS 10:13

▸▸ *Why does hope help you keep going when you're frustrated and exhausted?*

▸▸ *How does hope show up when you are connecting with other people?*

An Invisible Illness

*R*est Ministries aims to be an oasis for people who are struggling from chronic illness or pain. They have found there are millions of people who suffer from illnesses that don't even have any name or diagnosis. They started Invisible Illness Awareness Week as a way of "showing the world the little reminders that we have around us that give us hope! Hope that one day the pain will end; hope that God never leaves our side while we are in pain; hope that there is purpose in the pain. Hope that it is the little things God gives us throughout our day that remind us of His presence."[36]

They claim Romans 5:5 as a great source of that hope: "And hope does not put us to shame, because God's love has been poured out into our hearts through the Holy Spirit who has been given to us."

> But I am not ashamed, for I know whom I have believed,
> and I am convinced that he is able to guard until
> that day what has been entrusted to me.
>
> 2 TIMOTHY 1:12

▸▸ *How do you notice God's messages of his presence?*

▸▸ *How can a group of people suffering from the same illness bring hope to each other?*

Let It Ride

*T*here's something about hopelessness that can be paralyzing. It's a feeling of, *Why even try because nothing good will come out of it?* Do you know that feeling? I do, and I don't like it. Thankfully, it usually doesn't last.

Instead of fighting against it, sometimes I let it ride itself out. Sometimes I have too much going on or I'm thinking too much. Sometimes I'm tired and need rest. That's when the feeling of hopelessness can subside. It also helps that my sister is so good at reminding me that things always look better in the morning.

Hope says, *No matter how it looks, no matter how I feel, the story is still not finished being written. God is involved and is making something good out of it all.* If you're waiting for hope, it's on its way. You can count on it.

> For the weapons of our warfare are not
> of the flesh but have divine power to destroy strongholds.
> We destroy arguments and every lofty opinion
> raised against the knowledge of God, and take
> every thought captive to obey Christ.
>
> 2 CORINTHIANS 10:4–5

▸▸ *Who needs a remember that hope is on its way?*

▸▸ *How do extended times of struggle change your idea of hope?*

Power in Patience

A major element of living hope is having great patience. But it's so difficult, isn't it? I want resolution *now*. I want comfort *now*. I want answers to my difficult questions *now*. I want my pain to go away *now*. Hope says, *I am willing to wait, to rest and trust, knowing God is with me; he knows what's going on with me.*

Catholic Bishop Fulton Sheen said, "Patience is power. Patience is not an absence of action; rather it is 'timing'—it waits on the right time to act, for the right principles and in the right way." When you have patience, you grow in strength. When your patience is combined with faith, you grow in hope. Don't be afraid to not have resolution to your questions or your circumstances. God is using this time to help you grow and to help you know true hope that isn't based on circumstances.

> And he said, "My presence will go with you,
> and I will give you rest."
> EXODUS 33:14

▸▸ *Why does being patient feel like a waste of time?*

▸▸ *How can you find power in patience while you're waiting on God?*

Hope in a German POW Camp

*C*larence Stearns was a WWII pilot whose plane was shot down by the enemy. After telling his crew to bail, he stayed as long as he could before he jumped and opened his chute. He was stopped by the police on a road he hoped would take him to Switzerland. He was taken to a German POW camp.

Remarkably, he spoke of gratitude for the other men who were in the camp with him, and even about a German officer who treated the prisoners with kindness and respect: "To have someone treat you decent in a terrible time gave me hope for everyone." He told of a special time around Christmas where the guard shared a toast with him and some of his buddies. "Me and a German guard in a German POW camp, toasting together on Christmas! That gives you hope, doesn't it?"

> So we are always of good courage.
> We know that while we are at home in the body we are
> away from the Lord, for we walk by faith, not by sight.
>
> 2 CORINTHIANS 5:6–7

▸▸ *What allowed Clarence to find gratitude in a horrific situation?*

▸▸ *How can you restore someone's hope with unexpected kindness?*

Meeting Our Needs

*D*espite hundreds of prayers, some believers have difficultly believing God is meeting their needs, which makes it difficult to have hope. But sometimes we simply can't see how God is meeting our needs. Jesus taught the Lord's Prayer to be a guide for how we should pray. Theologian Martin Luther said, "When we pray the Lord's Prayer, we ask God to give us this day our daily bread. And he does give us our daily bread. He does it by means of the farmer who planted and harvested the grain, the baker who made the flour into bread, the person who prepared our meal."[37]

It may not appear that God is meeting our present needs, but he is providing through the work he calls each of us to do. We are all in this together, fulfilling his promises in ways we can't see. This makes it easier to believe that hope is about to show up in our lives.

> Let the thief no longer steal, but rather let him labor,
> doing honest work with his own hands, so that he may
> have something to share with anyone in need.
>
> EPHESIANS 4:28

▸▸ *What part do wisdom and accepting responsibility play in meeting life's needs?*

▸▸ *How much of it is God's responsibility to meet your needs?*

Trouble Seeing

I have horrible vision. I look forward to the day when I won't have to wear contacts or glasses again. Whether it's LASIK or getting new eyes in heaven, I'm good with either! But sometimes my spiritual vision gets hazy too. Occasionally, I can't see how God is working. This makes me long for a time when I'll be able to see God more clearly.

First Corinthians 13:12 says, "We don't yet see things clearly. We're squinting in a fog, peering through a mist. But it won't be long before the weather clears and the sun shines bright! We'll see it all then, see it all as clearly as God sees us, knowing him directly just as he knows us" (MSG). I have great hope that my vision will soon be made new, and that you and I will see God just as he sees us.

> Beloved, we are God's children now, and what we will be
> has not yet appeared; but we know that when he appears
> we shall be like him, because we shall see him as he is.
>
> 1 JOHN 3:2

▸▸ *What is something you can't wait to have made new?*

▸▸ *What provisions has God given you until that time comes?*

Who Does the Lord Have His Eyes On?

*P*salm 33:18 says, "The eyes of the LORD are on those who fear him, on those whose hope is in his unfailing love" (NIV). From God's perspective, Sarah Young writes, "To enjoy abundant life, it is essential for you to have hope. ... So I urge you to choose well the object of your hope."[38]

Then she continues: "The best choice is: My unfailing Love. ... My eyes are especially on those who are putting their hope in Me. Such people are ever so precious to me, and I watch over them vigilantly. This does not mean I shield them from all adversity. It means I bless them with My nearness in good times, in hard times—at all times. ... Look up to me in the midst of your moments, for my eyes are indeed on you."[39]

> So that by two unchangeable things,
> in which it is impossible for God to lie, we who have
> fled for refuge might have strong encouragement
> to hold fast to the hope set before us.
>
> HEBREWS 6:18

▸▸ *How have false hopes led you to discouragement?*

▸▸ *How is nearness with God during hard times better than having good times?*

Hope = Grounded in Faith + **Fueled by Love** + Guided by Vision

Lasting Hope

*D*o you ever find that your day starts off great, you're full of hope and trust in God … and then you get into traffic? Or you show up at work and are bombarded with chaos? How long does your hope last?

Psalm 25:5 says, "Guide me in your truth and teach me, for you are God my Savior, and my hope is in you all day long" (NIV). Easier said than done, right? It's easy to put our hope in God, confident and full of trust when things are going well. But we all know life doesn't always stay that way. The hard part is keeping our hope on God when things aren't going so well—when things appear to be out of control. Isn't that the time when we need God the most? It's not always going to be possible to have every detail in your life go perfectly, but keeping your hope continually focused on God, despite changing circumstances, is definitely a great goal to have.

> "With weeping they shall come,
> and with pleas for mercy I will lead them back,
> I will make them walk by brooks of water,
> in a straight path in which they shall not stumble."
>
> JEREMIAH 31:9

▸▸ *What are the regular moments in your day that threaten to steal your joy?*

▸▸ *How can you guard yourself against the challenges you expect to face?*

Hope = **Grounded in Faith** + Fueled by Love + Guided by Vision

Hope-Sized Vision

*H*ave you ever heard the saying, "Mile by mile, life's a trial. Yard by yard, it's not so hard. Inch by inch, it's a cinch"? This little proverb speaks volumes about how we can look at life. Speaking for myself, it's easy to look ahead and see how I hope life will be in the future. I can get lost in the fantasy of how great it's going to be, or I can get overwhelmed by all that it's going to take to get there that I end up not doing anything at all.

This saying is meant to be an encouragement to focus on the small things you can do today, trusting that you're going to end up where you're supposed to be. It's kind of like eating an elephant one bite at a time. When I have my hope properly placed in God, I am at peace and content with where I am.

> The plans of the heart belong to man,
> but the answer of the tongue is from the LORD.
>
> PROVERBS 16:1

▸▸ *What small things can you do today that are based on you trusting God for the outcome?*

▸▸ *How does discontentment pull you away from hope?*

Showing Up for the Hurting

*B*en was a young man who struggled with Hodgkin's lymphoma, which is a form of cancer. He said something powerful about the hospital he went to for treatment: "They treat the person as much as they treat the cancer. My doctor will remain near and dear to my heart forever. He also took great care of my mom, answering every one of her questions. That was important to me because she was battling along with me."

How can we show hope to people who are going through difficulties? It's easy to focus on the problem and lose sight of the person. It's also challenging to know how to reach out to family members of someone going through difficulties. When in doubt, ask. When in doubt, bring food. When in doubt, send a note or pray. Explore creative ways to live hope to those around you.

> "And the King will answer them,
> 'Truly, I say to you, as you did it to one of the
> least of these my brothers, you did it to me.'"
>
> MATTHEW 25:40

▸▸ *In what creative ways have people shown hope to you?*

▸▸ *Who is someone on the periphery of a difficult situation who could use some hope?*

Hope = Grounded in Faith + **Fueled by Love** + Guided by Vision

Rooted in God's Love

I'm convinced that a large part of living hope is being rooted in the unbelievable love of God, and knowing that nothing can ever separate you from that love. I believe this to be the core of the gospel message. That's why I love Romans 8:38–39, which says, "I'm absolutely convinced that nothing—nothing living or dead, angelic or demonic, today or tomorrow, high or low, thinkable or unthinkable—absolutely nothing can get between us and God's love because of the way that Jesus our Master has embraced us" (MSG).

Being rooted in God's unshakeable, unchangeable love makes me fearless. It allows me to know peace. It allows me to accept myself the way I am, knowing that's how God looks at me. There's nothing you can do today to make God love you any more or any less. You have the entirety of God's love right now. And that is hope.

> "For God so loved the world, that he gave his only Son,
> that whoever believes in him should not perish
> but have eternal life."
>
> JOHN 3:16

▸▸ *What makes you feel as if you're not experiencing all of God's love right now?*

▸▸ *What does knowing you are deeply loved motivate you to do?*

Are You Worn Out?

*L*ife can be so overwhelmingly difficult at times. My heart breaks for those who are struggling to take just one more step. If we find ourselves in this situation, Jesus offers us hope. He says, "Are you tired? Worn out? Burned out on religion? Come to me. Get away with me and you'll recover your life. I'll show you how to take a real rest. Walk with me and work with me—watch how I do it. Learn the unforced rhythms of grace. I won't lay anything heavy or ill-fitting on you. Keep company with me and you'll learn to live freely and lightly" (Matthew 11:28–30 MSG).

I love the promise of peace and rest that Jesus offers to us. He offers his constant companionship. God promised that he would be with us, helping us take our next step.

> Thus says the LORD:
> "Stand by the roads, and look,
> and ask for the ancient paths,
> where the good way is;
> and walk in it,
> and find rest for your souls."
>
> JEREMIAH 6:16

▸▸ *How do we "get away" with Jesus to know the rest he offers?*

▸▸ *What keeps you from resting in Jesus?*

Finding Hope in the Darkest Valley

*D*avid declares, "The LORD is my shepherd, I lack nothing. He makes me lie down in green pastures, he leads me beside quiet waters, he refreshes my soul. He guides me along the right paths for his name's sake. Even though I walk through the darkest valley, I will fear no evil, for you are with me; your rod and your staff, they comfort me" (Psalm 23:1–4 NIV).

You may be walking through what feels like the darkest valley of your life. God is walking with you in the midst of whatever you are going through. He offers you comfort and refreshment. There is hope in the darkest valley—it's in the fact that God is with you and leading you through it. There are green pastures and quiet waters just ahead.

> And I will lead the blind
> in a way that they do not know,
> in paths that they have not known
> I will guide them.
> I will turn the darkness before them into light,
> the rough places into level ground.
> These are the things I do,
> and I do not forsake them.
>
> ISAIAH 42:16

▸▸ *How have you felt God leading you through dark times in the past?*

▸▸ *How do the rod and staff of Jesus offer comfort?*

Hope = Grounded in Faith + Fueled by Love + Guided by Vision

Today's Blinding Pain

*L*ife is difficult for many of us. But it is during these unbearable times when the rubber meets the road in terms of what we believe about hope, and, ultimately, what we believe about God—who he is and how he looks at us.

Our hope rests on God's promise that even though we experience pain, one day we will be fully restored. He promises to complete the work he began in us. Philippians 1:6 says, "Being confident of this, that he who began a good work in you will carry it on to completion until the day of Christ Jesus."

Whatever you are going through today, I'm sorry—it's not fair. But you are never alone; God is doing a work in you that goes beyond what you can see or feel. And it is in that place where hope is found.

> And after you have suffered a little while,
> the God of all grace, who has called you to
> his eternal glory in Christ, will himself restore,
> confirm, strengthen, and establish you.
>
> 1 PETER 5:10

▸▸ *Which of God's promises can you hang on to when you are at the end of your rope?*

▸▸ *How does pain bring out what you really think about God?*

OCTOBER

Demonstrating God's unbelievable, unconditional love toward someone else is the best way to live hope. And we can spend the rest of our lives figuring out excellent, creative, and authentic ways to do that.

Seeing God in
the Changing of Seasons

I love saying good-bye to summer and hello to hooded sweat-shirts, cool breezes, and colorful trees in the fall. Scenes in nature help remind me of how God is always working, always going ahead and clearing a path for me. The truth is that I want to live with my eyes wide open. I want to be on the lookout for how God is working all around me. I don't know how many sunsets I've seen or how many beautifully colored trees, but I don't want to miss one chance to celebrate the handiwork of God.

There's great hope in beauty. Psalm 19:1 says, "The heavens declare the glory of God; the skies proclaim the work of his hands" (NIV). When I see the work of God's hands on display, I can't help but have great hope for the work he's doing in my life and in yours.

> For what can be known about God is plain to them,
> because God has shown it to them. For his invisible
> attributes, namely, his eternal power and divine nature,
> have been clearly perceived, ever since the creation
> of the world, in the things that have been made.
>
> ROMANS 1:19–20

▸▸ *How does the beauty of nature correlate to your own beauty?*

▸▸ *What does God speak to you through the wonder of nature?*

Growing Life

*I*just had two friends welcome their first children. There's so much hope for all the great things ahead for these tiny babies, the love they will share, the adventures they will go on. The miracle of new life reminds us that our lives are a small part of the grand story God is writing. There's a terrific illustration of hope during the nine months before the birth. Doctors confirm there is life growing, even before we can see anything. As the weeks progress, we see more outward signs of life.

Whether you are pregnant or not, hope says life is growing and moving and evolving, even when you can't see it. God is at work, turning you into the person he wants you to be. Trust his wisdom, let him have his way, and you'll be amazed at the beauty that emerges over time.

> "Consider the lilies, how they grow:
> they neither toil nor spin, yet I tell you, even Solomon
> in all his glory was not arrayed like one of these.
> But if God so clothes the grass, which is alive in the field
> today, and tomorrow is thrown into the oven, how much
> more will he clothe you, O you of little faith!"
>
> LUKE 12:27–28

▸▸ *How do you trust God is on the move when you can't see anything happening?*

▸▸ *What is God working to birth inside of your heart?*

Hope = Grounded in Faith + Fueled by Love + **Guided by Vision**

A Mustard Seed

*J*esus said, "What shall we say the kingdom of God is like …? It is like a mustard seed, which is the smallest of all seeds on earth. Yet when planted, it grows and becomes the largest of all garden plants, with such big branches that the birds can perch in its shade" (Mark 4:30–32 NIV).

Jesus' intended to show the great power of having a little bit of faith by comparing it to something as small as a mustard seed. A mustard seed is only one or two millimeters, but it eventually grows into a large tree. Hope doesn't say, *I only have this much faith.* Hope says, *Lord, take my tiny faith and grow it.* Offer your mustard-seed faith to God today and see what he grows.

> You cleared the ground for it;
> it took deep root and filled the land.
> The mountains were covered with its shade,
> the mighty cedars with its branches.
> It sent out its branches to the sea
> and its shoots to the River.
>
> PSALM 80:9–11

▸▸ *How does "planting a mustard seed" correlate to your life?*

▸▸ *Why is it so easy to dismiss having a small amount of faith?*

Ready to Give Up?

I wish it weren't the case, but sometimes when we're doing God's work, we get worn out and want to give up. Maybe you are getting tired doing the work you believe God is asking you to do. Let me encourage you that your work is not going unnoticed. People are watching how you are acting with grace, generosity, and love. God is working beside you, turning every one of your actions into something more beautiful than you could imagine.

First Corinthians 15:58 says, "Therefore, my dear brothers and sisters, stand firm. Let nothing move you. Always give yourselves fully to the work of the Lord, because you know that your labor in the Lord is not in vain" (NIV). To live hope means never giving up, even when you don't get the positive feedback or affirmation you desire. To live hope means being determined to keep loving even when you don't get much in return.

> Therefore, having this ministry by the mercy of God,
> we do not lose heart.
>
> 2 Corinthians 4:1

▸▸ *What is the value of feedback and criticism?*

▸▸ *How can we best care about others without being swayed by their opinions?*

A Living Hope

*F*irst Peter was written as a letter of encouragement to churches experiencing persecution in Asia Minor about a generation after the death of Christ. It's amazing how encouraging it still is.

The hope we talk about is rooted in Jesus Christ, and it finds its life through his resurrection. First Peter 1:3–4 says, "Praise be to the God and Father of our Lord Jesus Christ! In his great mercy he has given us new birth into a living hope through the resurrection of Jesus Christ from the dead, and into an inheritance that can never perish, spoil or fade. This inheritance is kept in heaven for you" (NIV).

What is living hope? It is a hope that is living, breathing, moving, and growing. It's at work within us; it's not static. It is a hope that believes with full assurance and strong confidence that God is going to do good, both now and in the future.

> For everyone who has been born of God
> overcomes the world. And this is the victory
> that has overcome the world—our faith.
>
> 1 John 5:4

▸▸ *In what way is your hope moving, growing, living, and breathing?*

▸▸ *How do you find hope in the resurrection of Jesus?*

In Spite of Your Imperfections

*T*he book of Ruth is a fascinating story. After Naomi's husband and two sons died, her daughter-in-law Ruth decided to remain with Naomi to help take care of her. In Ruth 1:12, Naomi says, "Even if I thought there was still hope for me …" (NIV). Just like Naomi, it's normal to feel like we might be beyond hope at times in our lives.

Someone may say that you're too old or you're too average, attempting to discourage you from believing that God can still do something great with your life. Don't believe the lies. The Bible is filled with stories of hope where God intervened in the lives of the most unlikely people—people like you and me who were filled with imperfections and weaknesses. Perhaps it's the broken people God finds easiest to use.

> I have been crucified with Christ. It is no longer
> I who live, but Christ who lives in me. And the life
> I now live in the flesh I live by faith in the Son of God,
> who loved me and gave himself for me.
>
> GALATIANS 2:20

▸▸ *Which lies are you tempted to believe about your ability to be used by God?*

▸▸ *How does God's view of us differ from society's?*

Growing Tired

*W*hen I wait for something I've been hoping for, it can feel as if my heart is going to rip out of my chest. Proverbs 13:12 tells me those feelings are quite normal. It says, "Hope deferred makes the heart sick, but a longing fulfilled is a tree of life" (NIV). Another translation says, "Unrelenting disappointment leaves you heartsick, but a sudden good break can turn life around" (MSG).

You might be dealing with unrelenting disappointment, and you're not sure how much more you can take. But try to remember a time when you experienced a sudden breakthrough in the past. It was *sudden*, right? You couldn't see it coming, and then suddenly, there it was. You are on the verge of a sudden breakthrough. Hold on to hope with patience and grace, knowing that God is with you. He is carrying you through this situation that you feel stuck in.

> "Behold, the former things have come to pass,
> and new things I now declare;
> before they spring forth
> I tell you of them."
>
> Isaiah 42:9

>> *Can disappointment hold you back from seeing the new things God is doing?*

>> *What's a good way to feel powerful emotions without letting them take you over?*

Cashing In

I met with a financial advisor who had great advice for me about what to do with all the money I don't have. He said that even a little bit invested now will help in the future. Having hope is a bit like making an investment. You might think you only have a tiny smidgen of hope, but you can put a little in the account today, and a little more tomorrow, and trust that it will grow over time. But you must put a little in today; you can't wait until tomorrow and expect your account overflow.

Whatever it is you're facing, place your hope in God, trusting that he will guide you to take the right steps you need to take to get you down the road he wants you on. We can't see the future, or even how God will provide, but he will. Hope believes that God is never going to leave you or forsake you.

> All the paths of the LORD
> are steadfast love and faithfulness,
> for those who keep his covenant and his testimonies.
>
> PSALM 25:10

▸▸ *How can you live out a tiny smidgen of hope today?*

▸▸ *How does hope grow as you make more deposits?*

Run without Growing Weary

*L*ife often feels like a giant race in which we all run from one place to another. Everyone is in a hurry. It's no wonder we feel so worn out a lot of the time. It's also common to get worn out doing God's work. But remember that God is with you and ready to give you a hand. Isaiah 40:29 and 31 says, "He gives strength to the weary and increases the power of the weak. … But those who hope in the LORD will renew their strength. They will soar on wings like eagles; they will run and not grow weary, they will walk and not be faint" (NIV).

God keeps us strong and encouraged. This isn't an excuse to say yes to everything that is asked of you. In fact, you may need to learn how to say no to some things. But as you seek God, he will lift you up and carry you through your circumstances.

> "For I will satisfy the weary soul,
> and every languishing soul I will replenish."
>
> JEREMIAH 31:25

▸▸ *How does hope help you get through tough times?*

▸▸ *How has God replenished your soul in the past?*

Stop You in Your Tracks

*D*ianne, from Minnesota, wrote to me about how fear threatens our hope: "Fear can stop us in our tracks. Fear can stop us from new experiences. Fear can stop us from fully enjoying our personal life. Fear can take over our lives. The more we let fear enter our being, the less we will move forward. We will be like a person driving a car with the brakes on. The car will eventually stop all together with the brakes useless. The car is useless then, too. God has given so much to us but we allow fear to slow us down, to stop completely, or to live with a sense of negativity our entire life."

The answer, she says, is found in Psalm 56:3: "When I am afraid, I put my trust in you" (NIV). Hope laughs in the face of fear, turns away from its tempting snares, and moves forward with faith and courage.

> And David was greatly distressed, for the people
> spoke of stoning him, because all the people
> were bitter in soul, each for his sons and daughters.
> But David strengthened himself in the LORD his God.
>
> 1 SAMUEL 30:6

▸▸ *When is fear a good thing?*

▸▸ *How has fear held you back from the life you desire?*

Hope = **Grounded in Faith** + Fueled by Love + Guided by Vision

Secured and Protected

I received a devotional from a lady in Australia: "Take a moment to stop and reflect on the nature of God our Father. Every promise in His Word is trustworthy. Psalm 139:5 says, 'You are all around me on every side; you protect me with your power.' Think of that in peace and quiet. This assurance of God's love, often expressed in art depicting the homecoming of the Prodigal Son, is meant for you. In God you are secure, protected on every side. Bring Him your troubles in the knowledge that He is the best and most loving of Fathers. The more you expect good things from your loving Father, the more you will taste His goodness. Tell Him what is on your heart, how you feel, what you long to receive from Him."

Hope expects good. Keep reminding yourself of his love, and watch hope come alive.

> But let all who take refuge in you rejoice;
> let them ever sing for joy,
> and spread your protection over them,
> that those who love your name may exult in you.
>
> PSALM 5:11

▸▸ *What do you long to receive from God?*

▸▸ *How does the parable of the prodigal son give you hope?*

What Is beyond Your Hope?

*C*lement of Alexandra, a Christian theologian who lived around 200 AD, said, "If you do not hope, you will not find what is beyond your hopes." Don't confuse this with the saying that something is "beyond all hope," which is used as a way of saying someone or something can't be redeemed. Clement was speaking about the power of hope to help us see beyond what we can now see.

Placing my hope in God will open me up to God doing what I never imagined. It's easy to place our expectations too low—to not dream big enough. When we hope, we are casting a vision, choosing to live facing a particular direction. When we hope in God, we're trusting him to lead us into a life of redemption and deeper communion with him. What could be better than that?

> "Behold, these are but the outskirts of his ways,
> and how small a whisper do we hear of him!
> But the thunder of his power who can understand?"
>
> Job 26:14

▸▸ *Why do we think we can understand what God is doing?*

▸▸ *How have you been aiming too low, trying to keep your hopes reasonable?*

Hope = Grounded in Faith + Fueled by Love + **Guided by Vision**

Close to Losing Hope

*Y*ou might be in the middle of a difficult spot, feeling as if there's no way out except by quitting. Elbert Hubbard, a writer from Illinois who lived around the turn of the last century, said, "A little more persistence, a little more effort, and what seemed hopeless failure may turn to glorious success."

It is easy to work at something, get tired, and then tell God the rest is up to him. And, in fact, God is waiting to help you to keep going; he is alongside of you, fighting through the challenge so you can get to the beauty ahead. Some of you have given up when you're actually very close to a breakthrough. Hope says that the story is still being written and that God's up to something good. Don't give up.

> To grant to those who mourn in Zion—
> to give them a beautiful headdress instead of ashes,
> the oil of gladness instead of mourning,
> the garment of praise instead of a faint spirit;
> that they may be called oaks of righteousness,
> the planting of the Lord, that he may be glorified.
>
> Isaiah 61:3

▸▸ *How has exhaustion stolen your vision?*

▸▸ *Could pushing Pause allow you to refresh and restart, rather than completely stop?*

Hope = Grounded in Faith + Fueled by Love + Guided by Vision

Because of Love

*F*irst Corinthians 13:13 says, "And now these three remain: faith, hope and love. But the greatest of these is love" (NIV). Love is the most important because it's the foundation of hope. We can only have hope because we know God loves us. If we didn't believe God loves us, then there wouldn't be any reason for hope. We can look at our circumstances and trust that God is working all things together for our good.

Living a life of hope must be fueled by love. We're loved, but how can we tell others they are loved? We tell them by demonstrating God's unbelievable, unconditional love. And we spend the rest of our lives figuring out excellent, creative, and authentic ways to do that.

> "And you shall love the Lord your God with all
> your heart and with all your soul and with all your mind
> and with all your strength." The second is this:
> "You shall love your neighbor as yourself."
> There is no other commandment greater than these.
>
> MARK 12:30–31

▸▸ *What are some ways you can show hope to the people in your life?*

▸▸ *How has God uniquely equipped you to offer hope?*

Do They Notice?

*C*an people notice that you're a person of hope? True hope shines the brightest when we go through difficult times. Hope says that no matter what I'm going through, whether good, bad, or indifferent, God is in the middle of it. Even though I might not be able to see him, he is there. All my questions will be answered one day.

First Peter 3:15 says, "But in your hearts revere Christ as Lord. Always be prepared to give an answer to everyone who asks you to give the reason for the hope that you have" (NIV). Hope is grounded in this great faith and fueled by unbelievable love. I hope you believe that, because somebody, sometime soon, may ask you where your hope comes from.

Blessed be the God and Father of our Lord Jesus Christ!
According to his great mercy, he has caused us
to be born again to a living hope through the resurrection
of Jesus Christ from the dead, to an inheritance
that is imperishable, undefiled, and unfading,
kept in heaven for you.

1 PETER 1:3–4

▸▸ *How would you explain your hope in a way a nonreligious person would understand?*

▸▸ *Why do so many people say they believe in hope but seldom show it to others?*

Hope = **Grounded in Faith** + Fueled by Love + Guided by Vision

The Utmost Courtesy

*F*irst Peter 3:15 is a great challenge to all of us. It says, "Always be prepared to give an answer to everyone who asks you to give the reason for the hope that you have" (NIV). But it also says we are to "do this with gentleness and respect." Other translations say that we are to do it "with the utmost courtesy" (MSG) or "with meekness and fear" (NKJV). It makes me chuckle a little, because this proves we haven't changed much as humans, even two thousand years later!

The author of 1 Peter knows that we are prone to *not* be gentle and respectful. Many translations leave off this last line, one that gives great insight into the timelessness of the Scriptures. This phrase also reminds us how important it is to be sensitive and thoughtful toward others, not making it all about us.

> Let your speech always be gracious,
> seasoned with salt, so that you may know
> how you ought to answer each person.
> Colossians 4:6

▸▸ *Why are we so often awkward in our attempts to express our beliefs?*

▸▸ *What might be the key to authenticity with those who don't share our beliefs?*

Called to One Hope

*E*phesians 4:4 says, "There is one body and one Spirit, just as you were called to one hope when you were called" (NIV). What does it mean to be called to one hope? Paul writes through most of Ephesians about union with Christ, and our call to be as one. This verse is a clarion call to unity. This statement echoes what Jesus prayed in John 17:21: "That they may all be one, just as you, Father, are in me, and I in you."

We don't experience unity as we focus on our differences, how we're right and they're wrong. Rather, we find unity when we focus on what we have in common. It's easy to find in others that which is difficult to forgive or even understand. But there is always one Christ in whom all believers hope, and one heaven we all hope for.

> Only let your manner of life be worthy
> of the gospel of Christ, so that whether I come
> and see you or am absent, I may hear of you that you
> are standing firm in one spirit, with one mind
> striving side by side for the faith of the gospel.
>
> PHILIPPIANS 1:27

➤➤ *What do you think causes the most disunity between people?*

➤➤ *How does your desire to have the right answers keep you from unity with others?*

Hope = Grounded in Faith + **Fueled by Love** + Guided by Vision

Where Is Your Suffering Leading?

*O*ne of the most difficult parts of my work is hearing the pain so many people are going through. I'm honored to hear their stories, but my heart breaks for them. I believe it's possible to live hope, even in the midst of our suffering. Romans 5:3–5 reminds us, "Not only that, but we rejoice in our sufferings, knowing that suffering produces endurance, and endurance produces character, and character produces hope, and hope does not put us to shame, because God's love has been poured into our hearts through the Holy Spirit who has been given to us."

I don't take lightly what you might be going through, but hope believes that God is up to something good, even in pain. God is guiding you through this to create even greater hope within you. Rest in the love that God has poured into your heart and cling to the hope that he is with you every painful step of the way.

> For this light momentary affliction is preparing for us an eternal weight of glory beyond all comparison.
>
> 2 CORINTHIANS 4:17

▸▸ *What has suffering produced in you?*

▸▸ *How can our struggles be used for growth and not personal destruction?*

Hope = Grounded in Faith + Fueled by Love + **Guided by Vision**

What You Have or Don't Have

*E*picurus was a Greek philosopher who said, "Do not spoil what you have by desiring what you have not; remember that what you now have was once among the things you only hoped for." And last week, my friend Tim said, "You keep waiting for what you're wanting, but you already have it."

These messages combined are as if God is trying to get me to be more grateful for what I already have instead of being focused on what I don't have. Longing for what one doesn't have makes a person anxious, depressed, needy, and closed off. But being thankful for what one has makes a person beautiful, graceful, and open to new things God has in store. That's the essence of hope.

> Oh come, let us sing to the LORD;
> let us make a joyful noise to the rock of our salvation!
> Let us come into his presence with thanksgiving;
> let us make a joyful noise to him with songs of praise!
> For the LORD is a great God,
> and a great King above all gods.
>
> PSALM 95:1–3

▸▸ *What role does gratitude play in your life of hope?*

▸▸ *In what ways has God already given you what you're hoping for?*

Hope = **Grounded in Faith** + Fueled by Love + Guided by Vision

Helping You Wait Patiently

*T*ertullian, a Christian author from Africa, defined hope. He wrote, "Hope is patience with the lamp lit." I remember an old commercial for a hotel chain that said, "We'll leave the light on for you." I thoughts about my parents who would leave the light on for me when I came home late so I could find my way inside easier. I also thought about the father in the story of the prodigal son, who, I imagine, left the light on for his wayward son. Leaving the light on implies that someone is waiting for you.

"Hope is patience with the lamp lit." Having patience is a huge part of hope, but it also describes how we wait. We wait patiently but expectantly. We trust God is going to show up, even though we're not sure exactly when—kind of like my parents when I was a teenager.

> Lead me in your truth and teach me,
> for you are the God of my salvation;
> for you I wait all the day long.
>
> PSALM 25:5

▸▸ *How are you keeping your lamp lit?*

▸▸ *What do you do when you get tired of waiting with expectation?*

How Does the Bible Give You Hope?

I've struggled to read the Bible. Sometimes it is difficult to understand, relate to, or *find myself* within. But Romans 15:4–6 says, "Even if it was written in Scripture long ago, you can be sure it's written for us. God wants the combination of his steady, constant calling and warm, personal counsel in Scripture to come to characterize us, keeping us alert for whatever he will do next. May our dependably steady and warmly personal God develop maturity in you so that you get along with each other as well as Jesus gets along with us all. Then we'll be a choir—not our voices only, but our very lives singing in harmony in a stunning anthem to the God and Father of our Master Jesus" (MSG).

Finding these verses that resonate so clearly within me gives me hope that I'll keep uncovering more truth and insight into God, *and myself*, as I continue to read the Bible.

> All Scripture is breathed out by God and profitable
> for teaching, for reproof, for correction, and for training
> in righteousness, that the [person] of God may
> be complete, equipped for every good work.
>
> 2 TIMOTHY 3:16–17

▸▸ *Where do you find hope in the Bible?*

▸▸ *Have you found a translation that you connect with more than others?*

Hope = Grounded in Faith + Fueled by Love + Guided by Vision

Your Hope Focus

*H*ope can have focus—like trusting that God is working in your circumstances, making you more like Jesus. Additionally, the Bible encourages us to keep our hope focused on the day of Christ's return. First Peter 1:13 says, "Therefore, with minds that are alert and fully sober, set your hope on the grace to be brought to you when Jesus Christ is revealed at his coming." Another translation says, "So roll up your sleeves, put your mind in gear, be totally ready to receive the gift that's coming when Jesus arrives" (MSG).

Keep your eyes fixed on the day when Christ returns. This kind of focus will help get you through any kind of circumstance while you wait for God to act.

> For the grace of God has appeared, bringing salvation
> for all people, training us to renounce ungodliness and
> worldly passions, and to live self-controlled, upright, and
> godly lives in the present age, waiting for our blessed
> hope, the appearing of the glory of our great God and
> Savior Jesus Christ.
>
> TITUS 2:11–13

▸▸ *How does an eternal focus carry you through life?*

▸▸ *When does being too heavenly minded make us no earthly good?*

Hope = Grounded in Faith + Fueled by Love + Guided by Vision

What Song Are You Singing?

*A*s a Christian singer, I choose what kind of songs to write and sing for others. A lot of my songs are messages I need to hear, while other songs are intended for others. What has emerged over the years is that much of my music is focused on the message of hope, which is found in the unconditional love God has for us. These are the kinds of songs I want to sing with my life.

What kind of song do you want to sing with your life? Don't fancy yourself as much of a singer? I get that, but we are all singing a song with our lives. All our words and actions are sending a message to the people around us of the kind of song we are choosing to sing. What kind of song would you like people to hear? Join me in singing a song of love that is filled with compassion and hope.

> Oh sing to the LORD a new song,
> for he has done marvelous things!
> His right hand and his holy arm
> have worked salvation for him.
>
> PSALM 98:1

▸▸ *Are people hearing the song you want them to hear with your life?*

▸▸ *In what way might you be singing dissonant songs?*

Hope = Grounded in Faith + **Fueled by Love** + Guided by Vision

Glass Half Full or Half Empty?

*S*ome feel that we are either glass half-full or glass half-empty people. Which one are you? I'm both—depending on the day. What holds us back from viewing life in a positive way? We can't control what happens to us, but we have an option on how we're going to respond to our circumstances.

Try to catch a vision for how God sees the world. He sees the world as his grand love story, and he's working to redeem the lost, the broken, and the hurting. He's asking us to join him in his mission to heal the world. Hope believes that good, not bad, is still to come. Even if the world says the sky is falling, we can trust even that is all part of God's good plan.

> "For I am God, and there is no other;
> I am God, and there is none like me,
> declaring the end from the beginning
> and from ancient times things not yet done,
> saying, 'My counsel shall stand,
> and I will accomplish all my purpose.'"
>
> ISAIAH 46:9–10

▸▸ *Are you ever without a choice to be either positive or negative? Explain.*

▸▸ *How do you think God wants to use you to help heal the world?*

Hope Leading to Action

*H*ope should lead us to action. A large part of living a life of hope is being fueled by love. When you know how incredibly loved you are by God, then you are free to give that same love away to others. First John 4:11 says, "Dear friends, since God loved us that much, we surely ought to love each other" (NLT).

Loving people is more than saying hello or giving a kind smile, though that's a great start. We love people when we extend to them the same grace and mercy we desire to have extended to us. We can be great believers in hope, but until we learn how to express that hope to a needy world, we're merely keeping our bright light under a bushel.

> By this we know love, that he laid down his life for us,
> and we ought to lay down our lives for the brothers.
> But if anyone has the world's goods and sees his
> brother in need, yet closes his heart against him,
> how does God's love abide in him?
>
> 1 JOHN 3:16–17

›› *How does living hope motivate you to move toward others?*

›› *Why do we usually only reach out to people we believe deserve our love?*

To Live Hope

*I*t's one thing to know what hope is, but it's another thing to show hope to the world around you—to *live* hope. If you choose to be a person marked by hope, how does that show itself to the world you live in?

One of the best ways hope shows itself is through peace. Peace comes from a belief in God that, no matter what happens, God acts in love toward you. When you are at peace while going through difficult circumstances, your hope in Christ will shine through. I wrote a song about this, called "Live Hope," which is on my CD, *The Messenger: A Journey into Hope*. It says, "To live hope is to believe, guided from above, when the world says just give up, God is in this. To live hope is to believe to have faith is enough, and to live this life with love, because God is in this. I will live hope."

> Therefore, preparing your minds for action, and being sober-minded, set your hope fully on the grace that will be brought to you at the revelation of Jesus Christ.
>
> 1 PETER 1:13

>> *What's an effective way to prepare your mind for action?*

>> *How can we encourage others to move beyond inspiration to action?*

Hope = **Grounded in Faith** + Fueled by Love + Guided by Vision

Staring into the Unknown

I long to uncover what it means to live hope—for us to know hope in the core of our being, and then choose to live it out to the world around us. As a singer/songwriter, I wanted to write a song that could be our anthem, to put words to what it means to live out the hope we profess. So I wrote a song called "Live Hope." The first line says, "To be brave, staring into unknown." Have you stared into the unknown lately? Maybe when you lost your job, or you finished school and you weren't sure what you were supposed to do?

We live out our faith by being brave, saying, "God, you've got me." Then we trust that he does have us, no matter what the circumstances might look like. I choose to live hope today. Will you join me?

> Then David said to Solomon his son, "Be strong and courageous and do it. Do not be afraid and do not be dismayed, for the LORD God, even my God, is with you. He will not leave you or forsake you, until all the work for the service of the house of the LORD is finished."
>
> 1 CHRONICLES 28:20

▸▸ *In what ways could you be braver?*

▸▸ *How does the fear of the unknown prevent you from being brave?*

Hope = Grounded in Faith + Fueled by Love + **Guided by Vision**

When You're Certain It's Over

*H*ave you ever reached the point where you were certain *it* was over? Whether it was a job, a relationship, perhaps a church you've been attending … sometimes things just end. In my song "Live Hope," I lay out a practical way of looking at what it means to live hope. One of my favorite parts says, "To keep on, when you feel like it's over. To get back up, when you've been knocked down. To reach out, when your past hurts so strong. This is what it means to live hope."

To live hope means you keep going even when you've been kicked, knocked down, dragged, or maybe even just ignored. Instead of thinking it can't get any better, hope says that God is in the middle of this pain and struggle. He's working all these circumstances for your good.

> For as we share abundantly in Christ's sufferings,
> so through Christ we share abundantly in comfort too. …
> Our hope for you is unshaken, for we know that as you
> share in our sufferings, you will also share in our comfort.
>
> 2 Corinthians 1:5, 7

▸▸ *How does hope allow you to get back up when you've been knocked down?*

▸▸ *How can you acknowledge the working of God in pain?*

Living out Your Beliefs

*I*t's important to know what we believe, but it may be even more important how we choose to live out those beliefs. Maybe I feel that way because I grew up learning doctrine and rules, and it didn't feel as if all the instructions had legs on them. I got lost trying to do the right thing. As a result, learning how to truly be the hands and feet of Christ hasn't been at the forefront of my life.

That's why I call this devotional and my radio feature the *Live Hope Minute*. Not only do I want us to know what hope is, but I also want us to know how to live it out. Sometimes it's through a testimony of what God has done for someone else, and sometimes it's through doing good for others. Matthew 5:16 reminds us, "Let your light shine before others, so that they may see your good works and give glory to your Father who is in heaven."

> "By this my Father is glorified, that you bear much
> fruit and so prove to be my disciples."
>
> JOHN 15:8

▸▸ *What are the fruits of your actions of love toward people?*

▸▸ *How have you been distracted from action by learning proper doctrine?*

To Simply Have Faith

I have grown up as a Christian and been bombarded with the importance of having faith. At the same time, I've been a bit of a control freak—I really enjoy knowing how things are going to go. I like everything to be well planned and thought out. But there's something about the life of faith that flies in the face of that kind of living. If you've lived life at all, then you probably know that life doesn't always go the way you want it to.

Living hope means believing that faith is enough to get me through. If faith isn't enough, then I'm going to be frustrated and confused by how life twists and turns. But trusting in God—that he's with me and loves me, forming me more into his perfect child—is truly enough, even when I don't get my way.

For in it the righteousness of God is revealed from faith for faith, as it is written, "The righteous shall live by faith."

ROMANS 1:17

▸▸ *How does trusting God allow you to go through life's challenges?*

▸▸ *In what ways is God leading you to let go of trying to control everything?*

Changing a Person

I have lived most of my life working hard to get others to see the truth, to get them to become more of who I wanted them to be, rather than loving them for who they are. I'm certain I ruined a lot of relationships that way. When I look at Jesus, however, I see that he desired to show love to the people who weren't doing it right according to those who knew better—the religious people. Jesus made a point: love is best communicated by compassion and understanding, not by rules and regulations. And yet Jesus never left anyone unchanged—his love made them better. Not his rules or principles … his love.

You have the power to change someone for the better, to reveal the goodness, the God*ness*, inside each person through your love. When you love like that, you can't begin to hold the hope that will fill your life.

> And above all these put on love, which binds everything together in perfect harmony. And let the peace of Christ rule in your hearts, to which indeed you were called in one body. And be thankful.
>
> COLOSSIANS 3:14–15

▸▸ *What have been ineffective ways you've tried to change others?*

▸▸ *How does tough love play into our mission to reveal God's unconditional love?*

Hope = Grounded in Faith + Fueled by Love + Guided by Vision

NOVEMBER

Live your life spreading hope by continually
saying thank you to God through prayer,
worship, and service to others.

Within Church Walls

*S*ome of you have given up on church; you've been burned. People are flawed, and broken, and most of us are hypocritical, at least to a small extent. But the church is also beautiful. Some of the closest friends I've had have been church friends. So much of my spiritual growth has come out of my church experience. I learned how to sing in a church. I learned how to think about other people more than myself in church. And I've seen people serve each other and the world with wild abandon in church.

People who have been hurt and broken by the church can find a place of healing and rest within a good church. I hope you can find one that allows for authenticity and doesn't require perfection, allowing you to be present with your questions and cheering you on during your quest for hope.

> And let us consider how to stir up one another to love and good works, not neglecting to meet together, as is the habit of some, but encouraging one another, and all the more as you see the Day drawing near.
>
> HEBREWS 10:24–25

▸▸ *Why are so many people hurt by their church experiences?*
▸▸ *What do churches excel at?*

A Formula for Hope

*M*any people talk about hope as if it's an elusive feeling that's great when you have it and challenging when you don't. But having hope is a choice each of us can make anytime we want.

Hope is a bit of a three-legged stool. One leg is *love*. We know we're unconditionally loved by God, and we're committed to sharing that love with others. Another leg is *faith*. We decide to put our trust in God; that he's with us and holding us and guiding us. We become a part of a bigger story than ourselves. And lastly, hope's third leg is *vision*. Having vision for a better future is important to keep us motivated and directed through difficult days.

Hope says that God is in this, he's got us, and something good is on its way.

> In your hearts honor Christ the Lord as holy,
> always being prepared to make a defense to anyone
> who asks you for a reason for the hope that is in you;
> yet do it with gentleness and respect.
>
> 1 PETER 3:15

▸▸ *When you feel hope slipping away, what piece of the formula might you be missing?*

▸▸ *What would your personal formula for hope look like?*

Hope = Grounded in Faith + Fueled by Love + Guided by Vision

Looking for Wisdom

*P*roverbs 24:14 says, "Know also that wisdom is like honey for you: If you find it, there is a future hope for you, and your hope will not be cut off" (NIV). When the writer talks about wisdom being like honey, I can't help but think about the stickiness of honey. When you find wisdom, it's difficult to lose it.

The first step in looking for wisdom is admitting you don't have the answers—you have a need for help outside of yourself—and then pointing your need in God's direction, asking, praying, studying, listening, and watching. You will find wisdom when you seek it. Then you will be met with hope and a bright future.

"Truly, I say to you, whoever says to this mountain,
'Be taken up and thrown into the sea,' and does not
doubt in his heart, but believes that what he says will
come to pass, it will be done for him. Therefore I tell you,
whatever you ask in prayer, believe that you
have received it, and it will be yours."

MARK 11:23–24

▸▸ *How does the search for wisdom run contrary to society's desire to know it all?*

▸▸ *What are good ways to develop and nurture wisdom?*

Hope inside a Rock

*M*artin Laird writes, "According to ancient theory of art, the practice of sculpting has less to do with fashioning a figure of one's choosing than with being able to see in the stone the figure waiting to be liberated. The sculptor imposes nothing but only frees what is held captive in stone."[40]

He compares sculpting to our spiritual life and how we should let go of the need to have our circumstances be a certain way in order for us to live, pray, or to be deeply happy. He adds, "With enough of this stone removed, the chiseling becomes a quiet excavation of the present moment. The emerging figure is our life as Christ."[41] This makes me want to hand over the chisel to God and say, "Have your way; turn me into Christ." Having that kind of faith is a great way to live hope.

> What you sow does not come to life unless it dies.
> And what you sow is not the body that is to be,
> but a bare kernel, perhaps of wheat or of some other grain.
>
> 1 CORINTHIANS 15:36–37

▸▸ *How can we hand over the chisel for God to shape our lives?*

▸▸ *What's the difference between being formed into Christ's image or the best version of ourselves?*

Hungry for More of God

*M*any songs are filled with an intense longing for God. Why do people long for more of God? I believe God is already with us—he's all in, not partly in. And Paul said that Christ lives within us. Theologically speaking, it sounds like we already have all of God we would ever need.

I received an e-mail devotional with these two lines: "We cannot *attain* the presence of God because we're already totally in the presence of God. What's absent is awareness."[42] So much of people's frustration comes from feeling they must earn God's presence instead of truly knowing grace, which is impossible when we think there's anything we do to get God. There's no such thing as "being far away from God." Don't let the Pharisees fool you into thinking there is.

> Where shall I go from your Spirit?
> Or where shall I flee from your presence?
> If I ascend to heaven, you are there!
> If I make my bed in Sheol, you are there!
> If I take the wings of the morning
> and dwell in the uttermost parts of the sea,
> even there your hand shall lead me,
> and your right hand shall hold me.
>
> PSALM 139:7–10

▸▸ *How can you increase your awareness of God's complete presence?*

▸▸ *What do we have to do to escape the presence of God?*

Hope = Grounded in Faith + Fueled by Love + Guided by Vision

Hope Underwater

*A*n old pipe in my apartment decided to burst one evening, causing water to gush throughout my whole place for about an hour. I felt helpless because there was nothing I could do to stop it. Finally, some firemen showed up and turned off the water. Then the cleanup crew arrived. I spent several days in a hotel, not knowing what I would be returning to. I had to prepare for the idea that all my stuff was ruined. That's when it hit me—it's all *stuff*.

My hope was in the fact that God would take care of me. But I also had many people who said they'd help me with whatever I needed. It was as if hope showed up in flesh through my friends. You can live hope today by finding someone in need and showing up for them like my friends did for me.

> Jesus … rose from supper. He laid aside his outer
> garments, and taking a towel, tied it around his waist.
> Then he poured water into a basin and began to wash
> the disciples' feet and to wipe them with the towel
> that was wrapped around him.
>
> JOHN 13:3–5

▸▸ *How can you show up for someone today?*

▸▸ *Where do you find hope when you're in an unknown place?*

Vision Adjustment

*T*here are many horrible things happening in the world today, tempting us to feel as if there's no hope. But you don't have to fall for those lies. God is at work and up to something *really* good.

Harold Kushner wrote in *When Bad Things Happen to Good People*, "We all have the power to give away love, to love other people. And if we do so, we change the kind of person we are, and we change the kind of world we live in."[43] If you look at the world and don't like what you see, it might be time for a vision adjustment. If you set out to be a person who continually gives away love and who looks through eyes of hope, then you will find that your world becomes a much more loving and hopeful place.

> Therefore do not pronounce judgment before
> the time, before the Lord comes, who will bring to light
> the things now hidden in darkness and will disclose
> the purposes of the heart. Then each one will receive
> his commendation from God.
>
> 1 CORINTHIANS 4:5

▸▸ *What increases your temptation to view the world as bleak and hopeless?*

▸▸ *How can you share the hope God has revealed to you?*

The Best about You

$\mathcal{M}$any people find it easier to believe the best about somebody else's life, but not about their own. It is easy to think that my circumstances are not going to get any better, knowing my history and how certain patterns repeat themselves. Someone posted on social media, "Believe the best about others." But could it be more helpful to say something like, "Believe the best about yourself"?

God is with you, living in and through you; what's holding you back from believing good things about yourself? When you believe the best about yourself, your whole outlook changes and you're able to stand tall and talk to others with confidence. Hope says that despite how the past has been, God is working to make all things good, new, and better. He's making you more like Jesus. I'm going to believe the best about God and in turn, the best about myself because of his promises.

> What is man, that you are mindful of him,
> or the son of man, that you care for him?
> You made him for a little while lower than the angels;
> you have crowned him with glory and honor.
>
> HEBREWS 2:6–7

»» *What holds you back from thinking the best about yourself?*

»» *How does your judgment of yourself spill over into your judgment of others?*

Hope = Grounded in Faith + **Fueled by Love** + Guided by Vision

Hope in Grace

I had a conversation with a guy who called himself an *almost* Christian. Something in him really wanted to become a Christian, but he wasn't exactly sure what he needed to do or believe. We had a great time together, sharing stories of experiences and how those shaped our thoughts about God and how much he loves us. The conversation revealed how foreign the concept of grace is to most people.

Grace says that God is extending his love and mercy to us, regardless of anything we do. Understanding grace opens to us a world of hope. It comes alive when we see the path in front of us isn't littered with checklists of what we must do. There was relief in my friend's eyes as he realized there was nothing he needed to do to earn God's favor.

> For all have sinned and fall short of the glory of God,
> and all are justified freely by his grace through
> the redemption that came by Christ Jesus.
> ROMANS 3:23–24 NIV

>> *What prevents you from believing grace is enough?*

>> *How does your covering of grace make a way to hold on to hope?*

When Life Doesn't Make Sense

Jennifer Rothschild, author of *God Is Just Not Fair: Finding Hope When Life Doesn't Make Sense*, tells why she wrote the book: "I was so tired of being blind. I wanted to quit more than I wanted to keep trying. I desperately needed to know God was enough when my life was a mess. I needed real hope because I had real pain and real questions.

"It is really hard to question God and still feel secure. It was hard for me to question God without feeling guilty … I wrote this book because I am still tired of being blind, yet, [I am] totally comforted in my darkness by God's companionship. I wrote this book because I don't want to quit anymore. Yet, I don't have to keep trying to feel better."[44]

> "And I will ask the Father, and he will give you
> another Helper, to be with you forever, even the
> Spirit of truth, whom the world cannot receive,
> because it neither sees him nor knows him.
> You know him, for he dwells with you and will be in you."
>
> JOHN 14:16–17

▸▸ *What's the difference between saying God is fair or just?*
▸▸ *How does God comfort you in the darkness?*

Stuck in a Tunnel

*A*s I travel the country, it is intriguing when a highway I'm driving on goes right through the middle of a mountain. I imagine the years of planning and excavating that went into blasting through a mountain, without destroying the whole thing, just so we could have the convenience of driving through it. There must have been days when the workers wondered if they were ever going to get through to the other side. But they knew there was another side. It wasn't going to be a dead end.

Do you ever feel like you're tunneling through a mountain in your life, but you're not sure if you are ever going to reach the other side? Let me be a voice of hope to you: There is an end to your tunnel. If you keep looking, the light is starting to peek through the tiniest of holes at the end of the tunnel. Don't give up hope—you will get through this.

> Commit your way to the LORD;
> trust in him, and he will act.
>
> PSALM 37:5

▸▸ *How would you encourage others to keep going through their dark tunnel?*

▸▸ *What in the past has God brought you through?*

What Does God Think about You?

*D*o you ever wonder what God thinks about you? People say all kinds of things in answer to this question, ranging from "Oh, how he loves me," to "I bet he's really sad or mad when he looks at me." But God is characterized by love—it's who he is and what he does. This is what he wants us to be characterized by as well.

Jeremiah 29:11 says, "For I know the thoughts that I think toward you, says the LORD, thoughts of peace and not of evil, to give you a future and a hope" (NKJV). God thinks thoughts of peace toward you; he wants you to know peace through his love. When I know I'm loved and am capable of loving others through him, then my life is overtaken by peace and hope. I wish the same for you too! Don't keep yourself from a life of peace because you're thinking incorrectly about how God looks at you.

> But the fruit of the Spirit is love, joy,
> peace, patience, kindness, goodness, faithfulness,
> gentleness, [and] self-control.
> GALATIANS 5:22–23

▸▸ *How does loving others create a life of peace?*

▸▸ *How do the thoughts you have about God affect how you view others?*

Hope = Grounded in Faith + **Fueled by Love** + Guided by Vision

Figuring God Out

*D*o you think you have God figured out? Have you ever thought that because you haven't seen him do a miracle, you probably never will? Or do you wait with hope and anticipation of what God might do, even yet today? First Corinthians 2:9 says, "Eye has not seen, nor ear heard, nor have entered into the heart of man the things which God has prepared for those who love Him" (NKJV).

I can't see the future. I have no idea what God is up to, but I do have a good feeling it's going to be something awesome, something that will continue to shape me into the person he wants me to be. When you are tempted to give up hope, thinking you've got God all figured out and that you know what he's going to do, remember 1 Corinthians 2:9 and be encouraged. God's love for you far exceeds your understanding.

> From of old no one has heard
> or perceived by the ear,
> no eye has seen a God besides you,
> who acts for those who wait for him.
>
> ISAIAH 64:4

▸▸ *How can you ever know what God is going to do in the future?*

▸▸ *How does the unknown future increase your fear or your faith?*

Hope = Grounded in Faith + Fueled by Love + Guided by Vision

Wish You Had More Money?

*Y*ou may be thinking, *What does money have to do with hope?* It seems like the equilibrium of our entire world is based on who has money and who doesn't. Is this how you view your own life? Hebrews 13:5–6 reminds us, "Keep your lives free from the love of money and be content with what you have, because God has said, 'Never will I leave you; never will I forsake you.' So we say with confidence, 'The Lord is my helper; I will not be afraid. What can mere mortals do to me?'" (NIV).

As a believer, I live my life according to a completely different set of standards than the world. No wonder it's been called "living upside down." When my hope is placed in God, trusting he is my helper, I don't need to look at my bank account to tell me my worth.

> I have been young, and now am old,
> yet I have not seen the righteous forsaken
> or his children begging for bread.
>
> PSALM 37:25

▸▸ *To what degree do you place your hope in the amount of your wealth?*

▸▸ *Besides God, what else threatens to determine your worth and value as a person?*

Outrunning God's Love

*D*o you ever feel as if God doesn't love you? This is often because we have various expectations on what love should look like. Gary Smalley, in his book *The Five Love Languages*, described how we each receive love in different ways. We can't base the reality of how loved we are by our feelings.

Even if you think you've done more wrong than God could ever forgive, I'm happy to say that you're mistaken. Romans 8:38–39 assures us, "For I am convinced that neither death nor life, neither angels nor demons, neither the present nor the future, nor any powers, neither height nor depth, nor anything else in all creation, will be able to separate us from the love of God that is in Christ Jesus our Lord" (NIV). That's a hope that says we can't outrun God or his love. We're constantly in the middle of it.

> So we have come to know and to believe the love
> that God has for us. God is love, and whoever abides
> in love abides in God, and God abides in him.
>
> 1 JOHN 4:16

▸▸ *Why do you think you can outrun the love of God?*

▸▸ *What part of God allows anybody to slip through the cracks?*

How Are You Seeing the World?

This world can seem a bit messed up at times. Does believing and trusting in Jesus actually overturn the hopelessness we experience in our world? While circumstances around us are constantly changing, sometimes feeling like our personal well-being is threatened, Jesus gives us a new perspective, a new set of eyes through which we see the world. And he gives us a new way to experience the world.

When everyone around you seems to be running crazy, Jesus says, "I give you peace." When everyone is shouting words of fear, listen to Jesus as he says, "Fear not." When peace is my state of being, I look at the world differently. I don't have to worry about missing out. God is in control, working his plan for my life and for all creation. That gives me great hope.

> When I am afraid,
> I put my trust in you.
> In God, whose word I praise,
> in God I trust; I shall not be afraid.
> What can flesh do to me?
>
> PSALM 56:3–4

▸▸ *How can you be like Jesus and live to overturn the world's hopelessness?*

▸▸ *How does worrying help you feel more aware of the true reality of the world?*

How Does Hope Grow?

*M*any people tell me they believe in God, even Jesus, but don't go to church. Unfortunately, it's usually because they had a bad experience in church, or they feel that what happens in church has no relevancy to them. My hope for these people is that, even if they don't want to be part of a church, they haven't retreated into isolation. Hopefully they have been able to establish a good support community, because hope grows in the context of relationship.

Hebrews 10:24–25 says, "And let us consider how to stir up one another to love and good works, not neglecting to meet together, as is the habit of some, but encouraging one another, and all the more as you see the Day drawing near." Hope is difficult by ourselves; we need each other to experience true and lasting hope.

> May the Lord make you increase and abound
> in love for one another and for all, as we do for you,
> so that he may establish your hearts blameless in holiness
> before our God and Father, at the coming of our
> Lord Jesus with all his saints.
>
> 1 Thessalonians 3:12–13

▸▸ *How can you encourage someone to find a balance of time alone and with community?*

▸▸ *What are the benefits you've experience by living in community?*

Hope = Grounded in Faith + **Fueled by Love** + Guided by Vision

Hope Leading toward Peace

*I*t is easy to find something to get stressed out about. I try to not watch the news, because it seems to be focused on creating fear and stress simply to keep ratings high! I want to live a peaceful, hope-filled life. This requires a bit of remembering what I believe.

I remember what role hope plays in peace. Second Thessalonians 3:16 says, "Now may the Lord of peace himself give you peace at all times and in every way. The Lord be with all of you." The God of peace is with us. When I remember God continually offers me peace, I catch myself when I'm tempted to be stressed or afraid.

Hope reminds me that God is with me through whatever I'm going through; he's working all things together for the good of those who love him (Romans 8:28). Being fully present amid my circumstances, just like God is, allows me to remember the truth about the peace God offers me.

> What you have learned and received and
> heard and seen in me—practice these things,
> and the God of peace will be with you.
>
> PHILIPPIANS 4:9

▸▸ *What are some good ways to remind yourself what you believe?*

▸▸ *In what situations do you find peace tends to leave you?*

Hope = **Grounded in Faith** + Fueled by Love + Guided by Vision

Making You Confident

*C*onfidence stems from a place of experience. You've done this before, you can do this again. You've gone down this road and you know it takes you where you want to go. In Hebrews 10:21–23, we read that "since we have a great priest over the house of God, let us draw near to God with a sincere heart and with the full assurance that faith brings. … Let us hold unswervingly to the hope we profess, for he who promised is faithful" (NIV).

As we place our confidence in God, our future is secure because God is in charge. How would this kind of living change your life? Would you stand up a little taller, knowing your Father in heaven has already paved the way for you? Would you courageously reach out to people with the love of God, knowing there's nothing anyone can do to harm you? Place your hope in God, allowing him to infiltrate every aspect of your life, and you'll see God working in ways you've never dreamed.

> Christ is faithful over God's house as a son.
> And we are his house, if indeed we hold fast our
> confidence and our boasting in our hope.
>
> HEBREWS 3:6

▸▸ *What is a way you would live hope if you had more confidence?*

▸▸ *How does God's faithfulness allow you to be confident?*

Two Powerful Words

*T*he hope-inducing discipline of gratitude has transformed my life. So you can probably guess that the two most powerful words that can transform your life are *thank you.* Most of us say, "I'm so grateful for everything I have. My life is so blessed." But how specific are you willing to get? How much thanks are you willing to express? When you see a beautiful sunset or have a great conversation with a friend, do you say thank you for that specific event? And even more importantly, who do you say thank you to?

God loves it when we point to him as the source of everything we have and everything we experience. When we show him we are grateful, it frees us to start seeing more how God is continually dumping his blessings on us. That's when hope comes alive.

> The trumpeters and musicians joined in unison
> to give praise and thanks to the Lord. Accompanied by
> trumpets, cymbals and other instruments, the singers
> raised their voices in praise to the Lord and sang:
> "He is good; his love endures forever."
>
> 2 Chronicles 5:13 NIV

▶▶ *Where do you usually point your gratitude?*

▶▶ *How does gratitude help someone out of hopelessness?*

When Gratitude Takes Over

*F*irst Thessalonians 5:18 says, "In every thing give thanks: for this is the will of God in Christ Jesus concerning you" (KJV). Throughout Scripture, God commands us to be grateful. When you become grateful, you will be amazed at how much there is in your life to be grateful for. When I'm grateful, I can't be depressed or resentful; I can't be focused on myself when I'm pointing to someone else and saying thank you.

There are more ways of saying thank you than with words. I want my life to be continually pointing to God, shouting thank you with my every breath. Everything I do, every conversation I have, every act of service I do, every song I write, every concert I perform, I want it to be a response of gratitude for all God has done. You might even call this worship. How you say thank you will shape the way you live your life.

> For it is all for your sake, so that as grace extends
> to more and more people it may increase thanksgiving,
> to the glory of God.
>
> 2 CORINTHIANS 4:15

▸▸ *How do you say thank you with your life?*
▸▸ *Why do you think gratitude is so important in the Bible?*

When You Don't Get
What You Deserve

*F*rom the time we were small children, we were taught the importance of saying please and thank you. It was all about manners and discipline. We aren't born grateful; we're born selfish and arrogant. While the gift of age can allow people to learn they aren't the center of the universe, some adults still have never learned this valuable lesson. This has led to one of the biggest social infections of our culture—entitlement, which is thinking, *I deserve this*, even at the expense of everyone else.

The missing piece in the selfish child and the egotistical adult is gratitude. It's like fire and water—you can't live your life fueled by gratitude and still be arrogant and selfish. But fortunately for both groups of people, the cure is the same. The answer is two simple words: thank you.

How can we be truly grateful and still hold on to expectations of what we think we deserve? We can't. Do you want to live hope today? Then say thank you.

> You will be enriched in every way to be generous in every way, which through us will produce thanksgiving to God.
>
> 2 CORINTHIANS 9:11

▸▸ *How can your gratitude help build hope in the lives of those around you?*

▸▸ *What would you have to surrender if you adopt a lifestyle of gratitude?*

Hope = Grounded in Faith + Fueled by Love + Guided by Vision

Gratitude's Power

*I*f you're looking for a way to truly live hope, being thankful might be the best discipline you can adopt. How does gratitude change a person? First, gratitude makes you happy. You can't say thank you and actually mean it without having a smile on your face. Unhappy people are driven by fear, bitterness, and misery, but happy people are driven by gratitude. Second, gratitude makes a person humble. A lack of humility says, *I did it; I'm responsible for this*. But gratitude continually points to God and others. Third, gratitude makes a person hopeful, much like how an optimistic person always looks for the good, so a grateful person always looks for the blessing in all circumstances.

Every person you meet and circumstance you encounter is an opportunity to be blessed. Every day is an opportunity for something beautiful to take place. A grateful person lives hopeful of continued blessings.

> "Out of them shall come songs of thanksgiving,
> and the voices of those who celebrate.
> I will multiply them, and they shall not be few;
> I will make them honored, and they shall not be small."

JEREMIAH 30:19

▸▸ *How does gratitude make you more hopeful?*
▸▸ *What have you forgotten to be thankful for?*

Say Thank You with Your Life

*O*ne of the ways God loved us was to take on the form of a baby and come live among us. He lived such a revolutionary life that the religious experts didn't recognize who he was. They were threatened and feared that his followers would try to overthrow the religious establishment, so they killed him. They hung him on a cross, buried him in a tomb, taking with him the curse of all our sin. But as he predicted, Jesus didn't last more than three days in that tomb. He rose from the grave, then ascended into heaven, giving his Spirit to live with us until the day we're together with him in eternity.

Your response to God's expression of love in Jesus shapes the essence of your life. Saying thank you to God for his gift of salvation is the ultimate act of gratitude. You can then live your life spreading hope by continually saying thank you through prayer, worship, and service to others.

> I will give thanks to the LORD with my whole heart;
> I will recount all of your wonderful deeds.
> I will be glad and exult in you;
> I will sing praise to your name, O Most High.
>
> PSALM 9:1–2

▸▸ *What attitudes besides gratitude have you expressed toward God?*

▸▸ *How would you like gratitude to change your life?*

Changing People

*L*ife is great when it's only me, but the minute I need to inter-act with other people, it gets tricky. I wish people would just do what I want them to do. I get frustrated when people do what is detrimental to themselves, and, in turn, make it more challenging for me to be their friend.

This is where I need to have faith and love—love that is unconditional and doesn't hold secret agendas for how others should change. It's a love that trusts God is in the changing business; I can retire from that job. Faith and love lead to hope. I can look at people I love and care about, and say, "God's got me. God's got you. And I don't need to intervene half as much as I think I do." When I release my desire to be in control, I make room for hope, and then God can have his way.

> But you, O Lord, are a God merciful and gracious,
> slow to anger and abounding in
> steadfast love and faithfulness.
>
> PSALM 86:15

▶▶ *How has your desire to change people kept you from loving them?*

▶▶ *Can you communicate love without having an asterisk next to their behavior?*

In Need of Rescue

*T*o be rescued means being taken out of a difficult situation, pulled out during the last minute, or the hero showing up at the right time—just when everyone thought the situation was hopeless. Zephaniah 3:17 declares, "The LORD your God in your midst, the Mighty One, will save; He will rejoice over you with gladness, He will quiet you with His love, He will rejoice over you with singing" (NKJV).

God is in the rescue business. That doesn't mean you're going to get pulled out or removed from a difficult situation. But my experience has shown me that God is a God of comfort in the midst of the storm. Knowing this kind of passion is being aimed in your direction makes it easier to get through whatever you're going through. Wherever you are and whatever you're going through, know you're not alone. God is walking with you to the other side; don't stop now.

> He delivered us from such a deadly peril,
> and he will deliver us. On him we have set
> our hope that he will deliver us again.
>
> 2 CORINTHIANS 1:10

▸▸ *Why are we prone to stop in the middle of what we're going through?*

▸▸ *How might God's rescue look different from how we want it to look?*

Turning You into Jesus

God is doing a work on us, changing us, fixing us, turning us more into the likeness of Jesus. Unfortunately, this usually comes through difficult situations where our character gets refined. First John 3:2–3 says, "But friends, that's exactly who we are: children of God. And that's only the beginning. Who knows how we'll end up! What we know is that when Christ is openly revealed, we'll see him—and in seeing him, become like him. All of us who look forward to his Coming stay ready, with the glistening purity of Jesus' life as a model for our own" (MSG).

You and I are already children of God, but we're on our way to something more. It gives me hope to stay patient through the trials I face, because they're all leading somewhere. And that somewhere is straight to Jesus.

> And we all, with unveiled face, beholding the glory
> of the Lord, are being transformed into the same image
> from one degree of glory to another. For this comes
> from the Lord who is the Spirit.
>
> 2 CORINTHIANS 3:18

▶▶ *What can we do to assist the process of becoming like Jesus?*

▶▶ *How have you seen God do his transforming work through the years?*

Rejoicing in Your Sufferings

I've been baffled by Romans 5:3, which says that "we rejoice in our sufferings." It seems like an upside-down way of looking at things. But let's look at the surrounding context: "We rejoice in hope of the glory of God. Not only that, but we rejoice in our sufferings, knowing that suffering produces endurance, and endurance produces character, and character produces hope, and hope does not put us to shame" (vv. 2–5 NIV). These verses are calling us to step back from the micro look at our lives and our sufferings, and get more of a macro view.

When we take a few steps back and see that God is up to something, especially when we go through various kinds of suffering, it makes it easier to get through it with a kind of alert expectancy. It doesn't make the pain or difficulty any less, but there's a grace, a living hope, that permeates everything we're feeling.

> I know, O LORD, that your decisions are right and
> that your punishment was right and did me good.
> Now let your loving-kindness comfort me, just as
> you promised. Surround me with your tender mercies
> that I may live. For your law is my delight.
>
> PSALM 119:75–77 TLB

▸▸ *How can you take a macro view of your life's circumstances?*

▸▸ *How do your struggles develop hope inside of you?*

Hope = Grounded in Faith + Fueled by Love + **Guided by Vision**

Willing to Wait

*O*ne of the most difficult aspects of living hope is waiting, living in the tension of the time between the vision and the fruition of that vision. Waiting, and not getting what we want right away, does something inside of us. It makes us grow and causes us to become stronger, and we become more whole people. A small baby doesn't have any understanding of the concept of waiting. The baby only lets the mother know when he wants something and doesn't stop until he gets it. In many ways, a lot of us are still like a baby.

Romans 8:25 says, "But if we hope for what we do not yet have, we wait for it patiently" (NIV). Paul authored this letter to the Romans to encourage them—and now us—that there is great value in waiting. To live hope means we wait with patience, trusting that God is at work, loving us well, and doing something bigger in us than simply adjusting our circumstances.

> "By your endurance you will gain your lives."
>
> LUKE 21:19

▸▸ *How is waiting changing you?*

▸▸ *Where is your hope found in the in-between times?*

Passing the Time

*I*n the concept of hope we can explore everything we believe about God: how he looks at us, and what we believe he's doing. When I'm living hope, I'm directing that hope toward God. Sometimes it has a specific thing I'm hoping for; sometimes it's just looking to God for whatever he's going to do. But it has a deep element of faith to it, a faith that believes God is permeating everything and is deeply interested in even the smallest details of my life.

We can hope well with confidence and faith. Psalm 71:14 says, "But I will hope continually and will praise you yet more and more." As you're living hope, exercise your praise muscle. Praise God for who you believe he is and for all he's doing in your life. Tell him thank you. As you grow in gratitude and keep directing praise toward him, you'll find that what God is changing you into is more valuable than anything you could ever ask for.

> O Israel, hope in the LORD!
> For with the LORD there is steadfast love,
> and with him is plentiful redemption.
>
> PSALM 130:7

▶▶ *How does your hope reveal what you believe to be true about God?*

▶▶ *How have you seen God change your life as you put your trust in him?*

Hope = Grounded in Faith + Fueled by Love + Guided by Vision

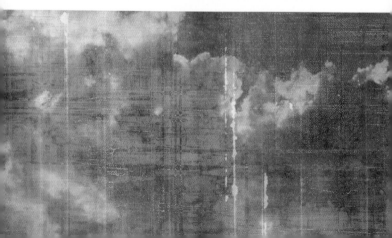

DECEMBER

You can have a hope that is no longer a fingers-crossed wish you keep holding on to, but rather a confident, brave vision for the future that is rooted in the everlasting promises of God and his love for you.

Being Joy to the World

*O*ne of the songs I wrote for *Hope for the Holidays* is called "Let Me Be Joy to the World." The song has turned into a mission statement of sorts for the life of hope I desire to live. The chorus says, "Let me be joy to the world, with a heart that sings your song of unconditional love for everyone to hear. Let my voice be a guiding star that will lead us to the King, shining loves pure light, 'til we all live in peace."

I want my life to be a song that shines light on our heavenly Father, and how it's possible to live in relationship with him. This way of living is rooted in the unconditional love that God demonstrated through his Son, Jesus. Once we know it for ourselves, we can then give it away to others. That's my great hope.

> Let them thank the LORD for his steadfast love,
> for his wondrous works to the children of man!
> For he satisfies the longing soul,
> and the hungry soul he fills with good things.
>
> PSALM 107:8–9

▸▸ *If your life was a song, what would people hear?*

▸▸ *How can you be joy to the world today?*

A Favorite Christmas Carol

*E*ach December, during my annual Christmas tour, I get to travel the country and sing songs everyone loves and deliver a message of hope found in the story of Jesus—his birth, life, death, and resurrection. Like the verse in "Hark the Herald Angels Sing," which says, "Mild He lays His glory by, born that man no more may die. Born to raise the sons of earth, born to give them second birth. Hark! The herald-angels sing, glory to the newborn king!"

This message of hope says Jesus was born so we would know what it truly means to live, and to destroy the power of death over us. It's a second birth, one that has no end. Perhaps you can find a song to sing about this Christmas season, one that conveys the hope you profess. And then sing it aloud wherever you go, using words only if necessary.

> But we see him who for a little while was made lower
> than the angels, namely Jesus, crowned with glory
> and honor because of the suffering of death, so that
> by the grace of God he might taste death for everyone.
>
> HEBREWS 2:9

▸▸ *How does Jesus show us what it means to live?*

▸▸ *What's a popular Christmas song that holds deep meaning for you?*

Hope = Grounded in Faith + Fueled by Love + Guided by Vision

Finding Joy in the World

*I*n 1719, Isaac Watts published a book of hymns called *Psalms of David Imitated*, taking the words of David and paraphrasing them. His most popular hymn, "Joy to the World," was based on the last half of Psalm 98: "Let the sea roar, and all its fullness, the world and those who dwell in it! Let the rivers clap their hands; let the hills sing for joy together before the Lord, for he comes to judge the earth. He will judge the world with righteousness and the peoples with equity" (Psalm 98:7–9).

Watts transformed the old Jewish psalm of praise for historic deliverance into a song of rejoicing for the salvation of God, and the birth of hope that began when Jesus came "to make his blessing flow far as the curse is found."

> The Lord will show the nations of the world his justice;
> all will praise him. His righteousness shall be like
> a budding tree, or like a garden in early spring,
> full of young plants springing up everywhere.
> Isaiah 61:11 TLB

▸▸ *How would you describe the elements of the earth praising God?*

▸▸ *What lyrics do you usually sing without ever thinking what they mean?*

Speaking Hope This Christmas

*H*ave you ever been told you can't say Merry Christmas? While I understand the need to be respectful to people of different religious beliefs, it's hard to imagine Christmas being only about presents and decorations, as great as those are. For me, it wouldn't be Christmas without Jesus. So I wrote a song about it: "They said I gotta say happy holidays, 'cause Christmas is just the wrong thing to say. Well, I sure gotta confess—this really is a mess, 'cause there's one thing I never will erase. You can't take Jesus out of Christmas, He is the reason we're making all this fuss. It's gonna be a Merry, Merry Christmas. But Jesus, it won't be Christmas without you."

Regardless of what I'm told I can or can't say, I'm going to continue to find ways to express love and compassion to those around me—with respect, gentleness, and compassion. Hope shows up when I put down my agenda and seek to connect with other people.

> My brothers, show no partiality as you hold the faith
> in our Lord Jesus Christ, the Lord of glory.
>
> JAMES 2:1

▸▸ *How can you share hope while being sensitive to other people's beliefs?*

▸▸ *Can you communicate hope more strongly through words or actions?*

Hope = Grounded in Faith + **Fueled by Love** + Guided by Vision

Hope for the Holidays

I love the holiday season. Despite how crazy everyone's schedules can get, we all can show each other how much we love one another, which is when hope shows up. First Thessalonians 5:11 reminds us, "Therefore encourage one another and build one another up, just as you are doing." This is the time of year when people are the most outwardly generous and intentional with their time together.

But it can also be the time of year when people are the greediest, focused on all they want as opposed to what they're going to give. Generosity connects us, but greed isolates us. There is a lot of hope to be found in the holidays, but anything you can do to connect with other people—giving a card, a gift, a meal, or maybe even just a cup of coffee—will reveal God's hope to the world around you.

> That their hearts may be encouraged,
> being knit together in love, to reach all the riches
> of full assurance of understanding and the knowledge
> of God's mystery, which is Christ.
>
> COLOSSIANS 2:2

▸▸ *How can you creatively deliver hope to someone this Christmas season?*

▸▸ *What's a good way to discourage greed during the holidays?*

Hope Defeats Cynicism

*M*any things in life don't turn out the way we hoped they would. When circumstances and people disappoint, it's easy to feel loaded down with discouragement and maybe even have a sense of hopelessness. I love the honesty of the psalmist in Psalm 42:5: "Why, my soul, are you downcast? Why so disturbed within me?" He doesn't stop there, however, saying, "Put your hope in God, for I will yet praise him, my Savior and my God" (NIV).

During this Christmas season, we celebrate the birth of Jesus and the fact that he came to give us something better than the disappointments of this life. When you choose to place your trust in him and all he's promised, you have a hope that is no longer a fingers-crossed wish you keep holding on to, but rather a confident, brave vision for the future that is rooted in the everlasting promises of God and his love for you.

> "Behold, the virgin shall conceive and bear a son,
> and they shall call his name Immanuel"
> (which means, God with us)."
>
> MATTHEW 1:23

▸▸ *How is this Christmas inviting you to a deeper level of hope?*

▸▸ *How does the presence of God help conquer your disappointments?*

Entering Your Darkness

*F*or many people, the Christmas season is a time of joy and celebration, filled with food, friends, family, and gifts. But for others, the holidays are a glaring reminder of love lost, relatives who have died, and broken relationships. It can be a lonely, dark, and isolating time. When God broke through time and space to enter our world, he entered a dark world, committed to shining the light and love of his Father.

Without Jesus we have no hope, but with Jesus, whom Paul called "our hope" in 1 Timothy 1:1, we can walk through the darkness of today with the light of God shining on the path before us. Once we know the hope that is found in Jesus, it becomes our pleasure to be that hope to the world around us.

It's our job to go into the dark places and shine the light of love to those who are buried in darkness, proclaiming the truth, "God is with us!"

> For there is one God, and there is one mediator
> between God and men, the man Christ Jesus.
>
> 1 TIMOTHY 2:5

▸▸ *Why did God enter our darkness two thousand years ago?*
▸▸ *How does God still come into your darkness today?*

Why All the Fuss about Hope?

*H*ope is everywhere these days. Just turn on the television or radio and you hear people talk about it. Companies are touting hope as the by-product that is received when you purchase whatever it is they're selling. I believe this is great. At Christmastime, it's culturally acceptable to talk about Jesus in a variety of settings, so our culture is primed for us to speak the truth about the meaning of hope.

Sometimes hope is shared as easily as a smile given to the person behind the counter at the coffee shop; sometimes it's in a warm coat given to someone living outside. But sometimes it's shown by how you live hope, especially in difficulties. If you can say, "My hope is based on nothing less than Jesus' blood and righteousness,"[45] when the world around you is falling to pieces, then people will see true hope in your life.

> Jesus said to him, "I am the way, and the truth,
> and the life. No one comes to the Father
> except through me."
>
> JOHN 14:6

▸▸ *What does it mean to have the righteousness of Jesus give you hope?*

▸▸ *Why are you on a quest to understand hope?*

Hope = **Grounded in Faith** + Fueled by Love + Guided by Vision

Joy in Hope

*P*aul wrote that we are to be "cheerfully expectant" (Romans 12:12 MSG). This makes me think about Christmas as a child, when I was excited about what my parents had planned for my sister and me. It was going to be something good, of that I was certain, mostly because I was convinced of their love for us.

Hope has a chosen attitude, as well as a focus. At Christmas, I focused my hope on my parents and what they had planned for me, being extremely excited about it. This is how I want to live in my relationship with God too. Of course, I'm keeping God as the focus—I'm looking to him, trusting him and what he has planned for me. And I'm excited about it, because I know it's going to be something good. I'm convinced of God's love for you and me. And I'm also convinced that he has something incredible ahead. I can't wait. How about you?

> But, as it is written,
> "What no eye has seen, nor ear heard,
> nor the heart of man imagined,
> what God has prepared for those who love him."
> 1 CORINTHIANS 2:9

▸▸ *How can you rejoice in hope today?*

▸▸ *How is the anticipation of Christmas an illustration of how we are to live all year?*

Sifting through the Rubble

*H*ave you ever heard someone say, "The older I get, I realize more of what I don't know"? I'm starting to get that, because it seems like the more I study, read, and pray, the less I seem to know. It's as if the message of God's truth gets winnowed down, like sifting a pan of sand and rocks while looking for gold.

The gold is in knowing that God is love, and his love is directed toward me. Truly, there's nothing more I need than that. The gold of the gospel helps me to be less distracted by all the extraneous rubble that can creep into my spirit—garbage that makes me think I have to do more or be more in order to claim my identity as the beloved. Because I am loved, I can show that same love to others. God's got us in his hands, and he's never going to let us go.

> And because you are sons, God has sent the Spirit
> of his Son into our hearts, crying, "Abba! Father!"
>
> GALATIANS 4:6

▸▸ *How do you experience God's love?*

▸▸ *What's a good way to sift through the unnecessary rubble that distracts you?*

Honest to God

*W*hen you talk to God, are you able to say how you really feel? I used to think that I could only say "nice" things to God, like words that were only full of gratitude or when I prayed for direction and wisdom. I believed that if I were to be completely honest with him, then God would be disappointed with me for not being spiritual enough. Inside I was full of many emotions and questions, but if I brought those thoughts to God, then I must be ungrateful or not very spiritual at least. I now know that was wrong.

Being honest with God means I believe God is big enough to handle all my thoughts and feelings. Let God hear from you, how you *really* feel. Let him have all your emotions, and never let go of the hope that he will deal with you only as the loving Father he is.

I say this not as a command, but to prove by the
earnestness of others that your love also is genuine.

2 CORINTHIANS 8:8

▸▸ *Why do we think we need to be spiritual with God?*
▸▸ *How could you speak to God with more authenticity?*

A "Why, God?" Moment

*H*ave you ever had one of those "why, God?" moments, where you can't see the reason behind what happened? It's more common to not see the why something happened than it is to be able to perceive the reason behind it. Hope says, *God, you're in this! Even when I can't see you working, I trust that you are in this and believe that you're making something good out of me in the process.*

I had a large project cancel recently, one I'd been working on a lot. I was looking forward to seeing what God was going to do through it. It's disappointing, but I choose to continue to hope in God. Romans 8:28 reminds me, "And we know that God causes everything to work together for the good of those who love God and are called according to his purpose for them" (NLT).

> I lift up my eyes to the hills.
> From where does my help come?
> My help comes from the Lord,
> who made heaven and earth.
> He will not let your foot be moved;
> he who keeps you will not slumber.
>
> Psalm 121:1–3

➤ *How do your "why, God?" moments help build trust?*

➤ *How do unanswered questions play into the development of your faith?*

After You've Been Burned

*I*t's great to be a person who thinks of others, serving them and lending a helping hand. But just because you serve someone doesn't mean the other person will be grateful for what you've done. I have given to people and never received back from them the thanks I hoped to receive. I had some strings of expectations attached, which only led to disappointment.

How do you respond when people let you down? Does it make you want to never reach out again? Hope keeps reaching out, regardless of what has happened in the past. Hope learns how to give and how to serve, without expectations of receiving anything in return. Hope trusts that God sees what you've done and knows the blessings will come, even if they show up at a completely different time and in a way you didn't expect.

> Instead of your shame there shall be a double portion;
> instead of dishonor they shall rejoice in their lot;
> therefore in their land they shall possess a double portion;
> they shall have everlasting joy.
>
> ISAIAH 61:7

▸▸ *How can you serve others without expecting to get anything in return?*

▸▸ *How does God repay us for what we've given to others?*

Into the Unknown

*H*ave you seen the film *Indiana Jones and the Last Crusade*? Remember that scene where Indy must cross a giant chasm and there's no bridge in sight? He remembers the phrase "leap of faith" and hears his father whisper, "You must believe, boy; you must believe." And with all the bravery he can muster, Indy takes a step off the cliff—and his foot lands on a bridge he couldn't previously see. It was constructed as an optical illusion to protect the treasure.

How can you be brave and take a step of faith? Keep your faith deeply rooted in the power of God, trusting in him. If you're facing something you don't think you can do, ask yourself why. Who told you that you couldn't do it? Close your eyes, take a deep breath, and take that first step. You'll be met with help and hope from above.

> But Jesus looked at them and said, "With man this is impossible, but with God all things are possible."
>
> MATTHEW 19:26

›› *How is God asking you to trust him at a deeper level than before?*

›› *Who are some voices of hope you can count on as you step out in faith?*

Hope = Grounded in Faith + Fueled by Love + Guided by Vision

A Different Kind of Story

*W*e're all part of the love story God is writing, each of us playing a uniquely created role to bring about his kingdom. Do you think that if God is the one writing the story, that everything should be fantastic and nothing should go wrong? Or is it possible that God is writing more a story of pain and death followed by resurrection? Your story is probably much more like the story of Jesus.

Hope doesn't ignore the reality of the situation—the pain and the difficulties—but it knows that it's not the end of the story. You're going *through* it. Keep going, and keep your eyes fixed on Jesus. He has shown you the way and promises to be with you through it all.

> But when [Peter] saw the wind, he was afraid, and beginning to sink he cried out, "Lord, save me." Jesus immediately reached out his hand and took hold of him, saying to him, "O you of little faith, why did you doubt?"
>
> MATTHEW 14:30–31

▸▸ *How does your faith help you keep walking through the storm?*

▸▸ *Where do you see hope emerging while you're in the struggle?*

Hope = Grounded in Faith + Fueled by Love + Guided by Vision

A Big Project

*H*ave you ever thought about starting a huge project, but can't even find the strength to get started? God puts awesome ideas inside of our heads because he wants us to bring them to life—to come alongside him in the creation process. It can be difficult to get started, but it's even more difficult to keep going when the task gets challenging. It's at times like these where we need to take heart from others who have gone before us.

For instance, Michelangelo spent four years painting the ceiling of the Sistine Chapel in Rome. And it took about twelve years for one of my favorite monuments, Mount Rushmore, to be carved out of the side of a South Dakota mountain.

Do you have a big project you want to work on? Don't give up. It might take a while to complete, but sometimes the vision is too big to bring to fruition overnight. It takes time and patience, a lot of faith, and a firm grasp on the vision.

> "For nothing will be impossible with God."
>
> LUKE 1:37

▸▸ *What is the "why" behind what you want to accomplish?*

▸▸ *What part do you think God plays in bringing your vision to fruition?*

All the Way Through

*I*t's incredible to think about the massive undertaking to carve a giant hole through a mountain. I've driven through tunnels where you can't see the light on the other end for quite a while, but you keep driving because you know the road isn't going to end in the middle—it's going to take you all the way through.

Is this where you are in life today? Are you driving in a tunnel and can't see the light at the other end? These are the days when your quest for hope becomes real. Hope shines brightest in the darkest places. Look ahead with hope—even if your circumstances look dark. Remember who God he is and that he loves you beyond what you can fathom. Remember how he works all things for your good. He's with you in the darkest of tunnels. And keep going, for the light is just ahead.

> For he will hide me in his shelter
> in the day of trouble;
> he will conceal me under the cover of his tent;
> he will lift me high upon a rock.
>
> PSALM 27:5

▸▸ *How does hope shine in the dark?*

▸▸ *In what ways can you find rest and shelter as you go through trials?*

Anchor of Hope

Someone gave me a wall hanging that says, "Hope is the anchor for my soul." I love the thought behind it and the verse from which it's taken: "This hope is a strong and trustworthy anchor for our souls. It leads us through the curtain into God's inner sanctuary" (Hebrews 6:19 NLT). Those are powerful words. You don't normally think of an anchor taking you someplace; usually, an anchor holds you down. Maybe that's what this verse is saying.

While the storm blows all around you and the waves are crashing on you from all directions, this hope holds you firm. It's strong and it's trustworthy. And when you find that peace in the midst of the craziness, that's when you can experience real intimacy with God. Don't worry about the storm; don't worry about the chaos. Hang tight to hope. God's got you, and he's not letting you go.

> For though I am absent in body, yet I am with
> you in spirit, rejoicing to see your good order
> and the firmness of your faith in Christ.
>
> COLOSSIANS 2:5

▸▸ *What does it mean to put down your anchor in the midst of the storm?*

▸▸ *What value does hope have when you're not experiencing a trial?*

Hope = **Grounded in Faith** + Fueled by Love + Guided by Vision

When Chaos Is Swirling Around

*I*t doesn't take long when watching the news to feel like chaos is swirling all around. It seems like the day's tragedies overpower any hope you have for the world. This is when it's important to remember what you're basing your hope on in the first place. It wasn't that everything in life would happen as you wanted it to, that the world would be chaos free and everyone would get along. Even though these are good aims to work toward, our hope transcends circumstances or else we're going to be continually blown by the wind—feeling hopeful and then not. Our hope must be rooted in the unchanging, ever-loving God.

Hang on to God's promises of presence and provision. Remember, our God is bigger than the storm. Your relationship with him is where the greatest hope is found; it will hold you through any amount of chaos.

> There is no fear in love, but perfect love casts out fear.
> For fear has to do with punishment,
> and whoever fears has not been perfected in love.
> We love because he first loved us.
>
> 1 JOHN 4:18–19

▸▸ *Why does the storm sometimes feel bigger than God?*
▸▸ *How do you press into your relationship with God?*

Hope = Grounded in Faith + **Fueled by Love** + Guided by Vision

Holding You Steady

*H*ope reveals itself in how we live, how we treat others, and how we interact with the world. This is especially true when going through storms. Our hope holds us like an anchored ship tossed by waves. This doesn't mean the boat doesn't move—it stays in one place. Do you feel steady in the chaos of life, or do you feel tossed by the waves?

If you desire to feel steadier, then consider where your hope is placed. An element of hope is being grounded in a belief that life is not up to you to manage or control; rather, it trusts that God watches and cares for us. Hang on to God as your anchor of hope. And remember Matthew 6:26: "Look at the birds of the air: They do not sow or reap or gather into barns. … Are you not much more valuable than they?" (NIV). Of course, you are.

> The eyes of all look to you,
> and you give them their food in due season.
> You open your hand;
> you satisfy the desire of every living thing.
>
> PSALM 145:15–16

▸▸ *What desires does God satisfy when you go through a trial?*

▸▸ *How do you live hope to those around you, even while you're struggling?*

Hope = **Grounded in Faith** + Fueled by Love + Guided by Vision

A Beautiful Time of the Year

*W*hat makes Christmas so great? I love listening to carols, especially the old classics, and looking at lights and elaborate decorations. I also love spending time with family and friends. But looking back over the multitudes of Christmases, especially as a kid, the best part has always been the hope of what presents I might receive. I loved making wish lists, going through the Sears toy catalog, and picking out what looked like the most awesome presents. And my parents always knew what to get me to make me so happy.

Christmas is great knowing that someone who loves you is planning something special, specifically with your joy in mind; they are preparing something to bring you happiness. This is hope—that someone who loves me is preparing something special for me, specifically with my joy in mind. God is that someone, and the gift is his Son, Jesus, whom we celebrate this Christmas.

> Joshua told the people, "Consecrate yourselves,
> for tomorrow the LORD will do amazing things among you."
>
> JOSHUA 3:5 NIV

▸▸ *How can you believe God has good things planned for you?*

▸▸ *How is Christmas a giant illustration of hope?*

Hope = Grounded in Faith + Fueled by Love + **Guided by Vision**

Holiday Exhaustion

*T*he holidays are one of the most stressful times of the year. Everyone's schedule gets put on overdrive, but expectations that everything has to be amazing can put an unnecessary burden on your shoulders. My secret for surviving the chaos of the holidays is gratitude. This is the most life-changing discipline one can adopt, especially during the holidays. It is impossible to be resentful when I'm grateful for all I have. When full of gratitude, I cannot feel entitled or that I deserve to be treated in a certain way. Gratitude stands up and looks pride in the face, saying, *You have no place in my life!*

If you start to feel overwhelmed by crazy relatives or an endless to-do list, stop for a moment and tell God what you're thankful for. Take time to demonstrate that gratitude to others. Tell your family what you're grateful for, showing them the power of gratitude and inviting them to tell God how thankful they are. God came to rescue us from the chaos of this world. Don't get trapped into thinking he didn't mean your own personal chaos.

> Giving thanks always and for everything to God
> the Father in the name of our Lord Jesus Christ.
>
> EPHESIANS 5:20

▸▸ *In what ways can you demonstrate gratitude without using words?*

▸▸ *How does hope allow you to get through stressful times?*

Hope = Grounded in Faith + Fueled by Love + Guided by Vision

Gotta Be Something More

S ometimes I feel like there has to be more to life than what I'm experiencing. There are days when I feel the pain, the uncertainty, the fear, the confusion, and the loneliness of life, and everything within me desires for it to be different. There is something in me that says, *This all* could *be different and it probably* should *be.* The difference between the way life is and the way I desire it to be creates a tension within me because I hope. I hope for things to be better, for things to make sense, for things to have some purpose.

God places hope in the hearts of believers to help us keep moving through the struggles of life. We're on our way toward our own resurrection. I know only a sliver of what that means, but I can't wait to fully see it. I have great hope for what God is going to do.

> Since we have the same spirit of faith according to
> what has been written, "I believed, and so I spoke,"
> we also believe, and so we also speak, knowing that
> he who raised the Lord Jesus will raise us also with
> Jesus and bring us with you into his presence.
>
> 2 CORINTHIANS 4:13–14

▸▸ *How does your hope create an inner conflict toward this life?*

▸▸ *Does the idea of your resurrection lead to hope?*

Hope = Grounded in Faith + Fueled by Love + Guided by Vision

A Crazy Dissonance

*T*he difference between the way life is and the way I want life to be creates a crazy dissonance within me. Life is a story of conflict, but it's also a story of hope and rescue. We're in the middle of a story with a hero waiting to rescue us—not to take us out of it, but to bring about beauty, purpose, and meaning. This is what God has been about for all eternity, showing us his love and desire to invade our stories—stories we've been thinking were up to us, or perhaps simply a product of chance.

If you want to acknowledge and receive all God has prepared for you, there is one gift you must first receive. The most controversial name in society today—Jesus—is the way God chose to physically enter our story. God thought, *How can I give them a gift they'll receive? Ahh…a baby!* Jesus is God's gift, a gift we as Christians celebrate on Christmas.

> For if many died through one man's trespass,
> much more have the grace of God and the free gift by the
> grace of that one man Jesus Christ abounded for many.
>
> ROMANS 5:15

▸▸ *Why did God choose to enter into the dissonance of life on earth?*

▸▸ *How is Jesus the hero the world was (and still is) waiting for?*

We Know How It Ends

*W*e celebrate the birth of Jesus every Christmas, but we celebrate with the incredible knowledge of what this baby was going to go through as an adult. Jesus entered into our darkness by a miracle, walked the earth, and died. Then his grandest act on earth was his resurrection from the dead. This man was tortured and hated, but he had a mission that allowed him to see the greater purpose behind it all.

When we have a greater vision beyond our present hurt and struggle, God will carry us through. Jesus demonstrates the way to his Father, but he also makes it clear that the way is going to be hard and difficult. But his great promise is that we're never alone, that he is with us—*Emmanuel*. Knowing he walked this path before us, we can trust he knows our every step, every pain, and every tear. And because of Jesus, we can take the next step. That's the hope of Christmas.

> For because he himself has suffered when tempted,
> he is able to help those who are being tempted.
>
> HEBREWS 2:18

▸▸ *Can knowing the ending bring greater meaning to the whole story?*

▸▸ *How does hope grow as you lean into the continual presence of God?*

When Your Prayers Don't Get Answered

*L*auren Daigle expresses a sentiment I have felt often. The song talks about continuing to trust in God even if he doesn't do what we want him to. When he doesn't move the mountain or part the waters as we think he should, we still need to trust him. We want to be people who trust, are marked by faith, and marked by the belief that God is in control. We trust that God is doing what's best and giving us what we need, instead of simply what we want.

To live hope is to trust, acknowledging that we don't see the whole picture from our vantage point; to accept that God is good and full of love for us; that he is continually acting on our behalf, even when it doesn't feel like it.

We look not to the things that are seen but to the things that are unseen. For the things that are seen are transient, but the things that are unseen are eternal.

2 CORINTHIANS 4:18

▸▸ *How can you keep unanswered prayers from shattering your hope?*

▸▸ *What increases your trust level in God and how he works?*

Churches Working Together

I was scheduled to do a concert in a small church in rural Nebraska. It seemed as if it was going to be a normal stop, until I found out the idea behind the concert. This small-town church decided to partner with three other churches in the area to help foster fellowship and community, despite their differing denominations. And they wanted to use my concert as a chance for them all to come together. I wish this wasn't such a radical idea!

What I find more normal is that churches are often territorial. They are more than happy to have people come visit their church, but they don't like their own people going to events at other churches. The churches of Hooper, Nebraska, that are choosing to live hope by tearing down denominational walls that usually keep us apart are a great example!

> Remembering before our God and Father
> your work of faith and labor of love and steadfastness
> of hope in our Lord Jesus Christ.
>
> 1 THESSALONIANS 1:3

▸▸ *What walls have been unconsciously built around you and your community?*

▸▸ *How can hope work to build bridges between different people?*

Can You Make Someone Change?

*I*t's challenging to love people who are caught up in something I don't agree with, or that might not be healthy for them. I wish they'd change. Instead, I want to love others based on the worth and value that Christ extends to all, not with an agenda or a hidden motive. Is it really love if there is always an asterisk attached to it?

If the changes a person experiences are not rooted in a knowledge of how loved they are, then they will always be works-based changes, and won't stick. Rules can change a person for a time, but love will transform for a lifetime. A person can't live in fear of the love of God being taken away based on his or her behavior. To live hope, to love like God, we need to love with no hidden agendas.

If I speak in the tongues of men and of angels,
but have not love, I am a noisy gong or a clanging cymbal.
And if I have prophetic powers, and understand all
mysteries and all knowledge, and if I have all faith, so as
to remove mountains, but have not love, I am nothing.

1 CORINTHIANS 13:1–2

▸▸ *How can we help someone without trying to get her to change?*

▸▸ *How convinced are you of God's unconditional love for yourself?*

In the In Between

*T*he time between Christmas and New Year's Day is a great time of personal reflection—to be grateful for the past year and think about what changes I'd like to see in the coming year. I look forward in hope, filled with courage and creativity. For me, looking forward must be rooted in gratitude. I can't look ahead out of lack or a feeling that I'm missing out.

First Thessalonians 5:17–18 is a great passage to remember during these days of introspection: "Rejoice always, pray without ceasing, give thanks in all circumstances; for this is the will of God in Christ Jesus for you." I am grateful for all that God has done in the past year—I want my life to be a giant thank-you to God—but I'm also looking ahead with enthusiasm to see what God has in store for the coming year. It's going to be something good.

> But thanks be to God, who in Christ always leads us
> in triumphal procession, and through us spreads the
> fragrance of the knowledge of him everywhere.
>
> 2 CORINTHIANS 2:14

▸▸ *Where do your times of introspection usually take you?*

▸▸ *How does gratitude allow you to dream about the future with hope?*

The Road Is Long and Exhausting

*P*erhaps the best-known American opera singer in the sixties and seventies was Beverly Sills. I can only imagine the thousands of hours of training and practice she put in before she ever made her first debut. She said, "There are no shortcuts to any place worth going."

Are you feeling like you want to give up hope because your road is long and the journey is hard? Does it seem like life is easier for other people than it is for you? Let me be the voice of hope today that says, *Don't give up.* You're climbing a big mountain that requires great courage, skill, faith, and persistence. And always remember you're not alone. When I get tired and it's difficult to go on, I fall on Christ with my simple prayer from Philippians 4:13: "I can do all things through him who strengthens me."

> That according to the riches of his glory he may
> grant you to be strengthened with power
> through his Spirit in your inner being.
>
> EPHESIANS 3:16

▸▸ *What helps you gather strength to keep going through challenging times?*

▸▸ *Who do you know who might need to hear, "Don't give up; you're not alone"?*

When You Know It's the End

We're at the end of another year. Looking back, mine's been filled with chaos and beauty, sadness and joy, frustration and surprise. Some of you are thrilled the year is over and are ready to move on to better days, while others of you will enjoy memories of great experiences.

Despite what happened this past year, we can't fathom the good God has in store for us. While we are never promised tomorrow, I want to continually find ways to live with hope for the days ahead. I'm going to choose to wake up with gratitude, living with a hopeful optimism that God has "got the whole world in his hands" and is working it all together for my good (Romans 8:28), making me more and more into the unconditional loving person of Jesus.

> To put off your old self, which belongs to your
> former manner of life and is corrupt through deceitful
> desires, and to be renewed in the spirit of your minds,
> and to put on the new self, created after the likeness
> of God in true righteousness and holiness.
>
> EPHESIANS 4:22–24

▸▸ *How would you explain to someone what it means to be a person of hope?*

▸▸ *What's the next step on your journey to live hope through your life?*

Hope = Grounded in Faith + Fueled by Love + Guided by Vision

Connecting

I'm so grateful you've chosen to go on this journey of hope with me. I pray it has been life changing for you as we've explored what hope is and how to live it out. How about we keep it going? I would love to hear your story, your questions, your insights into hope, and how you have used this book, either by yourself or with a group. Please take some time to explore the music, books, resources, and live events all based around the concept of hope that I talk about via social media and my website, livehopenow.com. Also, if you sign up for my newsletter (via my website), I'll send you a free collection of some of my favorite songs of hope that I've recorded and that you will be able to download for free!

The Live Hope Minute daily radio feature is currently heard on 250 radio outlets around the US, Canada, and South Africa. If you'd like your favorite station to feature it, please ask them! You can also hear it via my website and Apple Podcasts.

Finally, I'd love to work with you to create a live event to explore and build hope with your team, group, church, or organization. And if you know some people who could use hope, let me know so we can give it to them!

You can reach me at:

mark@livehopenow.com
Facebook.com/smeby
Instagram.com/tnwannabe
Twitter.com/msmeby

Notes

1   Jean Rhodes, http://www.thrivingnow.com/guidance-god-you-and-i-dance.

2   Ayn Rand, http://www.goodreads.com/quotes/119112-in-the-name-of-the-best
    -within-you-do-not.

3   Anne Frank, *Tales from the Secret Annex* (1949; repr., New York: Bantam Books,
    2003), n.p.

4   John Piper, "What is Hope?", Desiring God, April 6, 1986, http://www.desiringgod.org
    /messages/what-is-hope.

5   Samuel Rutherford, quoted in Sarah Young, *Jesus Today* (Nashville: Thomas Nelson,
    2012), 224.

6   Max Lucado, *Grace for the Moment*, 2 vols. (Nashville, TN: Thomas Nelson, 2000), n.p.

7   Harvey Mackay, "Sow Seeds of Hope," February 2, 2017, http://www.harveymackay
    .com/sow-seeds-of-hope.

8   Sara Hagerty, *Every Bitter Thing Is Sweet* (Grand Rapids, MI: Zondervan, 2014), n.p.

9   This quote has been attributed to Croatian pastor Peter Kuzmic.

10 C. S. Lewis, *Mere Christianity* (London: Collins, 1952), book 3, chap. 10.

11 J. R. R. Tolkien, *The Two Towers: Being the Second Part of The Lord of the Rings*
    (George Allen & Unwin, 1954), https://books.google.com/books?isbn=0547952023.

12 Decision Staff, "The Archaeologist's Spade Aids the Church," *Decision Magazine*,
    April 20, 2017, https://billygraham.org/decision-magazine/april-2017/55115-2.

13 Ken Hakuta, The Foundation for a Better Life, https://www.values.com/inspiration-
    al-quotes/6718-people-will-try-to-tell-you-that-all-of-the.

14 G. K. Chesterton, http://www.goodreads.com/author/quotes/7014283.G_K
    _Chesterton.

15 Eugene Peterson, *A Long Obedience in the Same Direction* (Downers Grove, IL:
    InterVarsity Press, 1980), 144.

16 Charles Allen, *The Miracle of Hope*, 48, as quoted in David Jeremiah, *Discovering
    God: 365 Daily Devotions* (Tyndale House, 2015), 102.

17 Barbara Cawthorne Crafton, *Let Us Bless the Lord, Year Two: Meditations on the
    Daily Office,* vol. 3 (Harrisburg: Morehouse Publishing, 2005), 149.

18 Santiago "Jimmy" Mellado, "The Power of Hope," *Compassion Magazine*, May 30,
    2014, https://www.compassion.com/magazine/fight-poverty.htm.

19 Sarah Young with Karen Lee-Thorp, *Receiving Christ's Hope*, Jesus Calling Bible
    Study Series (Nashville: Thomas Nelson, 2015), 3.

20 https://dcstevens1.wordpress.com/tag/al-sacharov.

21 *The G. K. Chesterton Collection*, 50 Books (Catholic Way Publishing, 2014), "Gilbert
    Keith Chesterton," n.p.

22 G. K. Chesterton, *The Collected Works of G. K. Chesterton, Heretics*, vol. 1 (San Francisco: Ignatius Press, 1986, 125.

23 Peterson, *A Long Obedience in the Same Direction*, 76.

24 Rutherford, as quoted by Young, *Jesus Today*, 224.

25 Charles Haddon Spurgeon, *Devotional Classics of C. H. Spurgeon: Morning and Evening I & II*, https://books.google.com/books?id=PrPH6E76RTAC, June 28.

26 Elane O'Rourke, *A Dallas Willard Dictionary* (Soul Training Publications, 2013), quoted by "Christian Mindfulness," http://christiansimplicity.com/christian -mindfulness.

27 Sarah Bessey, "Being Brave Together," SarahBessie.com (blog), January 12, 2016, http://sarahbessey.com/brave-together.

28 Oswald Chambers, as quoted by Dave McCasland, *Oswald Chambers: Abandoned to God* (Vereeniging, South Africa: Christian Art, 2006), n.p.

29 Karen Casey, *A Life of My Own: Meditations on Hope and Acceptance* (Center City, MN: Hazelden Publishing, 2010), January 5 entry.

30 Richard Rohr, https://www.goodreads.com/author/quotes/7919.Richard_Rohr? page=9.

31 Steven Curtis Chapman, as quoted by Shari Lacy, *Southern Exposure* (April 3, 2016), n.p.

32 Peterson, *A Long Obedience in the Same Direction*, 118–19.

33 Pete Wilson, *Empty Promises* (Nashville: Thomas Nelson, 2012), 44.

34 Barry Zito, as quoted by Tim Keown, "A Man in the Game," ESPN (December 1, 2012).

35 Oswald Chambers, *My Utmost for His Highest*, rev. ed. (Grand Rapids, MI: Discovery House, 2010), February 22 entry.

36 Lisa Copen, "Where is Hope? Those with Invisible Illness Share God's Reminders," Rest Ministries, August 31, 2012, http://restministries.com/blog/2012/08/31/where -is-hope.

37 Martin Luther, as quoted by Sebastian Traeger and Gregory D. Gilbert, *The Gospel at Work: How Working for King Jesus Gives Purpose and Meaning to Our Jobs* (Grand Rapids: Zondervan, 2013), chap. 4.

38 Young, *Jesus Today*, 256.

39 Ibid.

40 Martin Laird, *A Sunlit Absence* (Oxford University Press, 2011), 60–61.

41 Ibid.

42 Richard Rohr, "Staying Watchful," Center for Action and Contemplation, August 30, 2016, https://cac.org/staying-watchful-2016-08-30.

43 Harold Kushner, as quoted by June Cotner, *Looking for God in All the Right Places* (Loyola Press, 2004), 8.

44 Jennifer Rothschild, "The Story behind My New Book," *Living beyond Limits* (blog), March 7, 2014, http://www.jenniferrothschild.com/the-story-behind-my-new-book.

45 Edward Mote, "My Hope Is Built on Nothing Less" (1834).